THE BUTTERFLY
CONSPIRACY

ALSO AVAILABLE BY VIVIAN CONROY

CORNISH CASTLE MYSTERIES

Rubies in the Roses

Death Plays a Part

COUNTRY GIFT SHOP MYSTERIES

Written into the Grave

Grand Prize: Murder!

Dead to Begin With

LADY ALKMENE CALLENDER MYSTERIES

Fatal Masquerade

Deadly Treasures

Diamonds of Death

A Proposal to Die For

THE BUTTERFLY CONSPIRACY

A MERRIWEATHER AND ROYSTON MYSTERY

Vivian Conroy

CROOKED
LANE

NEW YORK

Copyright © 2018 by Vivian Conroy

Published in the United States by Crooked Lane Books, an imprint of The Quick Brown Fox & Company LLC.

Crooked Lane Books and its logo are trademarks of The Quick Brown Fox & Company LLC.

Library of Congress Catalog-in-Publication data available upon request.

ISBN (hardcover): 978-1-68331-765-4
ISBN (ePub): 978-1-68331-766-1
ISBN (ePDF): 978-1-68331-767-8

Cover design by Melanie Sun
Book design by Jennifer Canzone

Printed in the United States.

www.crookedlanebooks.com

Crooked Lane Books
34 West 27th St., 10th Floor
New York, NY 10001

First Edition: August 2018

10 9 8 7 6 5 4 3 2 1

THE BUTTERFLY CONSPIRACY

CHAPTER 1

"Merula!" Julia DeVeere's voice resounded from the other room. "Come in here and work your magic on my unruly locks."

Merula Merriweather leaned toward the mirror, half standing at her dressing table, putting a pin here and there in her exuberant dark hair. Whereas she had the patience to turn her cousin's hairdo into a real masterpiece, she didn't like to spend more than a few minutes on her own appearance.

Her chances for being the belle of the ball were minimal on most occasions, as she was untitled and a bit odd at that, an orphan with a shady past.

Merula only knew that her mother had run away from home and that five years later a baby girl had been delivered to her mother's family in London. That family, her mother's sister Lady Emma DeVeere and her influential husband Rupert, had taken great pains to convince the outer world that the baby had been born in wedlock, and on Merula's dressing table stood a silver-framed photograph of a smiling young woman and a stern man with light hair.

But when Merula looked at her own face in the mirror, at her features and her raven hair, she didn't believe the man in that photograph was her father. She wasn't even sure that the woman pictured was her mother.

Her head was full of questions about her family and the past, but she never asked. The truth might be worse than anything she could ever speculate about.

"Merula!" Julia appeared in the doorway, half dressed and with her hair done up on one side but not the other. "This new maid is abusing me in the most horrible fashion. Half my locks are either pulled out or scorched . . ." Julia fell silent as her gaze traveled from the feather-adorned comb in Merula's hair to the golden locket on her neck and down over the fiery-red dress with an edge of golden embroidery.

"You are going out!" she exclaimed. "Oh, you will be the night's sensation."

"Wrong, my dear," Merula responded at once, grabbing her black lace stole from the bed. "That honor will belong to *Attacus atlas.*"

"Who?" Julia queried with a frown that furrowed her otherwise flawless face. She was considered a true beauty, and every morning at breakfast her mother recited that Julia had to snare an earl, at the least, to get herself a title. Lady Emma hungered for her daughter to be called "Lady" as well, as the lack of a title for her only child was the one thing she regretted about her marriage to an untitled gentleman, no matter how much else Rupert DeVeere's wealth and esteemed position in society had given her. Julia, however, abhorred the candidates in line with her mother's social aspirations and longed for a dashing young diplomat who'd take her to Paris.

Merula explained, "My butterfly. It hatched this morning, and tonight I'm going to Sir Edward Parker's talk on a newly discovered tarantula, for the Royal Zoological Society, to show off the beauty and prove wrong all of those stiff gentlemen who didn't believe Uncle Rupert when he proposed that an ugly caterpillar could turn into a beautiful butterfly the size of both my hands."

Julia shrieked and pretended to be about to faint. "I have no idea how you can stand working with those horrible creatures. They'd give me nightmares."

"On the contrary," Merula parried, "they are the stuff of dreams." She draped the lace stole around her shoulders and reached for the drawstring purse to complete her ensemble.

Julia put a hand on her arm and pleaded, "Before you go, at least tell that silly girl how to do my hair. The maids only listen to you."

Merula sighed. "There is no secret to it. Since the maid is new here, she will probably do much better if you stop rushing her. Sit still, give her an encouraging smile, tell an amusing story to put her at ease, and you will see her abilities improve considerably."

Julia frowned. "Are you certain? Mother always says getting too familiar with the servants will just make them conceited and incorrigible."

"I tend to think a little kindness will encourage them to try their very best."

Julia shook her head. "Just like the time you gave your last penny to those dirty street urchins who claimed they had a sick mother. They ran straight off to the baker to buy biscuits for themselves. I saw them go in."

"They might have bought bread for the family. And even if they bought biscuits, I don't really mind. Those people have a hard enough life as it is."

Seeing such children never failed to remind Merula that if it hadn't been for her uncle's kindness, she herself might have grown up with perpetual dirt on her face and hunger in her stomach. Her privileged position hadn't been earned but given to her by someone who cared.

She smiled at Julia. "Just give the maid a fair chance and you will look spectacular. Oh, and my regards to Simon Foxwell, should he be dancing with you again all night, as he did last time. I don't know what you see in him though. The way he moves about the room and studies people, he's like a tiger sneaking through the high grass to jump the deer when it's least aware of the danger."

She shivered under her recollection of the intense look in Foxwell's amber eyes. "You think you're husband-hunting at those parties, but I feel like that man is hunting you."

"You can be so odd," Julia said, flushing. "It is not called husband-hunting. Besides, Simon will inherit his aunt's entire fortune. *He* is the prize catch."

"I just don't like him. I'm sorry," Merula said remorsefully and gave her cousin a peck on the cheek. Her distrust of Foxwell had been sharp and instinctive, like a child recoiling from the buzz of a wasp. But there was nothing to support it, and Julia wouldn't listen to reason anyway now that she could please her mother *and* herself by attracting a man who was well respected, rich, and handsome. At last Julia's dreams of seeing Paris might be within reach, if Foxwell's rich aunt took a liking to her and provided the young couple with funds to travel to the mainland.

A little melancholy at the idea of Julia leaving, Merula squeezed her cousin's arm. "I really hope you enjoy yourself tonight. Tell me all about it tomorrow over breakfast. Now I'm off to my grand reveal." And with that she dashed out of the room for the double staircase.

Of course, it would be *her* grand reveal only to her own mind. The guests at the lecture would just believe she had been allowed to unveil a creation of her uncle's. All Merula's zoological accomplishments were credited to him, an arrangement made by her own request, but one she regretted more and more as time went by. However, it had either been that or no research at all, and she had to count herself lucky her uncle hadn't outright forbidden her to engage in such eccentric hobbies.

He had even allowed her to make adjustments to the conservatory that was already in place for the keeping of tropical plants to turn it into a breeding place for her butterflies.

Although Uncle Rupert rarely set a foot inside, he generously paid all the bills sent to him for the changes and regularly asked her if there was anything more she might like. Used to having a demanding daughter who spent too much of his money in Regent Street, he considered it only natural that Merula also wanted things. That they were not dresses and hats but plants and a microscope, he seemed to find refreshing.

Not to mention how much it had enhanced his status with his peers that even members of the royal household took an interest in the work done by the Royal Zoological Society and might, one day, show up on his doorstep to see the work he was supposedly toiling away on.

Merula could only hope that on such an occasion the distinguished visitors would be even more ignorant about wildlife than her uncle so he wouldn't be exposed as a fraud. He didn't deserve to suffer humiliation in return for his generosity to her.

At the door leading into her sanctuary, Merula halted a moment with her hand on the doorknob, asking herself, for one fleeting moment, if it was really wise to take *Attacus atlas* with her tonight. Butterflies were delicate creatures, and to her mind it would be a disaster if something happened to it when she had had so little time yet to enjoy its beauty.

Then she decided that it was worth the wager and pushed the door open.

One of the adjustments she had made was that, right after this entry door, a second door had been installed, to prevent any butterfly that was flying nearby from being attracted by the draft created as the door opened and venturing outside. The double doors were like a mini corridor in which the butterfly could get caught before he flew toward what seemed like freedom but was, in reality, certain death.

Merula's arms suddenly crawled with gooseflesh. Her aunt's voice during their dinnertime conversation, when Merula had expressed an interest in seeing India, echoed in her ear: "India seems like freedom to you, child, but it would become the end of you. You'd venture into filthy markets full of poisonous fruit and snapping monkeys. You'd catch rabies and die a horrible death."

Uncle Rupert had laughed and winked at Merula, saying it was more logical she'd fall in with an expedition out to find the lost treasure at some sanctuary in the jungle. "How does the temple of the golden panther sound?"

"Must you encourage her?" Aunt Emma had asked with a hitched brow, continuing to Merula, "In that jungle you'd catch a poisonous dart from some incensed tribe who guarded that golden panther temple with their lives."

Merula smiled a moment as she realized that her aunt did have imagination, even if it was of the morbid kind, always predicting how every innocent pleasure could turn into immediate disaster. She would have bet that if Aunt Emma knew she intended to take the butterfly to the lecture, she'd come up with a scenario of mayhem and murder.

The heat of the conservatory slapped Merula in the face. She took a moment to breathe in and out, letting the humid air fill her lungs. Then she walked to the wooden contraption her uncle's secretary had built for her after her own design. Although Mr. Andrew Whittaker had a bit of a bookish look about him, he had been handy enough with his hands and interested in her research.

Lovingly, she touched one of the huge cocoons that hung suspended by a thin thread and a pin. They had traveled half the globe to get to her, having been taken from their native country in the Far East. The purchase of two of these had cost her most of the money she had intended to invest in caterpillars and plants for them to live on, but it was worth it.

Holding her breath, she looked up to where sat the creature that had crawled out of the first cocoon that morning. If Julia had been able to see it, she would truly have fainted. But for Merula it was a cause for excitement that made her feel more alive than ever.

As large as both of her hands held together with fingers spread like a flying eagle, the butterfly sat on the trunk of the small tropical tree, resting as it waited for the nocturnal hours to fly about. Each wing was the color of reddish brick, with colorful spots of yellow and blue. The structure seemed to be soft to the touch, almost as if dusted with powder.

But the greatest wonder of all were the patches, one in each wing, that were see-through, like glass, offering a view of the object the insect sat on. Right now, Merula could clearly distinguish the rough bark of the tropical tree through the patches.

It was a most amazing thing, and Merula sensed outright exhilaration coursing through her veins as she imagined the company of nature-mad men admiring her creature. Admiring her handiwork, as it were. She had purchased the butterflies, got them to hatch in her sanctuary, and she knew how to keep this rare animal alive. How long it would live, she had no idea, as the lives of some insects were very short. Another reason to take it with her that night and show it off. She might not have another opportunity.

Not even the knowledge that all the attention would be on Uncle Rupert, who would be congratulated on *her* success, could spoil this excitement for her.

From her workbench full of gardening tools, Merula picked up the large glass container she had previously pinched from the kitchens. It was actually meant to be put over cheese or other perishable foods when luncheon was served outside in the summer at the family's country house. As the item was not needed in the city, Merula figured nobody would miss it, and she carried it to the spot where the butterfly sat.

Climbing onto a stool, she held the container upside down and, with a leaf, gently scooped the butterfly off the trunk. It tried to fly off, but she held the container in its path, and immediately it attached itself tentatively to this new hold.

Careful not to disturb it, Merula stepped off the stool

and closed the container by placing it over a large wooden cheese board on which she had put some leaves with a pure-white flower. She couldn't resist presenting her natural wonder in the most attractive way.

And besides, the flower had to conceal the little holes she had hacked into the cheese board with a chisel to make sure the butterfly had fresh air.

Satisfied with the aesthetics of the end result, Merula covered the contraption with a sheet and carried it out of her workplace into the world.

★ ★ ★

Upon arriving at the house of their host for the night, Lord Havilock, Merula expected some surprised and even suspicious looks from the footmen attending to the arriving coaches.

But as her uncle assisted her out with the covered glass contraption in her hands, the two footmen didn't give her a second glance. Their attention was fully focused on the well-dressed gentleman striding up the house's blue stone steps ahead of them, carrying a monkey in his arms.

The beast was mounted on a wooden pedestal, its open mouth with its sharp little teeth giving it a ferocious look. The thin extended arms jerked up and down as the man jogged up the steps, as if the creature were still alive.

The butler at the open front door moved back a step, and Merula was surprised to catch a glimpse of disgust—or was it fear?—in his eyes. Servants were trained not to show emotions in front of their masters and their guests, but this man's instinctive response was stronger than all his years of careful grooming as head of the household. Apparently, his master's fascination with the animal kingdom was something foreign and perhaps even dangerous to his mind.

In the hallway, a three-tiered chandelier shot prisms overhead, and footmen were serving champagne to the arriving guests. The man with the monkey went straight for a tall, dark-haired man of the same age, greeting him with an amiable slap on the shoulder that made the monkey in his arms shudder.

Uncle Rupert looked the pair over with a slight twitch of his lips. This sign of disapproval was rare in her jovial uncle, who liked to believe the best of his fellow men.

Curious, Merula leaned over to inquire softly, "Who are they?"

"The one with the monkey is the Honorable Justin Devereaux. I met him before at one of these lectures. Unfortunately, he felt it necessary to regale me with all the gruesome details of mounting dead animals."

"Those taxidermists get better and better at what they do. Just compare that monkey to the pheasant we have at home. The poor bird looks like it was stuffed by an over-eager cook, and it doesn't even have eyes. This one looks so real. I wonder if the skull is still in there."

Uncle Rupert shook his head at what he probably considered a very inappropriate interest for a young lady and continued quickly, "The other gentleman is Lord Raven Royston."

He didn't have to say more. Royston had been the unfortunate focus of talk and speculation for weeks now, as he had invested heavily in the presentation of a steam-powered coach that had failed to ride even half a mile. Rumors claimed that part of the engine had exploded and that the flying parts could have harmed an innocent bystander.

"I suppose," Uncle Rupert whispered, "that after the earlier disasters with the coach and the hair tonic, Royston learned his lesson and is here tonight to show us he can be serious as well."

"Hair tonic?" Merula asked. This was new to her.

"Yes, apparently a friend of his developed a hair tonic that would give balding gentlemen their former locks back. Royston imagined it an overnight success, with thousands of vials selling throughout the country. However, those who volunteered to try this wondrous invention found that they lost the last of their remaining hair, gaining burns on their skulls in the bargain. The man who developed the dangerous liquid had to flee the country to escape arrest for fraud. Royston claimed he had never been involved in the actual creation of the tonic, so the police didn't pursue him further. That is the official story at least. But I guess his brother put in a word for him and might even have thrown in some money to persuade the police not to charge him with anything."

"Royston's brother *bribed* the police?"

"That's what some say. I suspect Royston's family wished he would leave the country as well to try his disastrous business ideas in a place they wouldn't hear of it. But he's still here and, judging by his appearance tonight, angling for a degree of respectability by focusing on serious science."

Her uncle's lips twitched again in that minimal betrayal of distaste. "Whatever he does now, he will always be associated with those incidents. Avoid him if you can, Merula. You don't have to be outright hostile to him, of course, should he happen to speak to you. After all, he is a lord. But don't encourage interest in any way, you understand? The man is a disaster magnet."

Merula nodded, inwardly hoping Royston would start a conversation with her so she could inquire as to what exactly had caused his steam-powered coach's engine to explode. After all, steam-powered train engines didn't explode, and they had to pull a much heavier load.

"Welcome, welcome." Their host Lord Havilock appeared by their sides. His gaze traveled down Merula's outfit, taking in every detail, and a wolfish smile appeared round his mouth. He gestured for a footman. "Someone must carry that for you, my dear. It looks heavy."

"No, I must handle it myself. The contents are very fragile." Merula was certain that Havilock wanted to rid her of her burden so he could kiss her hand. She wasn't fond of this French custom in general, especially not when the man in question was rumored to be looking for his third wife. With a three-decade age difference and Havilock's infamous roving eye, not even his beautiful house full of zoological treasures could persuade her to take an interest in him. It would take tact to remain polite and pleasant while dodging his attentions.

Glancing past her solicitous host, she caught the amused look of Raven Royston. For a moment it was as if he had read her mind and seen right through her excuse for wanting to hold on to the contraption in her hands.

Then Devereaux discerned a new arrival at the door and pushed his mounted monkey into Royston's hands. Before Royston could protest, he was hugging the grinning monkey while Devereaux strode away to greet a statuesque woman dressed in pearl gray.

Merula couldn't help smiling at Royston's murderous looks at his friend, who had saddled him with an ugly dead beast while Devereaux himself rushed to charm a female guest. A rich one at that, judging by the emerald necklace reflecting the light from the chandelier above. Merula wondered if some interesting history was attached to those jewels. Had they belonged to a German princess or the wife of the czar?

"Don't gawk." There was an anxious look on Uncle Rupert's face as he grabbed her elbow. "I hadn't expected her to attend tonight. It's better if we steer clear of her."

"Why?" Merula asked. "I don't even know her. I hadn't expected any other women to attend. Is she married to a member of the Royal Zoological Society?"

"She used to be. Come, quickly." Sounding rather nettled,

Uncle Rupert directed her firmly into the room prepared for the lecture. Merula wanted to ask what they were hurrying for, but the sight of the room took her breath away.

There were oil paintings of the English countryside on the walls, contrasting sharply with the exotic animals depicted in sketches standing on tables. She didn't know which one to look at first: the giraffe with its long neck and legs, the sleek jaguar that prowled the South American jungle, or the many colorful birds, each with even more extravagant plumage than the last. Long tail feathers, strange collars around their necks that could be puffed up at will. A world away from the simple dark blackbirds and brownish sparrows she knew. Could such creatures even exist?

Could they survive while being so conspicuous?

In a corner was Havilock's prize piece: a lion's skin with the head still on it, the wide-open mouth big enough to put your hand in, the eyes gleaming with a ferocious light. Merula resisted the urge to draw near, feel the skin, determine if the fur was soft to the touch like a dog's or stiff and resistant.

"You can put it here." Havilock cleared away a few sketches of birds to make room for her contraption. As soon as she had placed it, he reached for the sheet's edge, pretending to want to lift it for a playful peek underneath.

"Please don't, my lord," Merula said quickly. "I'd like everyone to see at the same time."

"Quite a natural wonder, hey." Havilock let his gaze travel her figure again.

Uncle Rupert distracted him with a remark about one of the bird sketches in which the bird didn't seem to have any feet, and Havilock laughed heartily. "Bird hunters a century ago removed the feet before shipping the birds here. No idea why, but it did cause some confusion. Ah, if you will excuse me for a moment, I must welcome my guest of honor." He strode to the door to welcome the woman in pearl gray and escort her through the crowd of men, who parted for her so she could stand right in the front. "You can see everything best, Lady Sophia," Merula overheard Havilock saying.

Lady Sophia was fanning herself with an ostrich-feather fan, her face reddish as if the room was too hot for her. Directly behind her came a brooding man in his midthirties whom Merula recognized at once. As his amber eyes brushed over her, she felt the chill that had touched her before when he'd confronted her. Why was Simon Foxwell here at some lecture instead of attending the ball Julia was going to? Her cousin would be so disappointed that she had missed her chance to waltz with him again.

Foxwell quickly assessed the zoological items on display. A patronizing smile played around his lips as if he considered them inferior, and Merula caught herself hoping her butterfly would wipe that smile away.

Havilock walked over to Merula, a glass in his hand, which he struck with a spoon.

Immediately the murmur of voices all around died down, and everyone present focused on their host.

"I'm delighted," Havilock said, leaning back on his heels, "to receive all of you here tonight for an outstanding lecture by my good friend and renowned expert on spiders, Sir Edward Parker. But before we enter the world of these ravenous creatures, we will first strengthen our hearts with a look at beauty. DeVeere . . ."

He gestured jovially at Uncle Rupert, who stepped forward, clearing his throat and fidgeting with his hands as if he didn't know quite where to put them.

Merula knew how much her uncle disliked being the center of attention and thanked him silently for doing this anyway.

He said, "Dear friends, we all share a fascination for insects, and tonight we will get a unique glimpse into the fascinating world of the butterfly. Although we know it comes from a cocoon, like a bird from an egg, many questions remain unanswered. Is it really true that this creature is born with wings, or does it have another form altogether at first? And if this is so, can we understand how it transforms from one into the other and truly accept that the caterpillar and the butterfly are one and the same animal?"

"Impossible," someone called, and another agreed with a tight, "They have been classified as different for generations."

The implication was clear. *Will you tell us otherwise?*

Among the disbelieving and even hostile expressions in front of her, only one face carried genuine interest. Raven Royston looked at Merula and her contraption with narrowed eyes as if trying to determine something. His failed investments suggested he was a gullible man, easily deceived into investing at the promise of a quick return. But as Merula looked into his eyes, she didn't see gullibility there, but rather intelligence and a challenge. As if he was quietly saying to her, *Prove it to me.*

Uncle Rupert continued, "I brought something special for us tonight, straight from my conservatory. My niece, Miss Merriweather, will present it to you. Please . . ." He gestured to Merula.

Her audience peered skeptically at the sheet cover.

"Underneath this is a glass case," she explained. She wanted her voice to sound strong, but it was breathless as her heart thumped under her breastbone. These men were experienced, jaded even, and what she considered a wondrous creature might not draw a second look from them. What had she been thinking when she had come here tonight?

But steadying her shaking hands on the sheet, she pushed on. "It contains a creature that came to life only this morning. In its present form, that is. Previously it was a caterpillar, green and hairy, unusually large, certainly, but nothing you'd admire. Now, however . . ."

She drew away the bed sheet with a flourish, and the light from the chandelier above fell on the glass container, illuminating the leaves and the large white flower inside.

The men closest to her gasped as they spotted the enormous butterfly with its bright colors.

People in the back whispered, asking one another what was under the glass.

"I don't see anything," Lady Sophia said in an impatient, petulant tone. "Just plants. What on earth is it, Simon?"

Simon Foxwell urged the woman to go closer, attempting to take her fan from her hand. But Lady Sophia continued waving it as she moved to the right, her steps hesitant.

Royston was already leaning over the container. A flicker of appreciation passed over his features. Turning his head this way and that, he studied what was under the glass. "A clever creation of paper or fabric."

"Excuse me?" Merula said.

"Collectors are duped on a daily basis." Royston held her gaze. "Merchants out for a quick dip in a rich man's purse stoop to anything, from painting feathers on birds to falsifying paperwork to prove an exotic 'new' find."

"You should know about being duped," someone called out from the back of the crowd.

Laughter resounded.

Royston didn't flinch, but Merula saw his jaw tighten. He spoke loudly, "The distortion of the glass gives it the illusion of life."

Merula heard him stall on the last word as the butterfly shifted a wing. He had seen that; he couldn't deny it. The furrow in his forehead told her he was trying to get a better look to determine how a creation of paper and fabric could possibly move.

The butterfly flapped its wings.

Merula couldn't suppress a smile of exultation at her luck. Skeptical Royston would have to believe this.

Lady Sophia stepped back with a gasp, raising a hand to her throat as if she was startled that the huge creature inside the container could be an actual living thing.

Royston's expression was still doubtful, and suddenly determined, Merula lifted the glass container off the wooden board it rested on. Without warning, the butterfly took off, lifting itself amid stares and exclamations.

Royston moved his head to follow the flight, even squatting to see the butterfly's wings from below.

"There are see-through patches in the wings," Merula explained quickly. "You can see the ceiling's gold leaf through them." Her hands were no longer shaking, but her voice was still high-pitched with excitement.

"I'm not looking for gold leaf," Royston retorted, unperturbed, "but for threads or other devices to make this creature fly."

Disappointment stabbed her. "You still think it is not alive?"

"It can't be, not at this size."

The butterfly lowered itself and sat on Lady Sophia's bare arm.

The woman gasped again, turning even redder in the face. She moved her free hand, but the movement was languid, not determined.

Havilock called out in a commanding tone, telling her to hold very still and let the other guests have their chance to see the creature up close.

From the excited murmuring, a few words could be made out: "Extraordinary." "Most novel."

The disbelief was fading to make way for amazement and even delight. Someone said a photograph should be taken for the newspapers.

Merula clasped her hands together, then relaxed them. Her heartbeat slowed, and a luxurious feeling of triumph spread through her. She had proven herself right, in the face of all these men. Her hard work had paid off.

Royston's voice sounded at her ear, low and determined, "Is this butterfly breeding really your uncle's doing? It always struck me as odd that Rupert DeVeere would spend time on zoology. History, yes; cartography, that he can talk about for nights on end, much to the annoyance of those who happen to be seated beside him at the dinner table. But when asked about animals, their habitats and customs, he is always vague, changing the subject quickly."

Merula's face was on fire now, and she didn't know how to respond. If she admitted it was her work, she'd humiliate her uncle. The man who had made all this possible for her.

But Royston's behavior tonight had also convinced her that he wasn't someone to fob off with a lie. He had already drawn his own conclusions from her uncle's evasive tactics. And if he had looked at her face just now, he might have glimpsed the elation that rushed through her veins, betraying her intense involvement.

Lady Sophia made a rasping noise. Her eyes rolled, and she staggered back.

The butterfly, startled, rose from her arm and fluttered away to sit on the back of a velvet chair. The bluish shine of the fabric filtered through the see-through patches in its delicate wings.

Lady Sophia crashed to the floor and lay still, her eyes staring up at the ceiling, seeing nothing.

Chapter 2

"She fainted," someone called. "Make some room, please, and bring smelling salts. Hurry."

A door slammed.

An elderly man with a cane said, shaking his head, "Women should not be allowed at these gatherings."

Royston scoffed, whispering to Merula, "Fainting spells have become fashionable among ladies of the upper classes and have very little to do with the occasion at which they take place."

Merula didn't reply, her eyes fixed on Lady Sophia's rigid body.

Simon Foxwell knelt beside her, touching her hand. The concern in his features convinced Merula that Lady Sophia had to be Foxwell's rich aunt. She had never seen them together before, as the aunt in question was rumored to keep to herself and avoid what she called frivolous activities such as balls and theater performances.

A footman carried in smelling salts and passed them to

Foxwell, who held the silver container under Lady Sophia's nose. Normally when the sharp scent of smelling salts invaded a fainting woman's nose, she immediately came to, gasping or sneezing, but Lady Sophia didn't stir at all. That horrible fearful expression seemed frozen on her mottled face.

"This is not working." Helplessly clutching the silver container, Foxwell asked, "Is there a doctor here who can see what ails her?"

Sir Edward Parker stepped forward. "I was a doctor in the army. It's been a while, but one doesn't forget."

"Good." Havilock nodded and added, "Let the footmen bring the screen from my library so Edward has some privacy."

At once, two footmen carried in a large screen of painted silk and placed it so as to shield the motionless Lady Sophia from further probing looks. Sir Edward disappeared behind the screen.

Merula stood with her hands folded together. A tickle of nerves danced in her stomach. When Lady Sophia had fallen, Merula had simply assumed the woman was of a nervous disposition and the confrontation with the giant insect had been too much. But the failure to respond to the smelling salts suggested Lady Sophia had not merely fainted. What had happened to her?

All eyes were on the screen and on the sounds coming from behind it: a rustle of fabric, slapping as if Sir Edward was trying to revive Lady Sophia by gently striking her cheeks, then a muttered curse.

Merula's heart skipped a beat.

Foxwell said, too loud in the silence, "What is going on behind that screen? How serious is it?" His amber eyes were narrowed, his hands clutched into fists by his side. Once again he struck Merula as being like a tiger waiting for his chance to pounce.

Sir Edward appeared at the screen. "She doesn't respond to any stimulus I've tried, and I can't find a pulse. Is there someone here with more medical knowledge who can have a look at her?"

Agitation had put red spots in his cheeks, and it was clear he wanted to relinquish responsibility to someone else as soon as he could.

Havilock said, "I already sent one of my footmen to get the doctor who lives down the street. He has a Harley Street practice. A very pleasant, talented young fellow."

Nobody responded to his reassuring remark. There was a deep chill silence.

Sir Edward glanced behind the screen again. "The mottled color of her face, her lips. I don't like it."

"What do you mean?" Foxwell asked. "Did my aunt have a heart attack?"

"That is . . . possible." Sir Edward's tone betrayed that he didn't really believe it himself. He knotted his bony fingers, keeping his gaze on the floor.

"What do you think ails her?" Foxwell pressed him. "I can assure you that when my aunt and I drove here tonight, she was in fine health."

He had barely finished his sentence when the doctor rushed in, carrying his big leather bag. "Someone is unwell here? I came right away."

The sight of him filled Merula with relief. Unlike Sir Edward, he was a professional who treated patients on a daily basis. He would no doubt establish that Lady Sophia was already coming to her senses again and that no harm had befallen her. He would suggest some fresh air or a few sips of water to help her regain her bearings. Then they could go on admiring the butterfly.

The doctor disappeared behind the screen. They heard his bag thud on the floor.

A few moments passed, stretching into what seemed half a day.

Then the doctor's voice called out, "Why have I been summoned? There is nothing I can do anymore. This woman is dead."

"Dead?" Havilock thundered. "Are you sure? Check again."

Merula pressed her nails into the palms of her hands to keep herself from showing her shock. She had never seen a dead body before, and the idea that the death had actually happened in front of all of them was quite disturbing.

The doctor appeared with a cold look on his face. "I can do many things," he said, "but I cannot revive the dead. This woman has no pulse. Judging by her facial expression and the bluish tinge of her lips, I'd say she died of suffocation. Has anyone harmed her?"

"Harmed her?" Havilock echoed. "Of course not. She was in full view of all of us this whole time."

"No one has harmed her," Foxwell spoke, slowly and carefully, "but she might have been stung by a creature. Could that have caused her to die?"

Merula blinked as she tried to work out what he meant.

The doctor's eyes went wide. "A creature? You mean, a snake or something?"

He glanced across the floor as if he expected a huge adder to come slithering up to him and climb up his leg. "You keep snakes in your home?"

"Of course not." Havilock looked appalled. "All of my samples are dead. Which cannot be said of the creature you brought here tonight, DeVeere. You should have known better." He turned to the door, which was still open following the doctor's entrance, and snapped his fingers. "Dispose of that thing."

Upon this signal, Havilock's butler rushed in, carrying a poker in his hand, with which he struck at the butterfly as it hovered over a sofa.

Its left wing smashed, it fell to the floor.

"No!" Merula cried. She felt as if she were caught in a dream where everything was happening very fast and she could do nothing to stop it. "Uncle, say something. It is not dangerous. The butterfly didn't cause Lady Sophia's death. No, don't . . ."

But the butler's shiny shoes had already trampled the fallen form. In moments the tender creature that had filled her heart with hope and happiness was reduced to dust on the carpet.

Merula raised a hand to her face, wanting to scream her razor-sharp disappointment into the crowded room. It had taken her so much time, effort, and money to make this possible, and her moment of glory had been ruined in a few heartbeats. Their host had ordered the beautiful creature's destruction without being certain it was even responsible for Lady Sophia's death.

"We need the police," Foxwell said in a cold tone. "That man"—he pointed at Uncle Rupert—"hated my aunt. He poisoned her on purpose."

Reeling under this second blow, Merula jerked her head to look at Uncle Rupert. His eyes bulged as the red spots on his cheeks faded to a chilly white. He looked as if he would be next to collapse and need the doctor's assistance.

"Stop this." Royston's words were a quiet command. Everybody looked at him. "Do we really want to be like those people in Limehouse who scraped off their wallpaper, believing it was killing their children?"

The doctor said with a tight expression, "Can you blame people for looking for a reason when four of their children waste away in just a few weeks' time? No cause was ever found."

"Exactly," Royston said. "Nobody established with absolute proof that those children died of poisoning, let alone that the alleged poison had come from the wallpaper."

Normally the idea of lethal wallpaper would have intrigued

Merula, but the presence of the dead body behind the screen chilled her to the bone. The end had come suddenly, without warning, and from what? How?

"There is arsenic in certain shades of wallpaper dye," Foxwell said in a weighty tone, apparently eager to demonstrate his knowledge of the subject. "And arsenic is indeed poisonous. Sir Edward here mentioned a mottled color and her lips. He thought it was poison right away. Foul play!"

Merula had to admit Sir Edward had looked flustered when he appeared from behind the screen. Upset by more than having to attend to an ill woman. Had he really realized at once that Lady Sophia had been poisoned?

Everybody stared at Sir Edward now, waiting for an explanation. He straightened up slowly as if trying to regain control of a situation that was too much for him. "Like I said, I was an army doctor years ago. During campaigns abroad, homesick or frightened young soldiers sometimes . . . took their own lives."

Merula swallowed. Such actions were usually kept very quiet for the sake of the families involved and the reputation of the army. That Sir Edward freely shared this proved he saw a need to do so.

Sir Edward said, "As they fell ill, I was called in to attend to them, but of course there was nothing to be done anymore. I must confess that some of the symptoms I saw with Lady Sophia just now could indicate . . . poisoning. Her behavior before she collapsed, gasping for breath, turning red in the face, can all show that a poison was causing speedy suffocation."

"Poisons are usually administered by ingestion," Royston said.

Havilock cried, "Are you accusing my champagne?" He took a step toward Royston as if he wanted to grab and shake him.

Royston held up a soothing hand. "I'm just saying we need more information before we draw any sort of conclusion about what happened here."

Merula was relieved that someone was trying to address this rationally, but Foxwell laughed grimly. "It is clear enough to my mind. I can testify that Lady Sophia drank nothing after we arrived here. We had just had dinner at her house, and she didn't want to drink anything when we arrived. Her symptoms started after the butterfly sat on her arm."

People murmured their agreement. They looked with disgust at the place where the butler had trampled the insect.

Someone said in a raspy voice, "Didn't the doctors in the case of the poisonous wallpaper claim that the victims inhaled the arsenic by simply being present in the room where the wallpaper was?"

At once people edged toward the door as if they feared some lethal residue might be left on the air.

Her heart pounding at the idea that her butterfly could have killed someone, Merula fought for composure. Royston was right: they had to stay calm and rationally work out what had happened. Was Foxwell's assertion even true? Hadn't Lady Sophia gasped when the glass container was still in place? Merula had then ascribed it to her shock at seeing such a large insect, but what if she had already begun to feel ill?

And, yes, now that she thought about it, Lady Sophia had also been waving cool air into her face with her fan while Havilock escorted her to the place of honor. Had she felt as if she couldn't breathe well? They should ask Foxwell if Lady Sophia suffered from lung trouble or the like.

Havilock was saying, ". . . for the police to figure out." He nodded at his butler and a footman, who closed in on Uncle Rupert and pinned his arms at his sides. Uncle Rupert didn't flare at this treatment but stood with his head down as if all life had ebbed out of him.

Merula swallowed hard. The police couldn't ask Lady Sophia exactly when she had started to feel ill. Would the officers be interested to know when the symptoms had begun or question Foxwell about possible causes for the death? There were dozens of witnesses right here who would declare that Lady Sophia had died after an insect of unnatural proportions sat on her bare arm.

An insect brought there by Rupert DeVeere, who, according to Foxwell, had hated the dead woman.

Merula had no idea why Uncle Rupert would hate anyone, let alone this particular reclusive lady, but he had acted earlier as if he'd wanted to avoid the lady in question, and right now he was not defending himself in any way.

A strong arm grabbed her round the waist, and she was shepherded out of the room as if she were near fainting. She tried to protest, but there was no way to fight Royston's persuasiveness, for it was he who held her. Her chest ached with sharp stabs of pain for Aunt Emma and Julia, who were innocently enjoying themselves at a ball, unaware that their husband and father was about to be arrested.

She gasped for breath to speak clearly. "How dare you? I am not leaving my uncle's side. That would be like an admission of guilt. The butterfly did nobody any harm, and I intend to stay and prove it."

"How? Nobody is going to listen right now. If you want to prove something, you must take another route," Royston retorted, pulling her to the front door. "Those fools just destroyed the evidence."

"Evidence?" Merula echoed, puzzled.

"You have more of these things, I presume?" he queried hurriedly.

"In my conservatory, there is another cocoon that has not yet hatched, but what—"

"Excellent. Just what we need." He had opened the front door already and yanked her into the cold night air outside.

Merula almost tripped as her companion rushed her down the blue stone steps.

Calling out to a passing hansom, he managed to halt it and drag her in with him. He glanced at her. "The conservatory is at your uncle's house?"

She nodded. He called the address out to the driver. The hansom lurched as the horse jumped forward under the coachman's urging whip.

Merula leaned back against the cushions and stared at the man beside her. He had simply forced her to come with him without even explaining what he had in mind. She had to admit there had been little time to explain anything, but still it wasn't her way to follow a man blindly. And Uncle Rupert had even called Royston a disaster magnet, urging her not to associate with him. In the current trouble, Royston might be more of a burden than a help.

"I believe I've made a mistake," she said, sitting upright. She put as much conviction in her voice as she could muster under the circumstances. Lady Sophia's flustered face and terrible staring eyes were seared into her memory. A woman who had wanted to attend a quiet night of scholarly discussion had died minutes after her arrival. Merula believed in earnest that it had not been her butterfly's doing, but deep inside she knew she couldn't be completely sure. After all, it was an animal from a wild and exotic place, about which they still had so little knowledge.

What if she herself was the guilty party, even if she had acted in innocence?

Resisting a shiver, she said, "Please ask the coachman to

turn around and bring me back to Lord Havilock's house. I must support my uncle." *I must accept my part in this, whatever will come of it.*

"Lord Havilock will not be able to protect you from his guests' wrath," Royston countered in a calm tone. "Lady Sophia was powerful and respected. Your uncle will be blamed for her death. Especially after their recent argument."

"What argument? I know Foxwell just said my uncle hated her, but that isn't true. My uncle doesn't hate anybody. He is the kindest and most soft-spoken man I know. He doesn't judge or condemn people on a whim and—"

Royston laughed softly. "You misjudge what happens to a man when he is humiliated. Even the meekest spirit can be taunted to retort."

"I don't understand."

Royston said with a sigh, "It seems that this Simon Foxwell, who is cast as her heir, was taking too much interest in your cousin, Julia DeVeere. He was even seeing her in secret, making plans to elope with her."

Merula stared at him. "Julia, run away from home? That can't be. She would have told me." Her mind was reeling at the possibility that her cousin had been about to change her life so drastically, for a man she had barely met, and had not even told her. Had not even betrayed herself by little things that . . .

Or had Merula perhaps been so caught up in her butterflies, her books, and her plans for tonight that she had not listened well? Had she missed the signs, had she . . .

Failed her cousin, and failed her family?

Royston continued, "Lady Sophia didn't consider Julia well-bred or educated enough for her nephew. Julia may be the daughter of a lady, but she has no title of her own, and Lady Sophia wanted her nephew to make a much better match. She told your uncle in no uncertain terms that he couldn't expect to profit from her fortune by an alliance."

Merula stared at Royston. "I know nothing of this. Lady Sophia hasn't visited our home to speak to my uncle, I'm sure of that. Is it not just rumors?"

"I was there when she told him. It was a scene if I ever witnessed one. At his club. As a woman, Lady Sophia should, of course, not appear there, but she never much cared for rules if she wanted to have things her way."

"She came to my uncle's club? She told him Julia wasn't good enough for her nephew in front of all his friends and relations?"

"Exactly." Royston held her gaze. "You understand what that means. Lady Sophia publicly declared war on Rupert DeVeere, and now she is dead. Died shortly after the butterfly that Rupert DeVeere supposedly hatched sat on her arm."

All strength ebbed from Merula's body, and she sank back into the hansom's padding. This was bad indeed. Her uncle had had a most compelling motive to wish Lady Sophia harm. To get even with her for the insult, yes, but also to pave the way for an alliance between his daughter and the nephew who would, after Lady Sophia's death, inherit her entire fortune.

Houses, land, stock, horses, jewelry.

Men had killed for less.

But Uncle Rupert would never kill. It wasn't in his nature.

Her mind raced to find a logical explanation for what had happened in that room. Anything other than that the butterfly had caused the death. "The doctor said it was suffocation. What can cause suffocation?"

Royston shrugged. "Strangulation with a scarf, for instance. But we were all with her when she collapsed. No one was strangling her."

"And how does poison cause suffocation? So quickly? Didn't the doctor mention that in this case you brought up, of the allegedly poisonous wallpaper, the children wasted away in a matter of weeks?"

Royston nodded. "Yes, but why is that relevant?"

"Well, I've heard about poisoning cases where people became bedridden and died, and their family and even the doctor believed it was something they had eaten or a contagious illness. Only later was it believed they'd been poisoned. But in all of those cases the people were ill for a few days or a few hours at least. How can a poison kill someone so fast as we witnessed with Lady Sophia?"

Royston held her gaze as if he wondered how she knew of poisonings, a subject kept well away from young ladies.

He didn't ask, though, but explained, "That depends on the poison. In India there are snakes whose bite can kill people in a matter of moments."

"But butterflies do not bite or sting. If they hadn't been so stupid as to destroy the butterfly, I could have shown everybody on the spot, under Lord Havilock's microscope, that butterflies have a tongue with which to drink honey but no teeth to bite and no stinger like a bee or wasp."

"Of course," Royston said in an ironic tone. "Those people would have just let you capture that thing to look at it under a microscope. I wager that they are right now clamoring for your head."

The idea of an incensed mob, not consisting of street rabble but of the most powerful men in London, was fearsome indeed.

But Merula wasn't about to despair yet. "Because I fled. Because *you* made me flee."

She gave him her best angry stare. "What was going through your head for you to do such a thing?"

"Your beautiful dress would only get stained in prison."

She stared at him in disbelief. "Excuse me?"

Was this some kind of ill-timed joke?

Some men of the higher classes who had never had a care in their lives made light of everything. Maybe this gentleman by her side even considered these shocking events a refreshing change from an otherwise dull evening?

At her expense!

Royston made a reassuring gesture with his hand. "What I'm trying to say is that I had no wish to see you arrested with your uncle and locked up while some incompetent constable does nothing to ascertain your uncle's innocence. The police might be capable enough of dealing with murderers who wield a knife or pistol, or even those who slip poison into someone's morning broth. But the subtleties of this case obviously go far over their heads."

Case? Who did he think he was? Some sort of lawyer or consulting detective?

Clenching her hands into fists, she shot at him, "First you tried to play inventor with your steam-powered coach and your hair tonic, and now you think you can dabble in solving crime? I won't let you wager my uncle's life, my family. This is not a game."

Royston threw her a dark look. "Far from it," he said between gritted teeth. "I've witnessed once before how a hasty conclusion destroyed a life. Several lives, in fact. I won't let it happen again."

She had no idea to what he was referring, but the tight lines in his face made it clear he was remembering something infinitely painful.

Something intensely personal too, more than just a case he had read about in the newspaper or a thing that had happened to a friend.

He continued, "Besides, I feel I'm to blame. I shouldn't

have been so skeptical, challenging you to release the butterfly."

He held her gaze. "I do realize you released it for my sake. To prove that it was alive. If you had just kept it behind the glass, Lady Sophia might have died anyway, but your butterfly would have had nothing to do with it. Now we need proof that it wasn't the cause of her death. And your second cocoon is that proof. A friend of mine has a laboratory and can establish without a doubt that there is no poison in the animal that can kill a human being."

Merula shook her head. "I will not let you dissect my other *Attacus atlas*."

"Not even to save your uncle's neck?"

"Lord Havilock will stand by Uncle Rupert. He is a level headed man; he knows butterflies do not kill."

Royston shook his head. "As soon as the word poison was mentioned, Havilock realized he might be accused. It happened in his home. He was so quick to deny his champagne had anything to do with it. If he can blame your uncle so nobody looks at him, he will certainly do so."

Royston held her gaze. "Everybody who was there tonight will point the finger at your uncle so they can all go scot-free. It's as simple as that. Their testimonies will be worthless because they won't say what they actually saw but what they *believe* they saw. I wager that, right now, people are declaring they witnessed Lady Sophia being stung. That they heard her cry out in pain or something. They will claim that they knew from the moment they detected the butterfly behind the glass that it was extremely dangerous. They will all have some story, if only to make themselves interesting, or because they are afraid. The police will be clueless about the butterfly's true nature and readily believe whatever they are told. After all, what else will they have to go on?"

CHAPTER 3

The hansom dropped them off in front of the beautiful home that had been her haven ever since she could remember. As she looked up to its warm stone and sleepy windows with their curtains drawn, Merula's chest contracted with remorse at what she had, unwittingly, set into motion

Royston moved as if to take her by the arm, as if he sensed her emotion and suspected she needed physical support, but afraid a friendly touch would unsettle her even more, she shook him off.

Her mind couldn't dwell on feelings right now, whether pain or regret, but had to be fully focused on finding the other butterfly and taking it to Royston's friend with the laboratory so they could learn more about its properties.

She wanted to march up the steps and ring the polished bell so the butler could let them in. But Royston caught her elbow and shook his head. "Let's go in by way of the servants' entrance, without announcing our arrival at the house."

"What for?" Merula asked.

He shrugged. "Word of the disaster will travel fast. If the butler knows we are in the house, we might not get away with the evidence to have my friend examine it. We need to buy ourselves some time."

She hesitated a moment, then acknowledged that he was probably right. She took him into a narrow alley beside the house. At the back, a few steps led down to a door. She tried it, and it was open. She shot him a quick look. "Aunt Emma would be upset to know this door is open at night. But then Lamb has to be able to leave and come back in without the butler knowing about it."

"Lamb?" Royston inquired.

"Her name is Anne, but we already had an Anne, so everybody calls her by her last name. She has an elderly mother who can barely take care of herself. Lamb's brother has moved away from the city, and she is now the only one this old woman can depend on. The butler is less than sympathetic to such needs, so Lamb made an arrangement with me."

"With you?" Royston hitched a brow. "You can decide such things in this house? But you are just a niece, I heard."

"And the only one who cares." She gave him a sad smile. "Aunt Emma is very good to the servants in terms of paying them fair wages and giving them their days off, but she wouldn't allow a maid to leave often, believing it sets a bad example for others. She is always afraid that something will upset the smooth operation of the household. So I discussed the matter with Cook, who agreed Lamb's old mother needs her daughter's help. As long as Cook doesn't get in trouble because of it. She can't afford to lose her position here either."

"Seems like a delicate balance to maintain," Royston said. "Are you such a diplomat?"

She studied his expression to see if he was teasing her, but he seemed to be in earnest. With a rush of surprise, she realized he had answered her questions about suffocation without saying it was no subject for a lady. He had even welcomed her suggestions about how the death could have come about. Now he seemed to admire her for her tactful treatment of the servants. What sort of odd man was he? To hide her confusion, she said quickly, "Let's go in now."

She pushed down the door handle and went in ahead of him.

Through a storeroom, they came into a large kitchen, where a thickset woman was dozing in front of the fire.

Merula put a finger to her lips, and they both tiptoed past the sleeping figure and came into a corridor. Merula's heart was beating fast, and all her senses seemed heightened. She heard every creak and tick in the house as if she were entering it for the very first time. As if she were a burglar coming in to steal a precious family heirloom.

"Here we are," she whispered and led him through the first door, then the second.

"It's not a dry heat in here," Royston said. "How do you create this high humidity? By letting water evaporate?"

"Yes, the orchids need it. They can't stand a splash of water directly on their roots. Then they die." She smiled at him. "The secret of good orchids is the right amount of water."

Royston reached up and loosened his necktie, then slipped out of his jacket and hung it over his arm. He looked around, quickly taking in everything from the tropical flowers growing on a dead tree trunk to the wooden contraption against the wall where her butterflies hatched. "You devised this?"

"There were plants here already. My uncle let me have it for my research. I mean, um, plants and things are not really his interest. He's not very practical when it comes to making things. So I designed that." She pointed at the pupa cabinet, hoping it would distract him from asking more questions that would expose her secret.

Walking closer, Royston studied the cocoons pinned to the back of it and the ledges on which hatched butterflies sat. Some of them had no wings it all, just tiny crinkled rudiments on their backs. In some, these were already developing into flaps, still flat and fragile, while others had full-blown wings and were trying them carefully.

Royston leaned over and let his eyes travel back and forth between the specimens of the different stages of wing development. "It's amazing," he cried out, "as if they are unfolding."

"I think it's more like filling with air, like when you

puff your breath into a glove and the fingers inflate," Merula said at his shoulder.

He glanced at her, taking in her expression with one probing look. "This is your work," he said with certainty, "not your uncle's."

She flushed, remembering his earlier observation to that point at the lecture. Her attempts to pretend she had merely assisted her uncle with some practical things, such as choosing plants and designing the pupa cabinet, hadn't been credible at all.

Royston continued before she could deny it, "Your uncle knows next to nothing about animals. Still he is praised for doing important research in which even the Royal Zoological Society is interested. He could be invited to meet the queen, while you do all the real work. Why on earth does he take credit for your accomplishments?"

"You can answer that question for yourself. Because nobody would allow me in. I am a woman. You heard them earlier. They do not even accept Uncle Rupert telling them anything, whether he has the support of the Royal Zoological Society or not. They would never listen to me, a mere girl with what they call fanciful ideas."

Merula knotted her fingers. "Perhaps it was presumptuous of me to think I knew anything about nature. I studied books, but I have no experience with live animals. I feel so responsible for the present trouble." As tears stung her eyes, she focused on a practical issue. "How do you propose to take the cocoon along? It's fragile."

Royston held up his jacket. "I can wrap it in this. The layers of cloth will protect it and also provide some warmth. My friend doesn't live far from here, and he has means to take care of it. While he investigates its possible toxic capacities, we can ask around as to who might have had reason to want Lady Sophia dead."

Grimly he added, "Apart from your uncle, of course. The scene at the club ensures that half of London knows about his argument with her. That is, unfortunately, a powerful motive."

Banging rang out in the nightly quiet.

Merula looked up, her heart skipping a beat at this sudden disturbance. "What is that sound?"

"I wager it is the police at your front door." Royston straightened up. "We have to leave."

Merula shook her head. "Impossible. There is but one way out of here, through the double doors, ending up in the corridor where they will see us. We must hide here until they have gone again."

She pulled out the pin from the back wall and transferred the large cocoon to rest in his jacket. Together they wrapped the cloth around it. Merula took him by his sleeve and directed him to a corner where there were several large bushes in pots. "Behind this. Quickly."

They crouched side by side, waiting, listening for sounds that would indicate feet coming for the conservatory. Merula knew that, if they were found here, their last chance of proving the butterfly was not the cause of Lady Sophia's death would be gone. They would then have to depend on the police to sort it out. And after the picture Royston had painted her about the false witness statements that would be given, she had little confidence in the outcome.

The banging came closer, and suddenly with a crash there were several men in the conservatory, shouting, asking where the poisonous creatures were. The edge in their voices betrayed their fear, reminding her of how little Merula had sung loudly every time she had to go up the deeply dark stairs in the DeVeeres' country estate where something evil might lurk to grab at her.

The heavily gilded family portraits of frowning gentlemen hadn't helped, or the gargoyles grinning under the roof's edges. Everything had seemed to breathe disapproval or malice there. She had always released a sigh of relief when they could go back to London and her nights of terror were over until the new summer season came around.

"There," a man called out. "A cupboard full of insects."

Merula didn't dare straighten herself to look at what they were doing. She might be seen. She might give away the man who wanted to help her and the cocoon carefully wrapped in his jacket.

A hacking sound resounded.

Merula grabbed Royston's arm, pinching. "They are destroying all my butterflies. The little ones have done nothing wrong."

She wasn't even sure he could hear her anguished whispering over the crashing as wood was torn away and splintered. She closed her eyes a moment to lock out the reality of these events.

Then a nervously high-pitched voice cried, "We have to burn everything in here to cleanse it of the evil."

Merula scooted closer to Royston. "Are they mad? They could set the whole house on fire!"

Should she rise and try to explain to them that they were taking this too far, that the butterfly hadn't killed Lady Sophia?

But she knew nobody would listen to her. These men were frantic. They'd rip the jacket out of Royston's hands and crush the cocoon. Then they'd set fire to the place anyway. Their fear would turn them into spooked horses that break into a gallop and thunder along, trampling everything in their path.

There came the hiss of a flame, then a shout. "Let's get out of here!"

There was a shuffle of feet and the thud of the doors.

Royston rose to his feet, clutching the precious bundle. Flames licked up the tropical plants and crawled across the floor, which was strewn with wood slivers. "It's pointless to try the doors," Royston said. "They will have secured them. Besides, if we try to escape that way, they may still catch us and destroy our evidence. We have to get out some other way."

"There is none," Merula said. Panic began to rise in her throat as she realized their position. They were trapped in a burning room, with the only exit closed off to them. Unless they were willing to deliver their sole hope of saving Uncle Rupert's neck into their pursuers' hands.

She looked up at her companion. "You should not have interfered."

He snorted. "On the contrary, my lady. My presence here will be your salvation. Hold this."

He pushed the bundle into her hands and moved to her workbench. With a giant sweep, he emptied it of tools and utensils. Glass broke as vials of liquid rained to the floor.

"Gently," she protested, upset with the rough way he treated her carefully collected work. But the metal clanging of the falling tools mixed with the crackling of fire reminding her sharply that her efforts were going to waste anyway. And this man she had just met tonight was trying to save her life.

Why? To make up for the lives destroyed that he had briefly mentioned on their way here? To do better than in a previous instance where he had been unable to act?

Royston grabbed the edge of the bench and moved it a few yards so it stood under the lowest point of the slanting glass paneling. "Give me that big pruning tool," he called to her as he clambered onto the bench.

She ran to hand it up to him.

He struck at the glass with one arm, using his other to protect his face. The normally moist heat in the conservatory was turning into dry desert air as the fire consumed everything that would easily burn.

Glass broke, shards raining over Royston. He tore off

his necktie and wrapped it round his hand for protection, then broke the remaining points of glass from the window frame. He reached down to her. "Come up with me. Be careful of the glass."

Holding the bundle gently against her chest, she let him pull her up to stand beside him. He took the coat from her and nodded at the window frame. "Pull yourself up and out."

She gave him a startled look, and Royston began to laugh. "Oh, please don't tell me you don't know how. Did you never climb out of your window at night to roam outside and look up at the stars?"

Or check in the stables to see if the foal had already been born, or make sure Uncle Rupert's rich friends had not abused the horses? Apart from her fear in the dark staircase of the impressive house, life had been sweet during long summers in the country.

"Try," Royston coaxed her, kneeling on top of the workbench so she could clamber onto his back. She hoped the heels of her dancing shoes wouldn't poke too painfully into his flesh. But he was strong and stable, an excellent support as she grabbed the frame and hauled herself up, then out. Her palms ached from gripping so hard and her heartbeat droned in her ears, but the cool air lapping at her face was delicious. She took two deep breaths before steadying herself and reaching back to him. "Give me the bundle."

In an instant she had it and crawled away from the hole,

pushing herself against the glass panels that were still unbroken. The heat radiating from the conservatory reminded her of the danger still lurking there, and she held her breath as Royston emerged. He looked around.

"If we go that way," she nodded with her head, "we can lower ourselves into a small backyard. It's closed off by a gate, but the lock is poorly maintained and easy to open."

As he hitched a brow at her, she added innocently, "So I heard from Cook when she instructed Lamb about alternative ways of entering the house at night after she had taken care of her ill mother."

Her cheeks flamed at the idea he might not believe her and think she herself was sneaking around London in the dead of night. What kind of idea did he have of her?

But what did it matter what he thought? He had helped her save the cocoon, and she was grateful for that. She would be more grateful still if his friend could prove Uncle Rupert's innocence in the matter of Lady Sophia's demise. But that was all. After that they need never see each other again.

In fact, she was sure she would prefer never to see him again, never to be reminded of this terrifying night and her shameful retreat from Lord Havilock's home.

Don't worry, she said to herself as she lowered herself into the backyard. *After this disaster, Uncle Rupert will forbid you to ever go out again. You won't research plants and butterflies anymore, nor attend lectures like Sir Edward Parker's. You won't even be allowed to read books on the subject. After all, your interest in zoology caused all this misery.*

In the distance, the bells of the fire brigade rang out.

Royston caught her arm. "Listen! At least they had the decency to call in the fire brigade, not risking the entire house and neighboring buildings. I'm sure the fire will be doused soon and your home will be saved."

He leaned over the lock on the door and *hmm*ed, then dug into his pocket and produced a small knife. As he put the tip of the knife into the lock, he said, "But the police will be looking for you very soon. The butterflies were hatched under *your* guidance. Your uncle may want to protect you and try to keep you out of it, but once they start questioning him thoroughly, he will have to admit he knows next to nothing about insects."

The lock clicked open, and Royston opened the door. Ushering her into the street, he continued, "All eyes will then be on you."

Merula swallowed. Her uncle had status and influential friends who could, to some extent, protect him. Who would hire the best solicitors to try to get him released. His case would look grim because of the influential victim and his recent argument with her, but it might not be completely hopeless.

However, once suspicion shifted to her, she would stand alone. Her interest in a male-dominated field would be considered unnatural. Her dubious parentage would make it even worse. The papers would start writing about the murderous foundling, the girl without a past who had caused the death of one of the most respected members of London society. Lady Sophia's family would call for her head, led by the arrogant Simon Foxwell, who had been quick enough to assume foul play to begin with.

Ashes from the burning conservatory wafted on the air around them, staining her precious dress. She was in the street with nothing but the clothes on her back. In an hour her life had spiraled out of control, and she had no idea how much worse it might still become.

"Come." Taking her arm to lead her into the darkness, Royston said slowly and insistently, "Proving *your* innocence and saving your future should now be our only objective."

CHAPTER 4

As they hurried through the darkened streets, Merula expected people to throw suspicious glances at them and stop to stare after them. But the elderly gentleman who came up to them, his cane ticking on the pavement, passed them with his chin on his chest, his eyes on the stone in front of him and his mind probably on some deep mathematical problem or perhaps the latest chess move in a game with a friend.

Merula enjoyed drawing conclusions about people from their appearance, and this man with his white beard and narrow chest had something bookish and scientific about him that placed him, in her mind, as a private tutor with a well-bred protégé or perhaps even at a college in Cambridge.

A little boy with dirty cheeks who should have been in bed by now ran past them, clutching an apple. Royston, securing his jacket containing the precious proof to clear her uncle, looked after him with a frown. "He probably didn't acquire that by honest means," he said with a nod.

Merula hitched a brow. "How can you know that? Maybe he is on his way home from his grandmother's house."

Royston shook his head. "You have an idyllic view of how these people live."

"What people exactly?"

"Poor people. You have probably never set foot in one of the poorer areas. Have never seen their houses or the way they have to scrape by to make a living. You think that when the servants at your uncle's house leave, they go to places with rooms as big as yours and bed linens just as white and clean."

"Absolutely not," Merula said. She didn't want to tell him how she had caught one of the youngest maids at the laundry cabinet running her hands over the silk sheets Aunt Emma adored and smelling each and every item to inhale the scent of soap so utterly foreign to the environment in which she herself had grown up.

This girl was the middle daughter of a family of seven children. The eldest son was at sea and two others were working as carpenters making coffins. She had told all that to Merula without shame, her cheeks flaming only because she had been caught red-handed.

Merula had told her that it wasn't a good idea to finger household goods, as it might get her dismissed, but had promised her in the same breath that she could have some soap to wash her own clothes at home to show her family how well off she was in her new position.

The girl had been delighted and reported back after her

day off that everybody had wanted to smell her clothes, not just her family, but all the children who lived along the street and even the grandmothers who sat out on their wooden chairs cleaning vegetables for dinner or making brushes from pig hair.

"That is not good," Royston said by her side.

Merula froze. "What is not?" she asked in a whisper.

Royston nodded ahead of them. "The tall house with the lights on in the upper floor is my friend's. But look who's guarding it."

Merula followed his glance to a policeman who was standing on the edge of the pavement like a sentry, letting his eye drift casually across the traffic that passed in the street: a hansom, an empty cart, a cyclist balancing precariously across the cobblestones.

She asked, "Do you think he is there for a reason? Does he suspect we are coming here?"

"I doubt the police can be so well organized in so short a time." Royston produced his watch and opened it, studying the hour with a frown. "The men who came to your uncle's house to set the conservatory on fire weren't with the police. They were probably Havilock's footmen, who were in a panic after the death at the lecture. Or, rather, who were made to panic by that irritating nephew of Lady Sophia. Foxwell was far too eager to accuse your uncle of murder."

"After what you told me during the ride, I'm not surprised. Foxwell must have known about the public row between his aunt and my uncle. He must really believe my uncle is humiliated enough to retaliate."

"But if he really cares for your cousin Julia, would he accuse her father and risk him ending up on the gallows?"

Merula frowned. "Who says Foxwell really cares for Julia? Perhaps he only flirted with her as he does with every handsome young woman and his aunt mistook the matter for a genuine affection. Perhaps the entire argument with my uncle wasn't necessary, but Lady Sophia didn't know that."

Royston nodded. "Possibly. Nevertheless, we have a policeman who might see us entering the house. Judging by the look of him, nothing escapes his eye. Two people who look . . . well, slightly disheveled will immediately have his undivided attention. And even though he won't know now that we are wanted, he might learn that later tonight and lead the police straight to us. He's probably eager to spot something—a pickpocket or a burglar prowling—to get a promotion. The last thing we need if we want to find refuge with my friend."

Merula bit her lower lip. "Doesn't he have an entire round to make? He can't stand here all night watching these few houses. He might miss something important somewhere down the street."

"There's another possibility," Royston said with a sour expression. "That he is not eager and out to spot anything but just acting like he's watching something so he doesn't have to walk about. For all we know he could be the laziest man on the force and determined to grow roots here for the rest of the night."

Merula sighed. The cold wind made her shiver, and she wasn't keen on staying out much longer in her stained dress. "What about the cocoon?" she whispered. "It needs constant high temperatures to hatch. We may be disturbing the process and hurting the only evidence we have to clear Uncle Rupert."

Royston nodded. Suddenly his expression lit, and he gestured. A tall boy with a hat pulled deep over his eyes sauntered over and looked at them. "You want me, governor?" he asked in a brass tone.

Royston dug his hand in his pocket and produced a coin. "This is yours if you can get that policeman away from there. Take him down the street or whatever."

The boy cocked his head. "How would I do that? If I stick out my tongue at him, he's not coming after me."

"I think a resourceful young man like you can think up something. Especially when the inducement is right." Royston produced another coin.

The boy's expression went from suspicious to tempted. He glanced at the policeman's broad, stern back, then at the coins in Royston's palm. Fast as lightning, he snatched them up and said, "You don't have much time, governor." And away he went, sneaking in the shadows of the houses to get behind the officer.

"What is he going to do?" Merula asked with a wriggle of excitement in her stomach.

"I have no idea," Royston responded, "but as he warned us, we won't have much time. We'd better be quick about our part." He kept his eyes on the officer, who was still blissfully ignorant of what was about to happen.

Suddenly, without warning, a figure shot from the darkness behind him and bumped into him. In an instinctive movement, the policeman grabbed at the boy's waist to arrest him, but he was too late. The boy already had the policeman's baton and rushed off with it, brandishing it like a sword. The policeman swore and ran after him.

"That's our cue." Royston put his arm around Merula to usher her quickly across the street and into the house of his friend. "The only thing that can go wrong now is him not opening the door."

Merula's exultation died a sudden death. "Not opening the door? You mean that we will be standing there on the steps in full view of everybody passing by to ring a bell that might not be answered? Doesn't your friend have servants?"

"He tries to have servants," Royston replied enigmatically.

They were at the foot of the steps already and walked up, Merula feeling as if she were going up to a podium or an auction block. "Hurry," she hissed.

Royston had already rung the bell. They heard it jangle somewhere deep within the house. On the ground floor everything was dark; only upstairs did bright light fill the windows.

Royston said, "He's probably experimenting, not listening to anything."

He rang again.

Merula glanced anxiously in the direction in which the policeman had vanished after the little thief. Did she already see his imposing figure coming back? Did she see the light from the street lanterns gleaming off the brass on his uniform?

The door opened and a tall man with long whiskers and a little scar under his right eye stared at them with mild surprise. "You need not have rung so often, my lord," he told Royston in a tone more rebuking than polite. "I'm not deaf."

"I didn't expect you here." Royston pulled Merula inside and closed the door. He exhaled a moment. "Now, Bowsprit, if somebody comes to the door asking for me or a Miss Merriweather, we are not here, you understand?"

Most servants would have thought this a rather odd command, even if they were too well trained to show it, but Bowsprit didn't even move a muscle. He just nodded. "Very well, my lord. Pleased to meet you, Miss Merriweather. You look cold. Shall I make a fire in the drawing room?"

"No, no fire or light in the downstairs rooms," Royston barked. "Upstairs."

"But . . . Galileo is conducting a rather . . . odd experiment."

Royston looked over Bowsprit's rolled-up shirtsleeves. "I take it you are assisting him? The things you do when I'm not around. Then again, it's most useful you're here so you can help us sort out this whole sordid affair. Up we go."

Bowsprit reconciled himself to the inevitable and walked ahead of them with the dignity of a first-class butler, even though his bare arms, covered with reddish-blond hair, and mud-caked boots didn't really fit the image.

Halfway up the stairs, Merula caught the smell. Her face scrunched up as she tried to determine what it was exactly.

Royston cast her an apologetic look. "Try not to pay attention to it."

That was almost impossible to do, as the smell was pungent and pervasive. When they entered the room, it wafted full at them, coming from the haze in which a shadowy figure stood with a vial in his hand shouting, "This is it! This is it!"

Bowsprit waved both his hands in the air to disperse the haze and even went to throw open a window, but Royston overtook him and gestured to him to leave it closed. He quickly pulled all the curtains shut so that curious people in the street couldn't see any figures moving inside the room.

Merula hovered near the door, holding a hand to her face to block out the smell and wondering if it was in any way dangerous to inhale. She hadn't forgotten the remarks of the frightened people at the lecture about poisoned wallpaper and inhaling poisonous scents or gasses. She knew a little about chemistry and how some substances when they became warm released gasses into the air that could, for instance, be explosive. She hoped it wasn't the case here, as a Bunsen burner was cheerfully flaming on a bench in the middle of the room, surrounded by all kinds of bottles, jars, and vials.

Some vials contained liquids, either brightly colored or pale like water; other had crystals in them that were deep purple or bright blue. On the floor were scratch marks and stains as if the wood had been burned away by something spilled. Still, the man holding the foul-smelling vial was not even wearing gloves.

Had Bowsprit just called him Galileo? Could that be his real name?

"You do realize what this means?" the owner of the house exclaimed, waving the vial. "What has been considered impossible for generations has been proven to work after all. I have to make notes of this sequence."

He inhaled exultantly, only to add with a sigh, "If I could remember exactly what I did. I've been at it since dawn, and somehow the attempts have become a little muddled in my mind."

Royston said, "You can help us with a more urgent problem." He cleared some books from a small table, under protestations from their host that he was ruining the order, and put down his jacket. Folding it open, he exposed the cocoon of *Attacus atlas*.

Their host, having put the foul-smelling vial in a holder, approached with narrowed eyes. "Must be imported from the East," he said in concentration. "No species of this size around here. New? Can I actually be the first to see it hatch?"

"We do hope it will hatch and you can see it," Royston confirmed, "but some precautions may be in order. The creature that crawled from one of these earlier today is under suspicion of murdering a member of the Royal Zoological Society."

"You are jesting," their host said.

Royston shook his head. "I was there when it happened. The butterfly sat on a woman's bare arm, and within moments she started to gasp, her eyes rolled back, and she collapsed. Smelling salts couldn't bring her back to consciousness. A doctor declared her dead shortly after. And everybody clamored that it was the butterfly's doing and that the person who had brought it to the lecture should be punished."

Galileo's pale eyes descended on Merula. "That would be you?" he asked. "I assume that my dear friend Royston has abducted both you and the twin of your alleged killer to have me establish there is no poison in the creature and you are not to blame for the lady's death? My, my, how gallant of you, Raven."

Royston flushed under his collar and said, "You have it all wrong. The police have the alleged guilty party in custody. Miss Merriweather's uncle."

"But you are right," Merula said hurriedly, "in the sense that I am the one hatching the butterflies in my uncle's conservatory. I took *Attacus atlas* with us to the lecture tonight to show it off. I released it because I was told it couldn't be a real, live creature. Then it descended on Lady Sophia's arm and . . ."

"Lady Sophia?" Galileo echoed. "Poor Albert Rutherford's widow?"

"I don't know if we should call him poor," Royston protested, but Galileo said, "He was a poor fellow for having to be married to her. She wanted to be in control of everything. Including his collection. Did you know he has the most amazing poisonous darts from Africa? They are projected by so-called blowguns. A very effective means of killing someone—if you can get close enough, of course."

"And Rutherford had those darts lying around the house?" Royston asked at once.

Galileo nodded. "That's what I heard."

Royston looked at Merula. "Maybe Foxwell found an ingenious way of introducing such an exotic poison from a dart into Lady Sophia's food or drink. Who says she can't have already been poisoned before she came to the lecture?"

Galileo looked doubtful. "The poisons on those darts work extremely fast. They were meant for hunting, you see. For taking down monkeys and all. If the poison took too long to work, the monkey could just jump away and the hunter would never recover his prey."

"A matter of minutes, you'd say?"

"Moments, sooner. That is why exotic poisons are so exciting. They do something to the human body that is quite extraordinary."

"I thought cyanide also causes a pretty quick death," Merula said.

Royston raised his hands. "Before we go into all kinds of violent death . . . Galileo, please put this cocoon with your other insects where it will be warm and safe until it hatches. Remember what I said, though, and treat the creature that will come out of it with utmost respect. I don't want to have it on my conscience to see you lying dead on the floor."

Galileo made a scoffing sound. He put on a glove and picked up the cocoon. He went to a door leading into another room. When he caught Merula watching him intently, he gestured for her to follow him.

Royston said, "You're not afraid of snakes?"

Merula hitched a brow at him. "Not as long as they are caged."

Galileo waited for her in the doorway, spreading his hands in an all-compassing gesture. "Welcome to my little sanctuary."

The room was hot, as it had been in her uncle's conservatory at home. The shelves were not lined with books but with glass containers holding branches, rocks, and sand. Glancing past the containers, Merula first had the impression they were empty, until in the fourth she spied a large black spider sitting in the shade of the branch in its cage. It was as large as the palm of her hand and quite hairy.

Suppressing her instinctive revulsion, Merula went closer and studied the creature, then let her gaze return to the cases beside it, which she had at first thought to be empty. In the first, a snake just as green as the leaves of the branch in its cage lay perfectly still between them, not even blinking its eyes.

In the second container, a bit of black body was visible in the back. Shiny, it seemed coated with something.

"Scorpion," Galileo said at her shoulder. "Really aggressive creatures. Kill quickly with a sting of the tail. I can explain better when he's showing more of himself."

"Where did you get all of these?" Merula asked.

"My first snake came from an importer of Eastern goods who actually found it in a crate with folding screens. It had slipped in and come all the way across the sea. The man was petrified and called me in, and I caught it and brought it here. Unfortunately, I have not been able to train it to respond to either whistles or milk."

Merula had to laugh. "I think Arthur Conan Doyle took a little artistic license there."

Galileo smiled in response. "I'm not complaining. The idea of killing someone by letting a snake in through a ventilator shaft is so brilliant I wish I had thought it up myself. Although I still believe a good doctor would have spotted the bite marks. Snakes have quite powerful jaws, and the injection of the poison would leave discoloration, bruises if you will. Conan Doyle's story says that they looked for signs of poison on the dead woman's body and found nothing. I readily believe that they wouldn't have found anything inside her body, as they didn't know to look for snake poison. But the bite marks!"

He raised both hands in desperate disbelief.

His expression turned thoughtful as he leaned over to her and said, "This lady of yours who died, Lady Sophia— was there a mark on her arm where the butterfly sat? Any sign that it bit or stung her, or some agent perhaps causing skin irritation?"

"Shortly after she collapsed, she was moved behind a screen, away from prying eyes. I don't recall seeing anything on her arm, but I didn't have a chance to look closely. Her face was very mottled in appearance. And she had difficulty breathing. The former army doctor who happened to attend the lecture said the symptoms all suggested poisoning."

Galileo nodded. "Our friend Raven has a point, though; it could have happened at her home. Before she left for the lecture. Not all poisons are fast acting. Well, I assume they will look into what she ate and drank before she left."

"*We* should look into that," Merula said. "We should do anything we can to gather proof that my uncle is not involved."

She looked around her at the cages with all the extraordinary creatures. "Suppose someone died and they said one of your creatures was responsible just because they don't know anything about them and are afraid of them. How would you feel?"

Galileo surveyed her from under his fine brows. His skin was pale, probably from spending all of his time indoors doing his experiments. Or could he be addicted to opium or other drugs? Uncle Rupert had warned her that some people in scientific circles induced their creativity by artificial means.

Galileo said, "Do you believe your butterfly was the cause?"

"No, but I can't be sure. In hindsight, I feel I should never have taken the chance of letting it fly free. I did it because Royston claimed it wasn't real, a mere fabrication of paper and threads."

"Ah, so that is why my gallant friend is now helping you out. He feels guilty for his part in it." Galileo went to a glass cage and stared into it. Without taking his eyes off the contents, he gestured with a narrow hand for her to come stand by his side.

Inside the glass case was a strange creature, much like a lizard but with brighter colors and eyes that looked as though they were inserted in tubes. As Merula watched it, she noticed that the eyes moved in different directions, as if the creature was looking both ways at the same time.

"It's a chameleon," Galileo said. "You see, it can observe its surroundings from various angles. It can also adjust its color. If I were to take it off that branch and put it on a red apple, its skin would turn red."

"Really?"

"It's a trick to escape predators who can't see him when he has the same color as his surroundings." Galileo glanced at her. "Most people live like that, blending in with their surroundings, adjusting themselves so as not to stand out. If you stand out, you are conspicuous and you might end up under attack."

Merula waited for him to go on. When he didn't, she said, "Your collection is rather extraordinary and your chemical work not without risk."

"I stand out, you mean," he said with a smile. "I chose to. I understand that your uncle is accused of murder and you feel guilty and compelled to look into his case. It will make you stand out, and it might even put you in danger. If I believe you, if only for the sake of argument, and assume Lady Sophia did not die because of the butterfly, someone poisoned her and is letting your uncle take the blame for it. That someone won't be happy when you start asking questions and casting doubt on what really happened to the unfortunate lady. So instead of feeling guilty and compelled to assist, you'd better ask yourself if you really want to stand out and get yourself into danger. If it is your conscious choice, it will be much easier to face whatever will come your way."

"I see your point," Merula said.

For a moment, the despair of being locked in the burning conservatory came back to her, and a shiver ran down her spine. Those men had taken an enormous risk and still they had done it, hastily, unstoppable. There had been but a few men who knew about tonight's events. Once more people knew about it—and if it made its way into the papers, the whole of London would soon know about it—more aggression would be aroused, more impulsive actions undertaken. She was a fugitive now and dragging other people into misery with her. Royston, this kind scientist by her side, and his rather unusual manservant with the mud-caked boots. People she longed to know more about, but people she also didn't want to put in peril for her sake.

She asked softly, "In bringing the butterfly here, I'm involving you. Do you mind? We can take it along again and leave."

Galileo shook his head. "I'm delighted with the chance to take a closer look at it. I have nothing of a reputation I can lose. You can stay here with me for the time being. If you don't mind all these creatures living under the same roof."

"As long as they are safely behind glass, I don't mind."

"Excellent." He looked over her stained dress. "I have nothing to offer you by way of clothes."

Merula flushed at his frank reference. The night was upon them, and she could hardly go to bed in this dress. There was also the morning to consider, and how could she conduct an investigation into Lady Sophia's death with nothing to wear?

"I have an idea," she said. "Your man Bowsprit, does he go all over London?"

"Naturally. But he is not my man Bowsprit. He's Raven's valet."

"Really? But what was he doing here tonight?"

"Helping me out with my experiments. He's fascinated by science, and I can't blame him. Inside vials, discoveries are made that will impact the future of mankind profoundly."

Galileo took a deep breath as if he was about to launch into an explanation of this lofty statement, but a look at her made him reconsider. She had to look every bit as exhausted as she felt. Galileo said, "Bowsprit can go wherever you need him to go."

"Good. Then I need to give him some instructions." Merula turned away and then added, "Thank you for showing me these fascinating creatures and telling me about how they live."

"Thank you for not fainting when I showed them." Galileo grimaced. "I can't get anybody to come and clean here. Not even for twice the wages others pay."

Merula laughed softly as she returned to where Royston was waiting. He was in deep conversation with Bowsprit but stepped away from his valet when he saw her. "How do you like his horror cabinet?"

"I had never seen a chameleon before. Or a live snake. Only pinned-up skins. Now, I have a request."

Royston smiled at her tone. "Out with it."

"Well, I have only this." Merula gestured at her clothes. "I need to sleep, and we have to get out tomorrow and investigate."

"Excuse me, but *I* have to get out tomorrow and investigate." Royston leaned back on his heels. "You will stay here and wait for the butterfly to hatch so you and Galileo can study it closer."

"We have no way of knowing when it will hatch. And we need so much information. We need to divide tasks. Galileo can determine whether the butterfly is poisonous or not. Bowsprit will need to talk to Lady Sophia's servants here in the city and find out what she ate and drank before she left for the lecture. If there was anything unusual: if she complained about not feeling well, anything arriving for her shortly before she left, a box of chocolates, anything that might have contained the poison."

Royston was listening with a frown, but he didn't interrupt her.

Merula continued, "You and I must go to Lady Sophia's house in the country. I know from my cousin Julia that Lady Sophia spent most of her time there. She didn't like social gatherings."

"Not to mention her husband's entire zoological collection is kept there," Galileo said. "It's worth a fortune, they say."

"And now Foxwell inherits it all," Royston said pensively. "We might be able to learn something useful about him from the servants there. The house is open for the public, I believe, because of its curio cabinet."

Merula clapped her hands together. "Perfect. We can pose as innocent travelers stopping off to see the curio cabinet we have heard so much about. News of Lady Sophia's death will not have reached them yet, so we must go there right after breakfast."

Royston made a mock bow. "Anything else?"

"Yes. I need clothes. Bowsprit has to meet our maid Lamb at her mother's. She always goes there to take care of her. Ask Lamb to pack a small case for me with what I need for a few days and take it out the back of the house, where she can give it to Bowsprit."

"After the fire, the police might be there," Royston protested.

But Merula looked at the big standing clock and said, "I think they will be gone by now. Maybe they have one man watching the house from the outside to see if I return. But Lamb should be able to get in and out."

"What if they also watch the back," Bowsprit said, "and they search the case she is carrying? As soon as they realize it's clothes for you, they will question her about your whereabouts."

"Yes." Merula frowned at this unwelcome possibility. "I can't get poor Lamb into trouble. She's a nervous little thing as it is."

Bowsprit's expression lit. "She can carry out the washing or items that supposedly need mending. She can put your clothes and what you need under sheets and pillowcases. The police are probably not watching the back of the house, but if they are, they will not consider her actions suspicious. She has to do it in the morning then. I will bring it here so you can change before you leave for Lady Sophia's country estate. You will have to sleep in that dress. I'm sorry about that."

Merula shrugged. "I'm already glad I don't have to sleep in the street." She yawned. "We'd better all turn in, because we have a long day ahead of us tomorrow."

CHAPTER 5

Merula slept fitfully, dreaming of butterflies that flew over her uncle's house, spreading a fine powder that set everything on fire. Through the haze, she heard Galileo call out to her about a chameleon and needing to adjust, while Bowsprit carried a basket with laundry that toppled as Lamb rolled out of it, clutching a bird without feet.

When she finally got up, stiff and uncomfortable in her crinkled dress, she felt as if she hadn't slept at all and that the weight of the world was on her shoulders.

But once she entered the room where Galileo lay on his stomach on the floor comparing formulas in notebooks while Royston poured coffee in cups without saucers, her mood cleared. The hot coffee filled her with pleasant warmth, and when Royston even managed to conjure up sausages with scrambled eggs, Merula dug in and soon felt like a new person.

"I have a perfectly good dining room downstairs," Galileo declared from his prostrate position, "but he doesn't want us to use it because of some exaggerated idea that someone might peep in from the street and see you."

"Well, your windows are at street level, and we can hardly keep the curtains closed all day," Royston said as he poured more coffee. "I won't feel at ease until Bowsprit is back here with Merula's belongings and we can be on our way out of the city."

Galileo didn't reply. He slapped a notebook, uttered a stifled "I knew it," and scrambled to his feet to make more notes on some papers on a desk in the corner.

Last night, Merula had been too distracted by their ordeal, the foul smells, and all the exotic animals in the other room to pay much attention to the furniture, but now she realized that the room was filled with pieces that would make an antiques dealer salivate.

Galileo's desk had beautiful ivory birds and flowers worked into the surface and decorated brass handles on the drawers, while the chairs on both sides of a tall cabinet had delicate twirled legs and embroidery with golden thread on the faded pillows. Little dents in the wood and tears in the fabric, however, suggested that no thought had been given to preserving these lovely pieces, as the owner was obviously more interested in his research than in his possessions.

Royston froze. He lifted a hand. "I hear footfalls on the backstairs."

"Must be Bowsprit." Galileo threw down his pen and

stared up at the ceiling as if he intended to catch another idea.

Royston said, "We can't be sure. Merula, go into the other room. If someone intruded, I don't want you to be there when we deal with him."

It sounded rather ominous, and once Merula was in the other room with the door shut, she had to fight the urge to open it a crack and spy to see what was happening. If someone had come in, who could it be? What would he want? And how would Royston "deal with him"?

She did hope he wouldn't use violence and get himself into trouble with the police. For now they might be fugitives, but they were innocent fugitives. If they started hurting people, intruders or not, they would be making themselves culpable and increasing Uncle Rupert's troubles.

The door burst open, and she shrank back. Royston stood on the threshold. "It's Bowsprit with your clothes," he announced.

Merula exhaled in relief and hurried out to meet the valet.

Bowsprit stood leaning over a big basket he had put in a chair. "Your maid," he said with a sour face, "was very hard to persuade that I could be trusted. She wanted to come here herself to see you. I told her she'd only be putting you in danger. She was shocked at all that had happened, even though she wasn't in the house when the fire occurred."

"How are Aunt Emma and Julia doing?" Merula asked, her throat constricting at the idea of the nightmare her family had been thrust into.

"I think your aunt had a nervous fit, but Lamb said she often has those and it's never serious."

Merula suppressed an involuntary smile at Lamb's frank assessment of her aunt's condition.

Bowsprit continued, "Your cousin Julia was more worried for you than for herself, it seemed."

"That's sweet." Merula picked up the basket, which was surprisingly heavy. "I will go dress myself. Oh . . . did you hear anything that might be worthwhile?"

Bowsprit shifted his weight. "Of course I took the liberty of asking Lamb a question or two. She doesn't like Foxwell, even though she has never seen him. But there is talk in the household that he's after Julia—and not because he really cares for her."

"Still, that is odd," Merula said. "Foxwell is heir to a fortune. He can get any woman he wants. Julia is charming, I daresay, but in the circles in which he moves, he must be able to do better. I mean, in terms of money or connections. Why would Foxwell have set his sights on Julia?"

"Another thing we need to look into." Royston rolled his shoulders back. Merula was gratified by this slight evidence that he too had not slept well. "Foxwell's reason for accusing your uncle of murder is tied to his interest in Julia, so who knows how it might all be connected? Why are you not changing?"

Thus admonished, Merula rushed away with her basket, still wondering at the weight of it.

In her temporary quarters, she laid the basket on the bed and looked through it, silently thanking Lamb for knowing exactly what she couldn't do without. She changed into a dark blue dress that was perfect for traveling and put on the pendant that she usually wore under her clothes. It had been left with her when she had been delivered to her aunt and uncle as a baby, and the engraving on the pendant contained the only clue to her parents' past. A name, perhaps of a place in Dartmoor.

Wearing it made her feel connected to her origins somehow, even if she didn't know what her parents had been doing in Dartmoor, if they had married there, or lived there, or whatever else the place name might mean.

If it was even a place name and not something else altogether. Aunt Emma had made it clear often enough that she didn't want Merula to ask questions about her mother and father, let alone try to find things out about them on her own.

Topping her neatly pinned-up hair with a small hat, Merula studied her features in the mirror. She couldn't deny that she was excited at the prospect of leaving London and taking a little day trip into the countryside, admiring its lush views, and exploring Lady Sophia's famous curio cabinet. It was rumored to contain mounted animals of some rare, recently discovered species, and Merula couldn't wait to see those.

Still, their journey had a very serious purpose, and she needed to prepare herself to ask the servants innocent questions that would reveal how relations had been between Lady Sophia and her future heir, Foxwell.

Maybe also between Lady Sophia and other members of the Society. Couldn't it be somehow significant that she had died at a zoological lecture? In any case, men with knowledge of rare animals might also know more about poison than other people did.

Pensive, Merula walked downstairs to find Royston waiting for her in the hallway. He reached out his hand to her, helping her down the last three steps of the stairs. "You look lovely."

"Not overdone for the occasion, I hope?" she asked quickly. She was never quite certain if he meant the things he said or was jesting in his semi-cynical way. She had heard Royston didn't have a high regard for women and had affronted his sister-in-law terribly the first time he had met her, but to Merula he had been nothing but kind and considerate, taking her ideas seriously and almost treating her like an equal. It was rather confusing, especially considering that, by working with him to solve the death, she was placing everything she held dear in his hands.

"Not at all overdone," Royston assured her. "We will have to introduce ourselves somehow, I suppose, so we will be Mr. and Mrs. Dutton from Walkingwoods, staying with friends in London who recommended the curio cabinet to us. I can't quite decide yet what my profession will be. There are so many exciting possibilities. I could, for instance, be an engineer working to bring electricity to every home."

Merula shook her head at his excited tone. "Better choose something general like merchant. You don't want them to remember you later on."

Royston's face fell. "I guess not," he agreed reluctantly. "That's a shame. When one goes to play a part, one should choose a part that demands rather good playing. A merchant . . . Bah!"

Merula suppressed a smile. Outside they found a hansom waiting for them. Royston grumbled, "I would have hired a carriage and let Bowsprit drive us if he wasn't needed here in the city. I hope we can discover something telling from his inquiries into Lady Sophia's last hours before her death. If we could prove she received a mysterious parcel that might have contained poisonous food items, we would be a long way toward diverting attention from your uncle."

Merula nodded. They climbed into the hansom, and the coachman urged the horse into motion. The morning air was fresh and clear and the sun was shining. The excitement Merula had felt about this unexpected journey returned full force. Why waste the morning worrying about her uncle being under arrest and her family in turmoil when she could try to do something to correct all of that while also enjoying the ride and hoping to learn something interesting at Lady Sophia's country estate?

"So Lady Sophia was married to an influential member of the Society?" Merula asked Royston.

"Yes. You should ask somebody else about him, really, as I never had much contact with him. I never visited him at his house, and I only knew Lady Sophia by name before I saw her last night."

"Yes, I heard she was quite reclusive. I wonder if that was just her nature or if there was a reason for her behavior. It might be telling if we knew what it was." Bad health? Or had Lady Sophia perhaps been afraid of meeting someone?

"*If* there was such a reason," Royston said in a warning tone. "From now on, as we are building theories to explain Lady Sophia's death, we must only introduce *facts* as basis for our assumptions. If we start building a theory with nothing but assumptions and speculations, it's bound to come clattering down around our ears, burying us under a ton of rubble."

"Maybe you can pretend to be an architect," Merula said sweetly. "Your comparisons already fit that occupation."

Royston shook his head, but she saw the hint of a smile around his lips and in his eyes. "I mean it, Merula. We are investigating the death of a woman we barely know. Every assumption we make about her character, habits, or daily routine might lead us further away from the truth instead of closer to it. We must make sure we find out all we can about her so that we are equipped to reconstruct what happened before she died and what could have caused her collapse."

"I believe that in cases where people collapse, doctors often don't know what caused it. They can establish that the heart stopped beating but not why. Do you think that we, mere laymen, can really find out what killed her?"

Royston said, "Maybe our ignorance works to our advantage. I've heard of cases where the police were led astray because some smart inspector immediately started to follow a clue, or what he believed to be a clue, ignoring other evidence that might have led him straight to the culprit. So thinking you know it all, or have experience, can actually sometimes be a disadvantage. We are coming at this with an open mind. We will look at everything we learn and try to see a pattern. Something that connects the how and the why."

"I think the how will be hardest," Merula said pensively. "Galileo asked me if I had seen a red rash on Lady Sophia's arm where the butterfly sat, any sign that it had stung or bitten her or otherwise caused her to react to it. But I can't say for certain. Do you know?"

Royston shook his head. "But I don't have to know. Before we left, I instructed Bowsprit not just to find out all he could about Lady Sophia's last hours but also to get in touch with someone who works at the mortuary and try to find out anything peculiar about Lady Sophia's body. Things like you mentioned: a rash, a response to a poisonous agent that might reveal to us how it was administered to her. She was in full sight of all of us the entire time."

Merula nodded. "It is very odd. She must have felt unwell already when she walked in. She was waving furiously with her fan."

"Aren't those fans just fashionable? I think she merely wanted to show off that she had ostrich feathers." Royston's face contorted in distaste. "Ladies walk about with entire dead birds on their hats to show off that they can afford to pay for it. I can't say I find it very charming."

"Do they kill the ostrich for the feathers?" Merula wondered. "Or does he shed them and then they are collected? I think peacock feathers are simply collected and the bird is not killed for them."

"I have no idea," Royston said. "I never made a study of the ostrich."

After a short silence, he added with a self-deprecating smile, "Or of any other bird, for that matter. I'm afraid I'm a zoology novice and you have the better of me."

Merula glanced at him. Again she didn't know if she should take him seriously or not. She had never before heard a man admit that a woman knew something better than he did. Royston had to be jesting somehow, feeling certain that he could play his part as experienced zoologist with verve.

But Royston just stared ahead with a serious, almost grim expression. She wondered what he was thinking about.

★ ★ ★

The driveway to the estate was lined with tall oak trees whose leaves rustled in the morning breeze. In the meadow to their right, a beautiful black horse tossed his head and trotted along with the hansom for a while, halting abruptly when the gate didn't permit him to go farther. Scraping with his powerful forehoof, he threw up clumps of grass and earth.

Merula gasped when she saw the house with its high facade, two wings, and turrets that each carried a small golden weathercock. A fountain in front of the house sprayed water high up into the air, and a gardener trimmed the box hedges.

In the distance, birds sang. Merula distinguished at least five different calls. This had to be a delightful place to live. No wonder Lady Sophia had hidden out here rather than staying in the bustling city.

As they approached, they saw a man of middle age standing on the front terrace speaking with someone through the half-opened front door. The person inside wasn't visible, as the door was kept at such an angle that the visitor couldn't get in. He seemed to want to enter desperately, as he had placed his hand on the door and was exerting some pressure, judging by his reddish cheeks.

Or perhaps they were red with anger, for as the hansom halted in front of the steps leading up the terrace, Merula heard the man shout, "I want my emperor penguin back right now. I have not come out here to be insulted. It is my property and I demand it back."

"His what?" Merula asked Royston.

He shrugged. "I thought he said emperor penguin. A penguin is a kind of bird from the deep south. They live in a world of snow and ice, I was told. And although they are birds, they can't fly. Their wings aren't developed enough. They walk upright, like we do."

Royston stepped out of the hansom and said, "Like this." He put his heels together, turned his feet out to form a V, clasped his arms closely to his body, and waddled forward in a strange, shuffling gait.

Merula suppressed a peel of laughter. "I can hardly believe that."

"You ask him." Royston reached out to help her out of the hansom. "He apparently owns an emperor penguin, so he should know."

He told their coachman to let the horse trot through the estate's park a little so he would stay warm while they went inside. The coachman nodded and let the horse walk.

Royston pulled Merula's arm through his, leading her up the steps. She had to remind herself that they were Mr. and Mrs. Dutton from Walkingwoods, out here for a nice little day trip to a curio cabinet. As a wife, she had to throw her husband admiring glances and hold her tongue while he spoke with the servants.

The man at the door said, "I demand to speak with Foxwell."

Both Merula and Royston froze. If Foxwell was there, he'd recognize them in a heartbeat. Their whole plan would go awry at once. But as the hansom was already moving away, it was too late to turn back now.

The person inside said something, and the door snapped

shut with a vicious click. The man banged on it with his fist, shouting, "You cannot do this! I will go to the police."

The door stayed shut. If Foxwell was in there, he didn't seem to want to show himself to this particular visitor.

The man, now deep red with rage at the treatment he had received, exhaled in a huff.

Royston called out to him, "Is the curio cabinet not open for the day?"

The man turned to them. He had a short white beard and lively blue eyes. He said with a scoff, "Curio cabinet. You're here for that? Full of borrowed items they show off as if they are their own. But they are not. Remember that when you go in there and have a look around. Just borrowed it is, all of it. And they refuse to return it. Stolen, it is!"

"You mean," Royston said, "that you lent this family some of your zoological specimens for them to put on display, but now that you want them back, they don't want to return them to you?"

"Exactly. My emperor penguin cost me a fortune. Newly discovered species. You might have read about it in the papers."

Although she hadn't, Merula nodded. "From the deep south, yes? A bird that can't fly because his wings aren't fully developed." She was just repeating what Royston had told her, but it worked.

The man nodded eagerly. "Exactly. You are a most astute young lady." He reached out his hand to Royston. "Newbury."

Royston grabbed his hand. "Dutton. I'm a merchant from Walkingwoods. We're just taking a little tour, and we heard that the curio cabinet here is very good. But if it is, as you say, stocked with borrowed items, I feel . . . uncomfortable visiting it."

Merula didn't like being ignored, but she realized it would be best to let the men discuss the situation and let Royston learn as much as he possibly could.

Newbury said, "I used to come here all the time when Lady Sophia's husband was still alive. I advised him on the curio cabinet. He wanted to set it up, but he didn't have the expertise to know what pieces to purchase. I advised him. How sorry I am now that I did! I said that it might be best to borrow some expensive specimens first and see how well the cabinet did at attracting visitors. He agreed, and I put him in touch with collectors, who were all eager to contribute. He was a very well liked man, and well respected. Unfortunately, after his sudden death, his widow refused to return our property to us."

"Why would you want it returned?" Royston asked. "If the cabinet was doing well, why not continue as you had before the death?"

"Ah." Newbury scoffed. He pulled a handkerchief from his pocket and dabbed at his hot face. "Death always changes things. New masters come around. Lady Sophia never had any children, you know, and when her husband died, his entire fortune fell to her to live off for as long as she lived, but with an heir already waiting in the wings, so to speak. Her nephew Foxwell. He is a very unpleasant person, believing he knows about zoology when he simply does not. When he saw the collection, he assumed it all belonged to his uncle, and he refuses to return anything to us who lent it to the cabinet. He turned Lady Sophia against all of us and made her suspicious of us. I come here to ask for my emperor penguin, and I am shooed away from the door as if I am a beggar. Asking for my own property! How dare they."

"But Lady Sophia isn't here right now. Can a butler or housekeeper just turn you away?"

"She instructed them. Or perhaps Foxwell did. I don't know. But I intend to take legal action against them. I can prove it's my emperor penguin, and I will get it back." Newbury nodded firmly and seemed intent on passing them down the steps.

Merula said quickly, "You spoke of having put Lady Sophia's husband in touch with other collectors as well. So there are others who have not had their specimens returned, I presume?"

"I am not the only damaged party, no. Far from it. In fact, I know that Lord Havilock had a fierce argument with Lady Sophia about it just last week. It seems a friend from the Americas is visiting him and wants to purchase some of his apes. But they are in the curio cabinet and thus out of reach. He was quite cross about it. Understandable. The friend will sail back to the Americas in a few days, and if Havilock can't liberate the apes before that, the chance for a sale will have passed." The man shook his head. "A sad business, really. Well, good day to you." And he marched off down the steps.

Royston said softly to Merula, "Well, well, so despite his friendly act with Lady Sophia last night, calling her his guest of honor and all, Havilock had also had an argument with her about specimens she didn't want to return. He had a buyer for them, a one-time opportunity that was about to slip through his fingers. Does that constitute a motive for murder?"

"It would," Merula said, "if Havilock expected Lady Sophia's heir to be more open to his pleas. But I don't really think Foxwell will be. Do you?"

Royston shook his head. "I don't think so, no."

"So what would killing Lady Sophia change then? Murder is so drastic. Why risk it when you aren't sure it will solve anything?"

Royston nodded. "You have a point. Still, we have to look into Havilock's dispute with Lady Sophia about his apes."

"You were with a man last night who was carrying a mounted monkey. Would he know more about it?"

"Justin Devereaux. Perhaps. I could ask him."

Royston turned to the front door. "Let's ring just to see what happens."

They rang, but nobody came to the door.

Royston said, "They must think it's Newbury again and don't want to open up and give him a chance of shoving his foot in. Well, that leaves us locked out as well. We could walk around the house and see if we can knock on a window somewhere and draw attention to ourselves."

They started to walk across the terrace that stretched all the way along the house's front, peeking into the windows. There was a sitting room with heavy oak furniture and paintings on the walls, a library with overfull bookshelves.

"I don't see a single mounted animal anywhere," Merula said, puzzled.

"Perhaps they are kept separate? Upstairs?" Royston hazarded.

Suddenly, from around the corner of the house, a man in a green jacket came at them. Ahead of him, a large mastiff strained on its leash. The dog barked at them and bared a set of excellent, gleaming teeth.

"Away from here," the man called. "Back to your hansom and off the grounds."

"Excuse me," Royston said, making sure he stayed out of reach of the snarling mastiff. "We came all the way from Walkingwoods to see the curio cabinet."

"It's closed at the moment. We don't like snooping about."

"We rang at the front door," Royston said coldly. "But no one appeared. We assumed there was another entrance."

"We are terribly sorry," Merula cut in, trying to sound anxious. "Could you restrain your dog? He looks so fierce."

"We don't like snooping," the man repeated. "Off you go."

Royston turned away, ushering Merula ahead of him.

"He means it," he whispered. "I've seen that fanatical look in men's eyes before. If he releases that dog, we're in serious trouble."

They hurried back to the steps and down onto the gravel. Their hansom appeared from the left and halted to let them climb in. "I think you're treating innocent visitors terribly here," Royston called to the man with the dog. "I will complain about it."

"You do that," the man said, grinning as meanly as the mastiff. "Lady Sophia won't mind."

"No, she won't, as she's dead," Royston whispered to Merula as he helped her into the hansom. "Apparently they don't know yet, as we expected. Still, we have not set one foot inside, and we have no idea how extensive the collection is or why they are so protective of it."

"Maybe it is no longer here," Merula said as she leaned back against the padded seat.

"What?" Royston said, sinking beside her.

The dog still barked, and the nervous horse began to pull with a jerk, throwing them against each other.

Straightening herself again, Merula explained, "Maybe Lady Sophia's husband sold off part of his collection even though some items weren't his. Maybe she couldn't return Newbury's penguin to him because she no longer had it."

Royston nodded slowly. "An interesting suggestion. But we've seen nothing to support it. It's a large house, so the fact that we didn't see any animals as we walked around doesn't mean anything. We'd need to know how many people lent specimens to the cabinet and how many of them actually got anything back. If any of them did."

"Would your friend Devereaux also know about that?"

"If it includes apes, he's interested, so who knows?" Royston leaned back, folding his hands in his lap. "Even though we didn't get inside, the visit wasn't without interest. We should find out just how angry Havilock was about his missed chance to sell. He's all smiles when you meet him, and still something in his eyes suggests he can get angry when he feels wronged."

"Most men do." Merula sighed. "That's exactly the reason people will believe my uncle capable of harming Lady Sophia, as she humiliated him. I know he'd never hurt someone, but who will believe that?"

Royston patted her arm. "We have another lead now. And who knows what Bowsprit may have come up with? I bet you we are making more progress than the police."

But as they rattled into London's inner heart, newspaper salesmen on every corner carried huge signs saying "Arrest in Sensational Butterfly Case" and "Butterfly Conspiracy Reaches Deep."

People rushed to buy the newspapers and stood talking in small groups, pointing out information on the front page to one another.

"Word is out," Royston said slowly. "We can't approach anyone who was at the lecture last night, because they will be reluctant to talk to us and might even try to turn us in to the police. What on earth does it mean that there is a

butterfly conspiracy? And why would it reach deep? Do
they think more people than just your uncle are involved?"

"I have no idea." Merula's stomach was filled with ice,
and she wanted the hansom to turn around and drive away
from all those people talking about her uncle and spreading
rumors that could ruin her family completely. "Perhaps the
newspapers just made something up? I can't imagine the
police giving such statements."

"Bowsprit will have seen this and will bring us the
newspapers when he returns," Royston said. "Let us hope
he has found out something pertinent about Lady Sophia's
last few hours alive."

He glanced at her. "With word of a sensational butterfly
conspiracy on the street, your uncle isn't likely to be released
unless we can deliver hard evidence of someone else's guilt."

CHAPTER 6

When they arrived at Galileo's via the servants' entrance and the backstairs, they found the chemist completely engrossed in releasing a clear liquid drop after drop into a vial filled with bluish liquid, apparently waiting for the instant when some momentous change would take place.

Royston studied his friend's intense concentration for a few moments and gestured to Merula to go into the other room. In passing, Royston picked up a blackboard and the easel it stood on, maneuvering it into the other room.

Merula followed at once. There, among the glass cages with the exotic creatures, Royston put down the blackboard, wiped away the chemical analysis that was on it, and started to write in a legible hand: *Lady Sophia dies.*

Underneath he made three rows marked *Suspects*, *Motives*, and *How*.

Under suspects he wrote *Foxwell* and *Havilock*. Foxwell's motive was *Money* and Havilock's *Return of property.*

The *How* column remained glaringly empty.

Tapping his chalk on the board, Royston said, "I guess the start to the how would be to know what exactly caused the death. Poisoning in general is not very helpful, as we have to know how the poison was introduced into Lady Sophia's body. Food or drink seems most likely. Foxwell assured us that she drank or ate nothing on the spot. Can we believe him?"

"I didn't see her eat or drink. But she was not in my sight all the time." Merula frowned. "She might have slipped a sweet into her mouth right before she entered. My aunt Emma always has something with peppermint with her to suck on during a performance or at a ball. She believes it keeps her mind clear."

Royston nodded. "It would be clever to put poison on something she would consume out of doors so the collapse would not happen in the family circle, where suspicion would automatically fall on those closest to her, that is, Foxwell or her servants. What do we know about her servants, anyway?"

"I assume Bowsprit will be able to tell us more about it once he is back."

"Yes." Royston consulted his watch. "I hope he won't stay out all day thinking we are at the curio cabinet. Bowsprit is very useful, but he has a mind of his own, and he doesn't like taking orders."

"Then why did you hire such an unusual type as your valet?"

"I wanted to give him a chance. He's too clever to just do manual labor at some factory."

"How did you meet?"

"In an opium den. I was asked by a female acquaintance to get her brother out. She had nobody else to turn to, as her friends weren't to know about the young man's addiction. She had arranged for him to go abroad to be cured."

Royston shook his head. "She had this rather annoyingly optimistic view of his situation. Just a change of surroundings, a little horse riding and vigorous walking, and he'd be himself again."

"You do not think it is that easy?" Merula asked. "I know nothing about opium addiction, and to be honest, I don't understand why anyone would try a drug that can make one aggressive or show one things that aren't real. I would be too afraid to try it."

"Count yourself fortunate," Royston said. "Those who don't know such fear and who experiment often find themselves in dire need soon enough. I found the young man in question in the third den I visited. He didn't want to come with me quietly but put up quite a struggle. Bowsprit came to my aid. I noticed he wasn't just strong and able but that he also knew how to deal with the matter without breaking anything in the den and getting into an additional fight with the owners. Once we had wrestled our reluctant charge into a carriage, I asked him to accompany me and help me deliver the man safely to his parental home, and he agreed. I won't shock you with the details of what happened when, upon reaching his home, we came across his father, who had returned early from a business journey to France. Suffice it to say he wasn't happy to discover the state his son was in. Coming home drunk is not a problem in many a rich family, but opium is a different matter."

"Do you agree with that assessment?" Merula asked. "It is far more dangerous, is it not?"

"In its addictive powers, yes, I suppose so. And while young men can indulge in alcohol and cards at reputable clubs, opium is usually found in places where you can get your throat slit. I talked to the father and tried to convince him that his son needed his help, but he turned the boy out of the house, denying he was even his son. There we were, in the street, with a raving young man and a crying sister who had come out after her father had dashed off in anger, with nowhere to go really. Bowsprit quietly said that he could find a place for the young man to sleep off his haze and we could try to send him abroad anyway, as had been the plan. So we did."

"Despite the father not cooperating?"

"He needed not. I provided the money for the crossing, and the girl's acquaintances would wait for her brother in the harbor where the ship docked. Bowsprit had been a sailor for many years, and he knew a few men aboard the vessel who would look after our imprudent charge to ensure he didn't get into trouble on the way."

"You provided the money. How generous. Did you . . . know this girl very well?"

Royston laughed softly. "Typical for a woman to see a romance everywhere."

Merula was indignant at his tone. "It is a logical assumption. Why else would you get embroiled in something so precarious to your good name and reputation?"

"Because I have no such thing," Royston said with a mock bow.

At that moment, the door opened and Bowsprit stepped in. His tight expression relaxed when he saw them. "You are back already. Good. I have someone you can talk to right away." He checked the time on the clock. "He should be in the coffeehouse in half an hour. Lady Sophia's butler. He can tell you everything you want to know about last night."

Royston nodded. "Well done. How about information from the mortuary?"

"I talked to a man who cleans there and saw them carry in the dead body last night. He said they were talking about it having been suffocation. Poisoning, but they don't know with what. He will let me know by way of a message delivered to a bookshop if he learns any more."

"To a bookshop. How discreet of you, Bowsprit," Royston said with a smile.

"I am not using this address, as we have to keep your whereabouts a secret for as long as we can. Have you seen the papers?"

Royston's smile died on his lips. "Unfortunately, yes. Have you purchased some for us to read?"

"Yes, but the information is no good. Just hysteria and no real facts." Bowsprit gestured over his shoulder. "I put them in the other room."

"With Galileo? He might accidentally mistake them for scrap paper and use them to clean his tools or light a fire in the hearth. Bring them in here at once. This is our official investigations room." Royston encompassed the blackboard with a wide gesture.

Bowsprit didn't seem impressed, but he dutifully fetched the papers and spread them out across the faded velvet sofa.

Her heart beating fast, Merula read aloud, "*Last night at a lecture for the Royal Zoological Society, at the home of reputed collector Lord Havilock, a member in attendance died after a poisonous insect sat on her arm.* What nonsense. We don't even know if the butterfly is poisonous or not."

"Go on," Royston said, having closed his eyes, apparently drinking in every word.

"*The lady in question collapsed and died within moments after the insect, a butterfly of inhuman proportions, was released from its cage. It was brought to the lecture by Rupert DeVeere, who is known for his butterfly research and his exotic imports, which he keeps in the conservatory at his home. After the death, the conservatory caught fire. The police are still looking into the cause of this, but it is assumed that frightened servants set the fire in an attempt to annihilate all the poisonous insects before they could kill again.*"

Merula spread her hands. "Can you believe this nonsense? Outsiders stormed in and set the fire, not our own servants."

Royston, his eyes still closed, gestured for her to go on.

Merula read, "*DeVeere was arrested on the scene of the death after the deceased's nephew, Simon Foxwell, accused him of foul play. He insists that DeVeere intended to kill the victim via the poisonous butterfly, as he had recently been embroiled in an argument with her about his daughter's reputation.*"

Merula cringed at the idea that more nonsense about Julia and Uncle Rupert's wishes for her to marry well would be spread around, but there the article took a turn in another direction: "*Foxwell claims that the death of his aunt is part of a conspiracy to defraud her of the extensive zoological collection built by her late husband, which is kept at her country estate. Although formerly always open to the public, the collection will now be kept behind closed doors and guarded to prevent the butterfly conspiracy from succeeding.*"

"No wonder we couldn't get in this morning," Royston muttered. "Foxwell must have sent word out to the estate at once."

"Maybe he went there himself?" Merula suggested.

She shivered and wrapped her arms around her shoulders. "He might have been there and seen us, from an upper story window. If he knows we are looking into the death . . ."

"Yes, then what?" Royston asked, snapping his eyes open. "He can hardly expect us to sit back quietly while your uncle is accused of murder. This newspaper article implies he planned it. Not an accident, not culpability for letting a dangerous animal fly free, no, a deliberate assault on Lady Sophia. The same as taking a club and bludgeoning her to death."

He took a deep breath. "Gross exaggeration or conscious misrepresentation, that is hard to tell. But it's clear
that Foxwell intends to start a war against your uncle and
have him convicted by public opinion before there is even
an inquest into the cause of Lady Sophia's death. He is moving very fast, not just pointing the finger, but also locking
the zoological collection away from prying eyes. You could
be right in your suggestion that it is no longer there, or
only partly. We have to find out more about that."

"But how? You just said when we saw the newspapers
spread all about the city that we can't openly approach anyone who was at the lecture last night. What sources are
then left to us?"

"I can try Justin informally. He won't believe just anything that is written." Royston nodded firmly. "For now,
we must focus on Lady Sophia's butler and find out what
she did right before she died. We have to find some other
way in which she might have been poisoned."

He pointed straight at the blackboard. "The suspects are
important and their motives carry weight, but the third
column is essential. The how. If we can resolve that, it will
lead us to the other information."

★   ★   ★

Merula had never been in a coffeehouse before, as it wasn't
a place young ladies went, alone or in the company of
others, at least not if they wanted to keep their reputation
intact. She had often longed to see more of London than

her visits to Regent Street with Julia allowed, but it had never crossed her mind to go out and venture into forbidden areas just because she wanted to. Her family's good name was dear to her, and she'd never embarrass them. But today those considerations no longer mattered, and as Merula stepped inside, she took in everything with a long wide-eyed look, wondering what kind of life these people had who regularly met here over the coffee served in wide cups without saucers and fatty pork pies not even offered on a plate but on a crinkled piece of paper.

In a corner, a nervous-looking man was waiting for them, rubbing his hands together and glancing around as if he didn't want to see anybody he knew. He got to his feet when they came over and bowed his graying head. "Buckleberry, my lord. Your valet said that if I told you all I know, there is something in it for me."

Royston threw Bowsprit a quick glance. "Of course I am willing to reward you for volunteering information in such an important case. I do hope that you will not adorn your tale in the hopes of a bigger reward. We are merely interested in the truth, not in fabrications."

Buckleberry's clean-shaven face flushed. "I swear to you, my lord, that I would never lie in such a case. My mistress's death is a terrible thing. Especially as she was so afraid of dying."

"Of dying?" Royston echoed, with a hitched brow. "She was under threat?"

The butler sank back on the simple wooden bench against

the wall, and the three of them seated themselves opposite him to listen to his tale.

Buckleberry said, "She wasn't under threat from people, my lord, if that is what you mean. It was her own imagination. She was always very particular, about food, things she did and did not want to eat. Small items, for instance, like peas, she avoided like the plague. She mashed everything that came onto her plate. The maids often joked she might as well just eat broth all day long, as she mashed everything into this unrecognizable mush."

"Was she afraid of being poisoned?" Royston pressed.

"How would mashing her food help then?" Buckleberry asked.

"How would mashing her food help in any way?" Merula wondered out loud. "Do you know when she started doing that? Was there a particular incident that caused it?"

"Not that I know of, Miss, but I have only worked for her for a few years now. And only in the city. She lived at her country house most of the time. I have never been there."

"Why did she keep a full household here in the city if she was rarely here?"

"Her nephew, Mr. Foxwell, is often here. He uses the house as if it were his own."

The slight disapproval in Buckleberry's tone could not be missed, but Royston didn't pounce on it. "So you had to maintain the house in the city mainly for Mr. Foxwell's stays there?"

"He loved the clubs, my lord, and came home late most any night."

"Intoxicated too?"

"Not that I noticed. I think he can either take alcohol very well or he doesn't drink quite as much as other young men do."

"Very wise," Royston said. "And did Mr. Foxwell eat with Lady Sophia last night before they left for the lecture?"

"Yes. They ate and drank all the same things. Lady Sophia mashed her food, of course, as she always does, but they both ate from the same dishes and drank wine from the same jug."

"Could the poison have been introduced into her glass or onto her plate before food was placed on it?"

"Not likely, my lord. She always checked her plate and glass as she sat down to eat. She claimed to be afraid something would be on it that she might accidentally swallow. She held up her glass against the light and checked her plate, even running her finger over it."

"So she was afraid of poison." Royston glanced at Merula.

Buckleberry said, "She was particular in many things, my lord. I heard from the maids who serve in her bedroom that she never slept lying down but sat upright, leaning back against her pillows. At least three pillows she wanted on her bed, else she'd make a terrible scene. She always wanted water beside her bed. Not just a glass full of it, but a jug with water beside it. She never ate chocolates or bonbons, claiming they stuck to her palate. But she used to love chocolate as a girl, I heard, and even when she was just married, her husband brought her boxes of chocolates often, as gifts."

Buckleberry looked pensive. Then, leaning over, he said, "If I can speak frankly, my lord?"

Royston nodded encouragingly.

Buckleberry said, "I think she was somehow sick in her mind. I can't quite define it, but you can sometimes see it in elderly people. They become quite possessive of their things and think everybody wants to steal from them. They claim items have gone missing when none have. I have seen it happen to my mother-in-law. Quite sad. She was such a kind woman all her life, but in her later years she became quite difficult to deal with. She even accused her own daughter, my wife, of stealing from her. Now Lady Sophia, she was the same lately."

"She accused people of stealing from her?" Merula asked. In light of the zoological collection, this might prove interesting. Was part of the collection missing and had Lady Sophia known this? Had she *not* been mistaken in believing she had been the victim of theft? Had she been right? Had it been a motive to murder her?

Buckleberry said, "Yes, she had a companion for ten years. A very competent woman who could deal well with all of her demands. Out of the blue, Lady Sophia accused Miss Knight of having stolen a gold earring. She threatened to dismiss her if it happened again. I had never seen the good woman out of sorts in all those years, but she was close to tears, confiding in me that with an accusation of theft to her name, she'd never work for a well-to-do family again. I can't understand how Lady Sophia could make such an accusation lightly. But then, she was changing. Becoming more aggressive and afraid."

"And this happened after her husband died?"

"It was becoming worse and worse of late."

Royston nodded slowly. "Was this companion, Miss Knight, with her last night?"

"You mean at the lecture? No, my lord, Miss Knight used to go everywhere with her, to the dressmaker's but also to balls and lectures inasmuch as her ladyship attended any. Until Foxwell came along. He then accompanied her everywhere. Miss Knight was quite upset about it at first. But she had to accept it, of course."

"Yes, of course. I think we need to speak with Miss Knight. Where is she now?"

Buckleberry said, "Normally she'd be at the house caring for her ladyship. But as Lady Sophia will never come home again, she is probably out and about."

The disapproval was thick in his voice. "She always had a reason to leave the house even though it was not her day off. Most disturbing to the household. The maids complained to me that they also wanted such freedom. I told them to become a lady's companion, then, and that shut them up, as they have no French and can't play music. But in my heart I did agree with them, my lord. Miss Knight should not have acted as if she was so high and above all of us."

"And do you have any idea where she went when she left the house?"

"On errands her ladyship sent her on, she claimed. But I have always thought she was seeing a man." Buckleberry nodded self-importantly. "She was always talking about men as if she didn't need them, but those women often have a secret lover."

"Yes, well, that still doesn't tell us where she is now."

Buckleberry shifted in his seat. "I might have an idea."

Royston hitched a brow. "Yes? That is what we are here for."

Buckleberry said, "Well, it's just a conjecture of course. But this morning she argued with Mr. Foxwell. I think there was some talk about her having to go now that Lady Sophia was no longer there."

"He was giving her notice? With her mistress dead for a few hours? After ten years of service?" Royston's voice rose more with every new, bewildered question.

Buckleberry said, "They never took to each other, those two. I think he was waiting for a chance to get rid of her. And now that Lady Sophia is gone, there is no need to keep a lady's companion about."

"He could have let her stay on for a few more weeks. That would have been decent." Royston glanced at Merula. It was clear he liked Foxwell less and less with every new thing they learned about him.

Buckleberry said, "As Miss Knight knows she has to find new employment, I can imagine she went to one of those agencies that help companions or nannies. I think I once heard her mention the name Grunstetter to my wife, claiming it is the most prestigious agency in the whole of London, maybe the whole of England." He grimaced. "You can count on her to come from the most prestigious agency there is."

Royston nodded. "We will go there at once. I have heard of it and know the address." He glanced at Merula again. He seemed to want to know if she had any more questions.

She looked at Buckleberry. "Are you sure that Lady Sophia and Foxwell ate and drank the same things and that there can't have been poison in anything she took?"

Buckleberry waited a few moments. Then he said, "It would be painful if this came out. In fact, it could be quite disastrous for me. But, as you are looking into my mistress's death and she has always been very generous to me, paying me very well, I want to tell you this. After dinner, when food is left, my wife and I sample some of it. She had bits of the veal from last night's table and I sampled the wine. Neither of us suffered as much as a stomachache. The third maid put veal on a sandwich for her beau who works in the harbor, and Cook's little girl ate the pudding. There was no poison in any of it, I am certain."

"Thank you for assuring us this way," Royston said with a half smile.

Merula asked, "Did Lady Sophia eat any sweets? Did she have anything in her drawstring purse that she might have eaten on the way over to the lecture?"

"Oh, no. As I told you, she mashed everything and she avoided any foods that were hard. She especially disliked sticky and coated things like sweets. I can ask the maids, but I am quite sure she never ate any of that."

"If you could ask if any of them know anything, that might help. Anything peculiar she did before she left the house last night." Royston sat up, leaning his palms on the table. "It seems she must have come into contact with the poison after she left the house. But where and how?"

Buckleberry said, "I will, of course, see if I can find out any more for you, my lord. For now . . ." He waited with an eager expression.

Royston dug through his pocket and handed him a few coins. "This is to show I have faith in you," he said. "I can make it a bearer bond if you have more to tell me. Ask your wife, the maids, any female who worked in her rooms and with her wardrobe if they know anything about her habits or peculiarities that might help us. I have no idea yet what we are looking for, so anything unusual could be of the greatest importance."

Buckleberry had looked disappointed at the sight of the coins, but the word "bearer bond" made him perk up, and he assured them he'd be thorough. They left him seated with his coffee cup clutched between his fleshy hands, a seemingly innocent servant having a moment to himself before he resumed his domestic duties.

"I have no idea if we are getting anywhere with this," Royston observed as they stood outside in the cool wind and mild rain of a grayish afternoon. "But that companion must be able to tell us something. When you've served someone for ten years, you know things."

CHAPTER 7

The Grunstetter Agency was situated on the third floor of a building that also housed a lawyer's office and a stockbroker. Even the stairs were carpeted, and neat brass plates spelled out the names of the various businesses. The solemn silence, however, was broken when they entered the Grunstetter premises. Female voices filled the air in an excited chatter. Six ladies were seated on simple wooden chairs along the wall, one of them in the middle of a tale about being at an exotic market when a hooded stranger placed a hand on her arm. The other ladies gasped and squealed, not even noticing the new arrivals.

Merula glanced past the faces, looking for one that would strike her as belonging to Lady Sophia's companion. As Miss Knight had served for ten years, she couldn't be very young anymore, so the two women who looked only eighteen were dismissed at once.

Four were left.

The woman telling the story seemed too animated and

outgoing for someone who had been described by Buckleberry as high and mighty. Three left, then . . .

Merula studied the faces, not sure whether the intense
brown eyes of the woman on the left or the cool blue ones
of the woman beside the storyteller seemed most likely to
belong to the character she was building in her mind.

Royston stamped on the floor and called, "Ladies! One
moment please."

The storyteller fell silent with her mouth wide open,
her excited expression giving way to regret and accusation
against the man who had suddenly disturbed her moment
of glory.

The others eyed him speculatively, not displeased with
what they saw. He was handsome, well dressed, and obviously well-to-do, so why not give him a moment of their
time? Perhaps he was looking for a companion for his sister
or his wife?

Royston said, "We'd like a quick word with Miss Knight
if she is here."

The woman with brown eyes rose to her feet. "I am
Miss Knight," she said in a pleasant voice. "How can I help
you?"

"Outside in the corridor, if you please," Royston said,
and without waiting for her answer he retreated, leaving her
to follow them.

Miss Knight came out with a flush on her face. She
crossed her arms over her chest and eyed Royston. "You
cannot command me, sir. Not unless you want to hire me."

She glanced at Merula. "Perhaps your wife is in need of a companion?"

Royston didn't admit or deny Merula was his wife. He merely said, "You used to work for the unfortunate Lady Sophia?"

The woman's expression changed from resistant to suspicious. "Who wants to know?"

"I am a consulting detective hired by an interested party. I'm looking into Lady Sophia's death."

"Isn't that the task of the police? I think they even made an arrest last night."

"They did," Merula said, "but we doubt that they arrested the right person."

Miss Knight gave her a cold stare. "And you are?"

"She is my client," Royston said. "I'm sure, Miss Knight, that you are a very observant person and that if your mistress was in danger for her life, you'd have known about it. We desperately need your help."

Miss Knight looked at him. "I have to find new employment because I'm being turned out like a dog. I never did anything to deserve such treatment. But here I am. Why would I help you?"

"Because even if Foxwell is treating you badly, your loyalty lies with Lady Sophia. You were with her for a decade. That is a long period of time to be with someone. You got to know her and you even came to care for her."

"She wasn't an easy woman to please."

"But still you tried. You were shocked when you learned of her death."

"Of course. She had this tendency to think she would get ill and would die, she was fearful like that, but she was in good health really. The idea that she had just collapsed was . . . unbelievable."

"You were not aware that she had a weak heart or anything of that nature?" Royston probed.

"No. As I said, she was easily convinced she might have contracted something, she believed every tale a friend told her about strange exotic diseases, but she was really as strong as a horse."

"Had a healthy appetite, you'd say?"

"She was fussy about food, wouldn't eat certain things. But I think she ate enough to sustain her health. She wasn't thin."

So Merula had been able to see for herself the night before. Lady Sophia had seemed like a strong, healthy woman, except, perhaps, for the reddish tinge in her face.

Merula asked, "Did she suffer from fainting spells?"

"She got upset about stories people told her, but she never fainted as far as I saw. I always kept the smelling salts at hand, though, just in case."

"You were usually with her when she went out?" Royston pounced at this opportunity to learn more. "Yet you were not with her last night."

"No. After Mr. Foxwell came to live with us, he started

to accompany her. He didn't like me to be present as well."
Miss Knight's lips compressed.

Royston said, "I barely know him, but he seems like a
very . . . determined man. Likes to have things his way."

"Exactly. He acted as if he owned her."

"Interesting choice of words. Can you expound?"

Miss Knight sighed. "I just told you that I am about to
be dismissed. I have no wish to speak ill of my mistress or
anybody else in her household."

"Come, come, Miss Knight," Royston said, "you are
about to be dismissed. You think that is unfair. We both
know Mr. Foxwell is to blame, as Lady Sophia would never
have let you go. Now you can tell us something about him
that will help us along, can't you?"

Miss Knight's expression changed from reluctant to
interested. "You think . . . he is involved in her death?"

Merula held her breath, waiting for Royston's response.
He could hardly openly accuse Foxwell of involvement. If
word of it got back to Foxwell, Royston might face a slan-
der charge.

Royston said slowly, "Let's just say that when a man
inherits everything, he has a reason to . . . wish the testa-
tor's death would not be too far in the future?"

"You have a way with words, sir. I will put it more
bluntly. Mr. Foxwell didn't just wait for Lady Sophia's
death. He was actively expediting the process."

Royston hitched a brow. "You must explain yourself."

"Mr. Foxwell knew that Lady Sophia was of a nervous

disposition and prone to believe even the most unbelievable things. She wasn't naïve or simple; she was afraid. That makes all the difference, believe me. She was clever enough to understand that some things were nonsense, but still she could not dismiss them from her mind, as she was certain they were going to harm her."

"Things or people?" Royston asked.

Miss Knight sighed. "One day she wanted lavender for her bedroom because she had heard it made you sleep better; the next she had heard from someone else that the scent caused headaches and she wanted it to be removed again. You never knew what she might come up with next. She had always been like that, but after her husband's death it became an obsession. He had a very good influence on her, you know, calming her fears. Left alone, she was devastated."

She looked down and muttered, "Poor woman."

"But then Foxwell came into her life." Royston encouraged her to go on with the story. "Then she wasn't alone anymore, so you'd think this would be good for her."

"You'd think so, yes, but the truth was something else completely. Foxwell soon noticed what state she was in. He realized that by playing on her fears, he could control her."

"Control her?" Merula repeated. "That is an odd word choice."

"Not at all. It was his intention all along. He realized that if he controlled her, he'd control her fortune. Her money and the collection."

"You mean the zoological collection?" Merula asked. "Kept at the country estate?'

"Exactly. It contains many rare and valuable specimens."

"Have you ever seen it?"

"Seen it? I know every bit in it." The companion pulled back her shoulders, her face lighting with something close to pride. "Lady Sophia didn't know a thing about animals. In fact, she loathed them and was even afraid to come near a mounted animal. She thought they were dirty and carried disease. I didn't feel that way at all. I found them fascinating. When my master was still alive, he showed me the specimens and we talked about them for hours."

"So you know the collection? So you know that items in it don't belong to Lady Sophia but to others who lent them to the curio cabinet."

Miss Knight exhaled in a scoff. "So that is what you're really after. Who are you working for? Havilock?"

"So you know Havilock is one of the men who wants to have his property back?"

"I could hardly *not* know that. He came to the house and threatened Lady Sophia."

"He threatened her?" Merula echoed, glancing at Royston.

Miss Knight said, "He demanded to have some items back. Lady Sophia denied having them. He got angry and reached out to grab her by the shoulders and shake her. She staggered back. I got up from the corner where I sat and approached them, trying to remind him of his place. He didn't even notice me and shouted that he'd solve the matter as he had in India."

"India?" Royston frowned. "Do you know what he was referring to? Has Lady Sophia been to India? Did she have dealings with Havilock there?"

Miss Knight shook her head. "Lady Sophia has never been to India, at least not since I've worked for her."

Royston *hmm*ed. "We must look into this," he muttered. "Very interesting. What could Havilock have meant?"

Miss Knight continued, "I asked him to leave and he did. I told Lady Sophia she should inform the police that he had harassed her, but she didn't want to. Foxwell also advised against it. Of course he didn't want the police to know."

"Because of damage to Lady Sophia's name?" Merula asked.

Miss Knight laughed softly. "Because his own thefts might come to light. He has been selling off items from the collection."

"What?" Royston said. "How could he do that?"

"As I said, Lady Sophia abhorred those dead animals and never set foot in the curio cabinet. She had no idea what her husband owned. Foxwell could easily sell things off without her ever knowing about it. And now that she's dead and he's the sole heir . . ."

Royston nodded. "Do you have any proof of things

he sold? Do you know for certain that a piece you once saw in the curio cabinet is now elsewhere?"

Miss Knight shook her head. "I think that's one of the reasons Foxwell didn't want me to accompany Lady Sophia anymore. Because he was afraid I would enter a home and discover a piece there that shouldn't be. He also tried to come between my mistress and me to isolate her and to make sure she did anything he asked. He controlled her completely by putting new fears into her head. He alienated her from all of her old friends."

"I see." Royston pursed his lips. "Last night you could not come, but you did help her prepare for her departure, I presume? Did she eat sweets or in any other way take anything that could explain her collapse?"

Miss Knight shook her head.

Merula suggested, "Did she take a calming draft before she went out, to steady her nerves? Laudanum, for instance? Could she have taken an overdose?"

Merula wasn't sure what symptoms this would have caused, but they had to try every possibility. "Perhaps poison was introduced earlier by someone, into the drops?"

Miss Knight shook her head. "Lady Sophia didn't take any laudanum or other drops. She ate dinner with Mr. Foxwell. I believe they ate and drank the same things. At least that is what he claims."

Royston didn't reveal what they had learned from the butler about this. He merely said, "If I asked you to conjecture, using your knowledge of the household and Lady

Sophia's actions before she left for the lecture, when and how the poison was introduced to her, could you tell me?"

Miss Knight shook her head. "I can't. I have been thinking about it, but I can't see how. It must have happened *after* she left the house. In the carriage, perhaps, when she was alone with Foxwell."

Royston looked at Merula. "He might have lied, of course, about her not taking anything during the ride to Havilock's. He could easily have given her something to suck on."

Merula expected the companion to deny this, as she must have known Lady Sophia never ate sweets as Buckleberry had told them, but Miss Knight said nothing.

Merula asked, "Is it true that Lady Sophia mashed all of her foods?"

"Yes, but it was just a passing whim like the other things. If someone had told her mashing was bad for her, she'd have stopped it."

Royston seemed to be growing irritated with the recital of Lady Sophia's peculiar manners. He said, "You are here looking for new employment because Mr. Foxwell wants to let you go. Because his aunt no longer requires your care, or because of . . . the missing earring?"

Miss Knight flushed. "There never was a missing earring," she hissed. "Foxwell took it to incriminate me. To isolate Lady Sophia even from her closest servants and make sure she didn't trust anyone anymore. It was all part of his plan. He took the earring so I would be accused."

She wrung her hands. "I've been afraid he would be so brass as to put it among my things, where it might be found and I would be turned out into the street. But he hasn't gone that far. I wondered why. Now I know. He intended to murder my lady and then I would have to go anyway."

Another woman might have burst into tears at this point in her story, but Miss Knight seemed too controlled to ever cry. She just stood there, rigid and indignant.

Merula said, "After this false accusation of theft, didn't you consider leaving of your own accord? Before the earring did turn up among your things and your reputation was ruined?"

Miss Knight looked at her with indignant eyes. "Leaving would have been an admittance of guilt. Never! Even now, I don't want to leave and let that bastard go unpunished."

She seemed to reproach herself for her outburst as she continued, calmer, "You must forgive me. Ten years of service should carry some weight, but apparently not with Mr. Foxwell."

"We understand," Merula assured her. "We intend to unravel the mystery of who killed Lady Sophia and bring that person to justice."

Miss Knight said, "That is very kind of you. Now, if you have no more questions, I better get back in or I will miss my turn."

"Thank you very much for your cooperation," Royston said.

Miss Knight smiled at him. "You have asked all the right questions. The police never bothered. Thank you." And she marched back inside the offices.

Merula said, "If she is right about Foxwell isolating Lady Sophia from her friends and about him selling off items from the collection, he had enough reasons to want her dead. Not just so he could inherit everything but also so he could cover up what he was doing."

"Still, there are problems with that theory," Royston mused. "People who lent specimens to the cabinet, people like Havilock and Newbury, whom we met this morning, will still want them back. They will not cease to ask for them just because Lady Sophia is dead now. What does Foxwell intend to do about them?"

"I have no idea." Merula frowned in concentration. "When we were there at the estate, we didn't see a single specimen on display. What if Foxwell has been removing them all? Miss Knight just told us that Lady Sophia never came near the mounted animals. She'd never know if he did remove them. He might have sold off some and removed all the others to some safe place. Maybe even abroad?"

Royston nodded. "And if Foxwell goes after them someday, disappears into the French countryside, the police will never catch him. I doubt they would even try. After all, he owns it all now. It's his word against that of Havilock, Newbury, and the other duped parties that some items did not belong to Lady Sophia's late husband."

Merula said, "Perhaps not. Newbury told us he had proof

that he owned the emperor penguin. If the others have proof as well, an agreement between them and the late Lord Rutherford for instance, then Foxwell will have to return the specimens."

Royston said, "Yes, but sorting out the legal details will take time, and if Foxwell has moved the collection abroad and intends to follow himself, he can still escape before the true owners have built a solid case against him. Clever. How unfortunate that we can't go see Havilock to ask for his side of the story."

"If he is the killer, he wouldn't tell us anything anyway. Consider this: it happened in his house. With his zoological knowledge, he must know about rare poisons as well. I'm still thinking about the poisonous darts Galileo mentioned. Could someone have stabbed Lady Sophia in passing with such a dart?"

Royston shrugged. "Perhaps, but we didn't see any such thing on the tables at the lecture. I also doubt that Havilock would leave poisonous darts lying about when guests come over."

"If he is the killer, he might have done it himself when he went up to Lady Sophia to greet her and usher her to the front," Merula said, excited at this idea.

"He'd be taking an enormous chance. There were so many people watching. Any one of them could have seen something."

Merula sighed, acknowledging he was right. "We need to find out what happened in India."

Royston nodded. "I should ask Justin when Havilock came back from India. I seem to recall it wasn't that long ago."

"But the companion just told us Lady Sophia was never in India while she worked for her. How can the two be related?"

"Maybe Havilock wasn't referring to something that happened when they were *both* in India, but to something in India that people here know about. Something that happened there."

"He used it as a threat, so it must be something ominous." Merula frowned. "Poor Lady Sophia. She was already fearful, and everybody was working to make her even more afraid."

"Still, she came out into the open for the lecture. A lecture about a tarantula too— not the most pleasant creature in the natural world. If she didn't like animals, why did she come?"

"Perhaps Foxwell pressed her?" Merula suggested.

"Then we have to assume he planned her collapse and wanted it to happen with plenty of people around. Witnesses. Especially with your uncle there, whom he could then conveniently accuse."

"But if we assume that Havilock wanted her dead because of the specimens, we can't assume at the same time that it was Foxwell planning an audience for her death."

Royston laughed softly. "They might all have wanted her dead, but I agree that probably only one of them did something that caused the fatal collapse. But which one?"

Merula stared ahead. "The thing is, nobody could have known I would bring the butterfly. It hatched only a few hours before the lecture began, and I decided on impulse to take it."

Royston shook his head and said, "For the moment, we must assume that the butterfly had nothing to do with it. It was there by accident. The killer just meant for her to collapse and die and for things to be obscured by people panicking or making wild accusations, which indeed is what happened."

"Thanks to Foxwell," Merula said. "He is at the heart of our case. Miss Knight said that he tried to isolate Lady Sophia for a reason. We have to find out if he did indeed sell zoological specimens from the collection."

"I think it's time we paid Justin Devereaux a visit," Royston said.

★   ★   ★

As the hansom turned into the street, Merula saw a policeman standing beside a lamppost, watching everything. He might have just been keeping an eye on the street vendors nearby or enjoying the faint rays of sunshine that broke through the clouds above, but she didn't trust that.

"That officer . . ." she hissed to Royston.

"I saw him." Royston called out to the coachman that he had changed his mind and wanted to go to the Strand. He let the coachman drop them off there, paid him hurriedly, and dragged Merula into the crowd. "We'd better walk to Galileo's," he said softly. "I have no idea if houses belonging to my known friends or acquaintances are being watched, but we must take no risks. We have to remain free to conduct our investigation."

"Do they know Galileo is your friend too?"

Royston shook his head. "I assume they are watching the houses of my friends from the same circles. People I spoke with last night and others I am known to associate with, like Justin. Galileo is a different matter."

"Good." Merula forced herself to breathe deeply. She had not imagined that it would be so nerve-racking to be hunted. She had always felt as if London was such an enormous city with so many people going about their business that it would be easy to disappear into the masses, to be anonymous. But it didn't seem to be easy at all. Her stomach was tight, and she waited unconsciously for a hand to fall on her shoulder.

It wasn't the police she was afraid of as such, or of being questioned, or even imprisonment, although she was sure it would be unpleasant. It was losing her freedom to move about and try to prove her uncle's innocence, as well as her own. If she was locked up and unable to act and just had to sit and wait and worry about her uncle, Aunt Emma, and Julia in this ordeal she had set upon them, though unwittingly, she'd go insane. She had to stay free and actively pursue answers.

In the street on which Galileo lived, everything was quiet except for a vegetable seller arguing with a woman about the freshness of his leeks. On the corner, a brewery cart had halted and the driver was checking the horse's hoofs. Some street urchins were gathering to see what was wrong.

Royston took in everything quickly, apparently searching for something out of the ordinary. As he saw nothing, they disappeared into the narrow alley beside Galileo's house to get to the servants' entrance. Going up the stairs, Merula listened to the silence in the house. Was something wrong? Was this a trap? Were the police waiting for them in that room?

She halted and put her hand on Royston's arm. "I don't feel right about this."

"About what?"

"I don't know. It's too quiet. What if they're waiting for us up there? How much do they know?"

Royston held her gaze. "You must not let the strain get to you, Merula. They don't know about this house, I'm sure. We have to stay level-headed to push on or we won't get anywhere."

Merula took a deep breath. "You're right. I'm sorry."

Royston walked on ahead of her. She clenched the stair railing tightly.

Upstairs the door opened, and Galileo looked out. "Hello there," he called. "The oddest thing happened."

Merula froze.

Even Royston tightened and called out, "What then? Can we safely come up?"

"Of course you can safely come up. It doesn't bite."

"What doesn't?" Royston took the steps two at a time to reach his friend.

Galileo said, "The parcel. It's a simple brown paper affair, tied up with string."

"What parcel?" Royston and Merula followed the disheveled chemist into his room.

He pointed at a chair. "That there was left on the steps in front. It is addressed to you."

Merula's heart skipped a beat. "To me? But nobody knows I'm staying here."

She felt beads of sweat forming on her back.

Royston muttered under his breath. "Who left it there? Did you look about you? Didn't you think it could be dangerous when you just took it in?"

Galileo shrugged. "I guessed it came from Merula's family. They might want to get in touch with her."

Merula looked at Royston. "Bowsprit! Did he tell Lamb where I'm staying?"

"I can't imagine he would. He knew he'd have to act as go-between. He also knew the risks of telling her anything."

"Lamb can be trusted," Merula said. "Maybe she left the parcel on the steps."

"With your name on it for everyone walking by to see?" Royston shook his head. "That would be madness."

He hovered over the parcel, studying the handwriting. "Very neat and legible. The string is dirty, though. Probably already used a few times."

"Could come from our kitchens," Merula said. "Cook is very efficient and never throws out anything she can still use."

"Better see what's inside," Galileo said.

"Not just like that," Royston objected. "Have you got your extra-thick gloves here? I'm not taking any chances with what might be inside."

"I see." Galileo looked about him, located the gloves, which were stained with chemical spills, and threw them to Royston, who caught them deftly and put them on. Then Royston used a knife to cut the string and took care unwrapping the paper.

Merula wasn't sure what he expected to be inside, but she couldn't stand the tension building under his careful approach. Even the rustle of the paper jerked her tight nerves. She wanted him to open it fast so they could see what was in it.

It was a small cardboard box.

Royston folded the flaps open. The box was filled with straw. He pulled out a handful, spreading it across the table. It looked very ordinary. Digging his hand back into the box, his expression tightened. "There's something in here," he reported, carefully pulling it out and holding it up to the light between his gloved fingers.

It was a glass bottle, marked with a skull and crossbones, the warning symbol for poisonous materials. Underneath was written in the same neat handwriting as the outside address label, *Stay away from the butterfly conspiracy.*

Merula went cold. She felt as if the room around her expanded for a moment, turning into a wide universe in which there was a roaring sound that blasted in her ears. Then the room turned small and suffocatingly close around her and she believed she could not breathe.

Someone knew she was here and had sent her a threat. Stay away or else . . .

"What is in the bottle?" Galileo asked. His expression was tense.

Royston tilted the bottle to the left, then to the right. He scrunched up his face. "Nothing, it seems."

"*Nothing?* But it's marked to contain poison. Let me see it. I can do tests on it. I can determine what residue is in it." Galileo clapped his hands together. "The killer sent us the bottle in which he kept the poison used to murder Lady Sophia. He is daring us to analyze what it is."

Galileo laughed softly. "You reckless bastard. But I'm taking you up on the challenge. I'll find out what it is and we'll hang you with it!"

Merula shook her head. She heard her own voice in the distance as she spoke, "You will find absolutely nothing in it, not a drop, a crystal, a trace. It's clean. The killer sent this bottle to taunt us. To show us that his method is so ingenious that we can never detect it. He's certain he's safe."

"If he's so certain he's safe," Royston said, pale with anger, "then why does he feel the need to warn us to stay away from the butterfly conspiracy, as he calls it? He must think we can discover something or he would not warn us.

The murder happened not even a day go. What can he think we have discovered already?"

"Maybe we touched a nerve somehow." Merula was staring ahead. "Maybe we've come close to a vital bit of information already. But where? How? This morning at the country estate? Does the killer know we went there? Is that dangerous to him somehow? Or did it happen here in the city? Our meeting with Buckleberry? With Miss Knight? Is the killer watching us? Does he know our every move?"

Her voice broke as she said the last words. Nerves filled her to the point of shaking.

Royston took her arm and directed her onto the sofa in the corner. "I'll get you a drop of brandy."

"I'm fine. I just wonder how much the killer knows. Is he following us? Does he know what we're doing, what we know? Is he keeping track of every move we make?"

"How would that be possible? I didn't see a carriage follow us to the estate. I saw no one I know when we spoke to Buckleberry."

"No one you know, no, but what if whoever it is has a person following us? Someone inconspicuous who just blends in wherever he goes?" Merula shivered as she thought of the people in the coffeehouse, the newspaper vendors and the telegram boys, so many people she would never look at twice because their presence was natural, nothing to feel suspicious about.

Royston shook his head with conviction. "A killer who killed so ingeniously would not involve other people who can then betray him. It must be a shot in the dark, trying to scare us."

"It worked." Merula pushed her hand to her throat. Her heart beat heavily in the artery running there. "I feel as if he is very close to us."

"In any case, he knows you are here," Galileo said softly. "And in sending you the empty bottle, he said more than that you do not know how he killed Lady Sophia."

They both looked at Galileo's serious expression.

The chemist continued, "He's also saying that, if he wants to, he can use this unknown method to kill again. To kill *you*."

CHAPTER 8

"Are you sure you want to continue investigating?" Royston asked.

Merula sat on the sofa, her head in her hands.

Galileo's words had shocked her to the core. The idea that she herself could suffer the same gruesome fate as Lady Sophia was terrifying. She had no idea how the poison had been introduced to Lady Sophia, so she could not defend herself against an attack on her own life.

Did she have to give in to the killer's demands?

Did she have to stay away from the case, leave London, flee into the countryside or wherever she might be safe? Abandon Uncle Rupert in prison, Aunt Emma and Julia devastated at their home?

Could she abandon them after *her* butterfly had played such an unfortunate part in the whole affair?

As if Galileo knew she was thinking of the butterfly, he said, "Your cocoon hatched, by the way. What a gorgeous creature. I have not been able to study it in detail yet, but it has fascinating aspects I have never seen before. It doesn't seem to have a mouth or anything like a mouth. That means it can't feed and it will live only a short period of time."

"Does it also mean it can't bite or sting?" Royston asked eagerly.

"A sting can be given with other body parts. I'm still looking closer. And in the end, I will have to use tissue to look for poison."

"Meaning you will have to kill it," Merula said softly.

Galileo nodded with a sad expression. "It's the only way."

The knowledge that he also didn't want to do it cheered Merula. Sitting up straight, she said, "Everything must be done to clear my uncle."

Looking at Royston, she added, "And yes, that also includes us continuing our investigation. We must have come close to something vital already. Why else would the killer feel the need to threaten us?"

"I thought," Galileo said, "that this butterfly conspiracy was just some fabrication from those newspapermen. But now it seems there really is such a thing. Why else would the killer refer to it? Can it mean he isn't working alone?"

"I hardly expect him to have put the parcel on your doorstep in person," Royston said. "Still, I keep thinking that involving other people is a risk. There is always a chance they will talk or start pressuring you to give them money to keep silent. Why would the killer take those chances?"

"Probably because there is a lot at stake." Merula folded

her hands in her lap to hide that they were shaking. "Lady Sophia's fortune, for instance. If we can prove Foxwell is her killer, he will never touch any of it. That could drive him to take risks."

Royston nodded. "Agreed. We must concentrate on what we've learned so far."

He went into the other room, and she heard the chalk squeak on the blackboard. He must have been writing down the information they had gathered on his suspect list. Miss Knight's revelations supported the case against Foxwell, as it seemed he had been working on some plan to isolate Lady Sophia for a long time.

The door opened, and Bowsprit came in with an exultant expression. "Miss! I found someone who has the key to solving the murder."

"You did?" Merula frowned, perplexed at his certainty.

"Well, he says he does. He wants to meet you and tell his story in person." Bowsprit seemed ready to storm off again. "Where is his lordship?"

"In the other room, writing down some information." Merula rose and smoothed her dress. Her hands were still quivering. "Are you certain this man's tale is genuine?" She gestured at the parcel on the table. "Someone sent me an empty poison bottle with a threat."

Bowsprit looked at it. His normally lively and florid face turned pale. "Is this the bottle from which the poison came that killed Lady Sophia?"

Before Merula could reply, he said to Galileo, "Can you

find anything on it? Doesn't Scotland Yard search for fingerprints these days? Can you find some?"

Galileo leaned back on his heels as if insulted by the question. "Of course I can. Unless the killer handled the bottle while wearing gloves. But what is the point? Scotland Yard has fingerprints of known criminals to compare their findings with. I have no such thing. Besides, we are thinking the killer might be Mr. Foxwell or Lord Havilock or some other member of society who has never been in touch with the police and whose fingerprints won't be on file."

"But they don't have to be," Bowsprit enthused. His color was returning, and he waved with his hands to underline his point. "If you do find fingerprints on this bottle, I can work with members of the various households to bring you things like a drinking glass that were touched by the owners. You can then compare the fingerprints."

Galileo looked at Bowsprit with a whole new respect in his eyes. "That is a very clever thought. Genius, in fact. If I do find prints on the bottle, that is. I will have a look."

Bowsprit nodded. "Very good. Then we can go out and meet this man. I spread word among the servants that I'm willing to pay for information about Lady Sophia's past, anything that can throw light on her sudden death. Every maid has a sister or a cousin who cleans at a boarding house or works in a shop. The butlers and footmen all know coachmen, telegram boys, and hotel clerks. Word spreads fast if a reward is at stake. The message arrived at the bookshop that I am using for our communications. This gentleman claims to have known Lady Sophia well, some years back. He is waiting for us at Charing Cross Station. He wanted a busy meeting place where we would not be spotted."

"Sounds as if he is afraid," Royston said, entering. He seemed to have caught the conversation from the other room, for he stood ready to go out.

Bowsprit nodded. "He must know something really important."

Royston was at the door already. "Let's not waste another moment, then."

★   ★   ★

At Charing Cross Station, the newspaper sellers were still shouting about the butterfly conspiracy, impressing with urgency upon Merula's mind that she was at the heart of a dangerous affair and, judging by the mysterious bottle, a potential target of the killer.

Despite the many people bustling about them, each completely absorbed in their own business, Merula felt uncomfortable, as if eyes were watching her from all sides. She stayed close to Royston and Bowsprit and was relieved when, next to a pillar, they met a short rotund man with a pale sweaty face and watery eyes. His clothes were old and often mended, his elbows almost poking through the sleeves. He looked the three of them over and whispered hurriedly, "Have you brought the money? I need the money first, else I won't say a word."

Royston took Merula by the arm and moved her a few paces away from the man who waited with Bowsprit by his side.

Royston said, "He looks as if he just waddled out of an opium den. This man is addicted, either to drugs or to alcohol. I doubt we can get anything useful out of him. He must have heard the word 'reward' and made up a story to earn some money to feed his addiction."

"Still, he could know something. We must let him speak. Just give him the money."

Royston sighed. "Are you sure? If he doesn't reveal anything relevant—"

Merula waved a hand. "He asked for a busy meeting place, so he seems to feel he is taking a risk in meeting us. He must know something."

"Or the ruse from his addiction makes him believe he is being pursued. Whatever he will tell us could be utter nonsense, fabrications from an overactive mind. I can't see him as a reliable witness."

"Even so, we have to pursue each and every lead."

She leaned over to Royston and added, "Consider our position since the murder happened last night. We are on the run, the police want to find us, and the killer knows where we are. We can't afford to waste any time or any chance for information."

Royston released a deep sigh. "You're right. I'm sorry. I just don't like people who make themselves important. But perhaps he knows a great deal."

They returned to the man, and Royston asked him, "Who are you, anyway?"

"I used to live next to Lady Sophia. I have important information regarding her health. It might explain why she collapsed."

Merula felt a rush of excitement. At last they would be able to fill in something under *How* on their blackboard! She nodded at Royston. He reached into his pocket.

"Five pounds," the man said.

"Excuse me?" Royston asked.

"Five pounds or you get nothing,"

Royston made wide eyes at Merula, but he did pay. The man clutched the money to his chest and said in a rush, "I lived next to her, like I said, and three years ago there was a garden party at her house. I was also invited. Everything was very pleasant, nice people there and delicious food. Then suddenly she seemed to be choking and turned all red in the face. I thought she would die."

"She had some sort of attack like that last night," Royston said eagerly. He glanced at Merula. Her heart was pounding, and she couldn't wait to hear more. Now they were getting somewhere.

The man said, "It turned out there was a whole almond in the pastry she was eating. It got in her throat, and she almost choked to death. She was livid at her cook, and I think she even dismissed her on the spot. The cook claimed it was not her fault, but Lady Sophia was too angry to listen."

"That is it?" Royston asked. "She almost choked on an

almond and sent off her cook for it? That is your vital information about her health?"

He burst into disbelieving laughter. "Everybody has had such an experience at one time or another. A fish bone, a nut, seeds from an apple going down the wrong way. You cough a few times and that's it. Unpleasant but nothing earth-shattering. Yes, powerful people might even dismiss their servants for it, but it has absolutely nothing to do with Lady Sophia's death last night. She wasn't eating or drinking anything as she stood there. She never ate sweets, we've heard, so she can't have been sucking on something that got caught in her throat. This information is completely irrelevant."

He was talking louder and louder, and Bowsprit grabbed his arm to control him.

The man shrank back, clutching his reward. "Good day to you then, sir. Miss." He turned and vanished among the crowd of people rushing to catch a train or waiting to meet with travelers who had just alighted.

Royston said, "An almond! Did you see any almonds last night? Or any kind of nuts or other things anybody might choke on?"

Merula shook her head. "You can't blame the poor man. He thought it mattered. As he started to describe her symptoms, I thought it was the same thing as well. He only wanted to help."

"Yes, help himself," Royston scoffed. "He's off now to find an inn or opium den to indulge in his addiction. And I paid for that!"

"You did it for the case," Merula said, patting his arm. "I encouraged you to try it. We have to do all we can. I'm sorry."

"It's not your fault. But I'm tired now of talking to sources. I want some real, tangible information. I'm going to send a telegram to an old friend of mine. If I remember correctly, he came home to England from India on the same ship as dear Havilock. Perhaps he will know what happened in India that Havilock used to threaten Lady Sophia."

"Excellent," Merula said. "I want to meet Julia."

"What?" Royston said, freezing. "How do you want to contrive that?"

"Bowsprit can contact Lamb, and she can convey a message. Julia wanted to go to the art exhibition in a gallery on Bond Street. I can meet her there. We will both pretend to be studying paintings on display while we speak. I want to know what Julia knows about Foxwell that can help. If what you told me last night is true, they must have been much closer than I ever thought they could be."

Royston said, "The argument between Lady Sophia and your uncle at his club did happen. I can't be certain, of course, if her accusations were true. She might have heard of Foxwell dancing with your cousin and made more of the attachment than was necessary. She seems to have been very protective of Foxwell."

Merula nodded. "In any case, I want to speak to Julia."

She ached to talk for a few minutes to her cousin, to ascertain that she was all right, to ask about Aunt Emma and about what was being done for Uncle Rupert. She ached to feel a part of their family still, even after she had brought disaster upon them.

Royston said to Bowsprit, "Help her set up this meeting at the gallery. And stay near her to keep an eye on her while she's in there. That parcel has me worried."

CHAPTER 9

Merula stood in front of a painting called *Summer After-noon in the Meadow* and tried to determine whether the white smudge in the middle was a sheep grazing in said meadow or perhaps a young lady in a summer dress picking flowers. The pink spot on the left could have been a hand.

She tilted her head to the right, then to the left to see better.

"Perhaps it is hanging upside down," a voice said softly at her ear, and there was Julia, smiling weakly, her hair neatly done up as always and her dress impeccable. She even wore a new hat, perhaps because it gave her confidence, or because it conveniently shadowed her face and changed her appearance.

Merula resisted the urge to hug her cousin. They had to keep up the act of being strangers standing next to each other at an exhibition.

"Yes, it is a rather mysterious affair," she agreed and added in a whisper, "How are you? How is Aunt Emma?"

Julia came to stand so close their shoulders touched, and she said just as softly, "Mother is in bed. She says this is the worst disaster that has ever struck us in her entire life, and for once I tend to agree with her. What on earth happened last night? We have only heard it from the police, and they had this bizarre story of a butterfly killing someone and it being Father's fault."

"It was *Attacus atlas*," Merula confessed. "I brought him and released him. Just to show that he was really alive. He sat on Lady Sophia's arm. Then she collapsed and died. Sir Edward Parker, who has some medical experience from his army days, claimed it was a poisoning, and then your Foxwell cried that Uncle Rupert had done it."

Julia looked horrified. "Simon would never say such a thing. Not about Father."

"Well, he did. I was there." Merula lowered her voice even further. "Royston suggested to me that there is something between you and Foxwell and that his aunt, Lady Sophia, didn't agree. That is why Uncle Rupert had a grudge against her, a reason to kill her."

"Royston? You mean, Lord Raven Royston? How do you even know him?"

"He was at the lecture last night. He helped me to get away before they also arrested me. He told me that Lady Sophia caused a terrible row for Uncle Rupert at his club, claiming you were far too friendly with Foxwell, and Lady Sophia wouldn't accept that." Merula thought it better not to repeat Royston's words about Julia's supposed shortcomings.

Julia seemed to know Royston, if only by reputation, and her opinion of him wouldn't be improved by hearing herself described in terms such as "not well bred enough."

Julia protested, "How absurd. Simon was going to introduce me to Lady Sophia. He said she'd think me perfectly charming."

"Lady Sophia had already told Uncle Rupert in no uncertain terms there would never be anything between you and her nephew. It was a humiliating scene, Royston assured me."

Merula wanted to convince Julia that the accusation of murder rested on a solid motive, but Julia scoffed, "What does Royston know? Why believe him? It is highly improper that you ran off with him. You have to come home."

"Hush." Merula glanced about her, but the other visitors to the gallery didn't seem to be paying attention to them. "I can't come home right now. Royston is helping me solve the case. He wants to prove who did it so Uncle Rupert will be released again. Have you already engaged a solicitor for him?"

"I think our family lawyer was going to do something. Mother won't go see Father in prison. I just hope they will realize it is all a mistake and let him go again." Julia fumbled with her bracelet. "This is so distressing. Guests for our musical soiree have already canceled. It's in a week's time, so they seem to think Father won't be free again. Or perhaps it doesn't even matter. Perhaps the fact that he was in prison is enough, guilty or not."

Her voice rose in frustration.

Merula warned her again, "Hush. Not so loud. We must move to the next painting."

They went to stand in front of a mainly red canvas that was called *Sunset Over a Lake*.

"I can't see which are the skies and which is the water," Julia complained. "I think I could make art like this. Of course, Mother would have a fit. She'd say it's not appropriate for a young lady of my social standing. If I still have any now. What do you think?"

On the one hand, Julia sounded anxious and on the verge of crying; on the other, she also seemed oddly excited by the situation.

Merula said, "I need information about Foxwell, Julia. He is Lady Sophia's sole heir. He gets it all now that she is dead."

"You think he could be involved in her death? How mean! He loved her. He grew up without a mother and she was . . ."

"Like a mother to him? That is not what I heard. People claim he was quite manipulative toward her and only interested in her property, particularly in the zoological collection, selling off items he doesn't own."

"Who said that? Miss Knight, by any chance?"

Merula was taken aback that Julia would name the companion. "You know her?"

"Simon told me about her. It seems that when he first came to live with Lady Sophia, Miss Knight made it very clear to him that she was interested in him. In having an affair with him, you understand. Simon told me it was quite despicable because she is very plain and can't make conversation."

Merula wouldn't have called the woman with the lively brown eyes plain, but in his circles, Foxwell had his pick of much younger girls who refined their faces with makeup and changed their figure with corsets and expensive dresses. Naturally, his aunt's companion couldn't compete with that.

Julia whispered, "Simon said she was pathetic, but also vengeful, and that ever since he turned her down, in the politest terms, as he is a real gentleman of course, she has tried to find ways to make him look bad with his aunt. She would tell his aunt he was seeing certain unsuitable women or . . . Yes! That's it! If Lady Sophia did argue with Father about Simon and me, it must be because that horrible Miss Knight put it into her head that there was something sordid going on."

"So Miss Knight was manipulating Lady Sophia to turn her against Foxwell?" Merula asked. It was the exact opposite of what Miss Knight had told her and Royston, namely, that Foxwell had been trying to isolate Lady Sophia by turning her against her companion and even against her old friends. Who was telling the truth?

"You must admit," she said to Julia, "that when someone dies unexpectedly, the sole heir is the first suspect to come to mind. He needs the money."

"He doesn't need any money," Julia protested. "Simon has a fortune of his own. He told me in the deepest confidence because he didn't want me to think he was after my money. He has far more."

"How gallant of him to point that out." Merula wrinkled her nose.

Julia poked her with an elbow. "Simon meant it well. He really cares for me." She wrapped her arms around her shoulders and sighed. "I wish I could see him. I need him now. I need him more than ever."

Her face contorted a moment, and Merula hoped she would not start to cry. How could she act as if she were standing next to a stranger when that stranger wasn't really a stranger and was heartbroken for a family tragedy she herself had caused?

But Julia pursed her lips, took a deep breath, and said, "I will prove to you that Simon had nothing to do with it. I will get information that he has a fortune of his own. And that he never sold off items from the zoological collection either."

"But where is the collection?" Merula asked. They moved to a new painting, this time all blue with a few smears of green. "*Canadian Forest*," read the card beside it.

Merula had always wanted to see faraway places, like Canada, or America, and as she stood there staring at the blue dashes, she wondered if this situation meant she'd have to leave her homeland, not because she wanted to but because she had to.

Could she stay here if Uncle Rupert wasn't cleared? If he died on the gallows, because of her?

She'd have to run, leave, never come back.

She swallowed hard, fighting the despair churning beneath the surface of her purposeful attitude, waiting to break free and swallow her whole.

Julia whispered, "I thought the zoological collection was in the curio cabinet at Lady Sophia's estate."

"Royston and I were there this morning, posing as visitors, but they wouldn't let us in. Us or anybody else. A man asked for his emperor penguin and was brushed off as if he were there to sell something. Very odd indeed."

"I can try to find out something about that too," Julia said. Her pale face had color now. "I want to help. For Father, of course, but also for Simon. Poor darling. He must feel so alone now without his aunt. And then to be suspected. You are all wrong about him, I'm sure. All wrong."

"You find out what you can and send me word through Lamb." Merula looked at her. "But be careful. These people are not to be trifled with."

"People? Plural?" Julia queried with a hitched fine brow.

"Have you not seen the newspapers? It's a real conspiracy." Merula half smiled. "They are exaggerating, I think, but still, be careful. I saw Lady Sophia die, and it was terrible."

Julia looked her in the eye, and Merula saw the same urge there that rushed through her own chest. The need to embrace and hold the other tightly.

But it wasn't possible. She whispered, "Good-bye," and rushed off, blinking against the burn behind her eyes.

Outside in the fresh air, she inhaled deeply and clenched her hands into fists to regain her composure. At least Julia wanted to help her. The information about Foxwell's alleged fortune and the zoological collection might prove very useful to them.

And even if it wasn't useful at all, the idea that her cousin didn't hate her but wanted to help her with the case filled her with a rush of relief and joy. Finally something good and stimulating on this long hard day.

"What is that on your dress?" Bowsprit asked as he stepped up to her.

She glanced up at him in surprise. "On my dress where?"

"There's something on the back of your dress. As if it's stuck to it."

Merula's heart skipped a beat. *A poisonous dart,* the thought flashed through her mind. *I have been pricked and I didn't even notice.*

For a moment it seemed as if everything around her stopped moving: the carriage in the street, the telegram boy running behind it, the old woman with the basket on her arm.

Merula could only hear the sound of the blood rushing in her ears as she held her breath, waiting for her heart to stop beating.

Bowsprit had already leaned around her, and Merula felt a slight movement on the small of her back as he removed something. He showed it to her on the palm of his hand. It was a normal-size butterflylike creature. Brownish and gray-ish with markings on its back and wings. Forming a skull pattern.

"Death's-head hawk moth," Merula whispered. "Por-tent of death." Her mouth was dry, and her tongue seemed unwilling to obey her orders.

Bowsprit frowned at her. "How did it get on your dress? Did you lean into anything in there? I didn't know the art gallery had a butterfly display."

"It does not." Merula tried to sound level. "This comes from someone's private collection. It was pinned to my dress while I was in there. Somebody must have passed me, brushed me, and . . ."

She swallowed hard. Someone had brushed her and stuck the portent of death on her back. As if death itself had passed her, touching her for a moment with an ice-cold finger.

She had survived.

This time.

But it was another warning. Proof that whoever had killed Lady Sophia was watching her every move and wouldn't tolerate her interference. They would stop her before she arrived at the truth.

Bowsprit said, "His lordship must hear about this at once. Come." He wrapped a supportive arm around her and ushered her along.

Merula came willingly, her legs wobbly and her palms covered in sweat. If someone could just walk past her without her even noticing who it was, or what had happened, and pin the death's-head hawk moth on her dress . . .

She hadn't seen anyone she knew inside the gallery. So how was this possible?

Who had done it?

★　★　★

"Can the leak be inside your own household?" Royston half leaned over her as she sat on the sofa, a glass with a drop of brandy in her hand. She had never drunk strong liquor before, but Royston had insisted on it this time to steady her nerves.

Royston continued, "How did they know you were here so they could send the parcel with the poison bottle in it? Lamb knew, didn't she? And now we set up a meeting between you and Julia at an art gallery, with Lamb delivering the message, and again our adversaries turn up there. It must be Lamb who gives them information."

"No." Merula shook her head fervently. "I know Lamb. She would never be involved in anything to hurt my family. Especially not me. I helped her with her mother, remember?"

"Perhaps they are pressuring her to cooperate via her mother. These people might stoop to the lowest means to achieve their aim." Royston shrugged. "What do we know?"

He straightened up and paced the room, his hands on his back. "This has to stop. They're just taunting us. They know everything about us, where we are, what we do, and we know nothing about them. Nothing!"

Galileo said, "We know they are familiar with butterflies and have access to a collection that holds a death's-head hawk moth."

Merula nodded in appreciation. "Not everybody knows—"

But Royston cut her off, snarling at Galileo, "The murder happened at a lecture for members of a zoological society. They *all* know about butterflies, and most of them have specimens in their homes as well."

Merula's shoulders sagged. He was right. The clue in itself meant very little. It was just chilling how it had been done. The killer or an accomplice coming so close to her . . . She could have slapped herself because she hadn't noticed a thing. She prided herself on observing people well and drawing inferences from their appearance, but at the exhibition she had been blind. Probably because she had been so distracted by Julia's emotions and her own. Never before had she felt quite so clearly that Julia was like a sister to her, and the idea of their bond being broken by the current trouble was unbearable. But such feelings were distracting and leading her away from a solution to her problems.

She exhaled to compose herself and said, "At least Julia is willing to help us with information she can gather better than we ever could."

"What can Julia do?" Royston barked. "Foxwell lied to her, I wager, and he will do so again. If she even gets to see him. And other acquaintances, will they want to get involved? The matter is splashed across all the newspapers. No . . ." Royston shook his head violently. "We are on our own."

He halted and looked at her. "We aren't safe here. We have to leave London."

"Where can we go?" Merula felt her cheeks heat as she added, "We can't pose as a couple as we did this morning. We can't just pretend to be Mr. and Mrs. Dutton and take rooms somewhere. It would be . . . highly improper." So far she had disregarded any concerns about her reputation, but if Royston and she were to leave the city to stay somewhere together, she could no longer ignore the implications. She might consider him a friend, a helper she could trust, but to the outer world they were just a man and a woman associating far too freely.

"I have a place." Royston stared ahead as if speaking to himself more than to her or the others. "I haven't been there in years, but I think we can stay there for a few days. We have to resolve the matter as quickly as we can. Nobody will guess we have gone there. It is isolated, so there is no risk of neighbors keeping an eye on us. We just have to make sure we aren't followed from London. Bowsprit, you get a carriage for us. Make sure you get it from someone who doesn't know you work for me. There must be no connection. You will be our driver. I'll explain the route to you. You must make sure we are not followed."

Bowsprit nodded as if such tasks were an everyday matter. "I'll go right now."

"Good. We must leave London as quickly as we can." Royston looked at Merula. "You cannot tell anyone where we are going."

"How could I when I don't know myself? You haven't mentioned the name of the house or the location." Merula held his gaze, trying to gauge his mood. "You do trust me, don't you?"

"Of course, but I don't know if your family and the servants at your house can be trusted. We have to be extra careful." Royston glanced at Galileo. "Can you come with us? We might need your chemical expertise, and reaching out to you here would pose an extra risk."

Galileo sighed. "I could come for a day or two. I can't leave my animals for a longer time. I will pack some items that might prove useful." He began to walk about energetically, collecting equipment.

Royston nodded and looked at Merula again. "We leave at nightfall."

CHAPTER 10

It was a night with a strong silvery moon in a deep-black sky. Merula had lost all sense of place and time as they moved along a winding country road, hearing nothing but the sound of the horse's hoofs and the wheels rattling as they turned and turned.

She might have dozed off for some time, until she jerked awake and looked out the window to see the silhouette of an elegant country house. Rubbing her eyes, she asked Royston what time it was. He didn't reply. In the light of the lantern, his features were grim. The flickering light sparked in his eyes, which seemed to burn with an intensity of their own. In a low voice, he said, "Welcome to Raven Manor."

Merula eyed him. "You were named after the house?"

He shook his head. "Raven is a name well documented in our family line. Dating back to a medieval warlord who rode the land on a big black horse, his garb dark as well."

"But this house can't have been built in medieval times," Merula said, puzzled. "It is far too elegant."

"As was my mother. She didn't have anything in common with plunder and darkness. If only she had never come here."

Royston opened the door even before the coach had come to a full halt and stepped out. Staring up at the house for a moment, he muttered, "We meet again."

Then he reached into the coach to help Merula get out.

Galileo said as he clambered out on his own, "I never knew you owned a place in the country. You sly fox. Must be ideal to hide out at in the summer. Take a friend or two."

He was obviously a little piqued that he had never been invited here, but Royston didn't respond to his light teasing and just stood with the lantern in his hand. In the weak light his expression was suddenly weary, and Merula resisted the urge to touch his arm, draw his attention, smile at him. She had to keep reminding herself that he was a man, used to handling his own affairs, not in need of her support.

Bowsprit had climbed down to get the luggage and placed it at the steps leading to the house's front door.

"I assume you don't keep servants here?" Galileo asked.

Royston said, "I don't think anybody has been here in twenty years."

Galileo stared, and Merula felt her own jaw sag. If one had a place in the country to go to when summer turned hot and London was full and oppressive, why not go there?

Royston produced a key from his pocket and went up the steps to unlock the front door. He then came back to take the luggage inside. Bowsprit took the horse and carriage to the stables.

Inside the house, a deep silence permeated everything. It was as if she could feel the lack of human habitation. Wherever the feeble light of Royston's lantern fell was covered with cobwebs and dirt. A door he opened creaked in protest, and a cold draft seemed to pull around them, sending a shiver down Merula's spine.

In London they had not been safe, but at least Galileo's place had been comfortable and cheery, a far cry from this hollow, soulless place. The emptiness that echoed in every footfall on the wooden floors seemed to creep inside her.

"We'd better go to bed right away," Royston said. "I'll show you your rooms."

He went up the stairs, holding the lantern ahead of him.

Merula followed, clutching the damp railing. There were no family portraits here that could stare at her in dark disapproval, but still she felt as if eyes were watching her from the darkness. Even the sound of her own swallowing made her jerk.

Galileo said behind her back that he wished he had brought his creatures because the place could use some life.

Upstairs Royston opened a large oak door to their left and showed Merula into a room that hung full of shadows. The bed was covered with heavy blankets, and there were curtains on the windows. Royston tried to pull them shut, releasing a wave of dust into the room. Galileo was lighting the many candle stubs in the room: in a chandelier, on the dressing table, beside the bed. The wavering lights made the room look even more unappealing.

Merula almost jumped when she saw a pale face in the mirror, then realized it was her own.

"Whoever lived here all those years ago?" she asked in a whisper.

"I did." Royston sounded curt and dismissive. "I grew up here. I'll get the luggage."

Merula looked at Galileo, who made a face at her. "Don't ask me. He never told me anything about his life, let alone about his childhood. I had no idea this place even existed."

Merula didn't want to be alone, but she knew it was pointless to say it. She ached for company and meaningless chatter, but Galileo couldn't stay with her, and Royston was obviously eager to avoid her company. She had to get into bed and sleep. If she could at all after that day's terrifying events.

Royston brought her case into the room and said, "Sleep well, then."

"Are you sure no one followed us?" Merula glanced at the windows. "No one can try to come in?"

"No one followed us," Galileo said quietly. "You are quite safe here."

Royston looked as if he didn't share the sentiment, but he turned away from her and walked to the door. "Good night." Both men left and the door was shut behind them.

Merula stood in the middle of the room, looking around

her. Outside she heard the call of an owl, long and lonely in the darkness. She shivered, walked to the bed, pulled the blankets away, and lay down without undressing. Pulling the damp heavy blankets over her, she squeezed her eyes shut and tried not to think of the hand that had stuck the death's-head hawk moth to her dress.

The same hand that could also have slipped a dagger into her back.

★   ★   ★

She awoke with a start, certain she had heard a sound at her window.

Or was it at her door?

Her heart pounded, and she wanted to crawl under the blankets and burrow a way out of this room, this house, this situation, back into her old life where everything had been normal.

The sound repeated itself, and she forced herself to stick her head up over the blankets and listen better. It was not at her window.

At her door, then?

Was it a signal of someone asking for entrance?

Royston, having had a brilliant thought about the murder case?

As she was still dressed, she slipped out of bed and walked to the door. Most candles in the room had died, but two still spread a feeble light. She put her hand against the wood and called out, "Who is there? Is it you?"

After a silence, she repeated, "Hello? Raven?"

She hadn't called him Raven before, but as she was now a guest in the house he had lived in as a child, their fates inexplicably intertwined by the murder case they were caught up in, it seemed odd to call him Lord Royston or just Royston or anything formal. In the darkness around her, she desperately needed a friend.

But there was no reply.

With a deep breath, Merula opened the door a crack and peeked out. The sound seemed to come from farther down the corridor. From one of the rooms there.

She thought for a moment. It was none of her business what was going on in there and, if she was smart, she'd just dive into bed again and try to sleep some more.

But how could she sleep in this mysterious place?

Merula grabbed one of the two candles still burning and walked out of her room, across the corridor, and then to the door from behind which the strange sounds emanated. It sounded like wood being moved across wood.

She took a deep breath and reached for the door. She turned the knob. She pushed it open and peeked inside. In the middle of the room, a figure stood looking at the opening door. His face was pale, his eyes wide as if he expected to see a burglar with a club.

It was Royston in shirtsleeves. Around him were many wooden crates, which he was apparently moving about.

He exhaled and said gruffly, "Almost gave me a heart attack. Must you sneak about in the night like that?"

"Must you move things around like that? It woke me."

"I'm sorry. I was just looking for something." He reached up and rubbed his forehead.

Again it struck Merula how tired he looked.

"You should be in bed," she said. "You can look in the morning."

"No, I can't sleep until I have ascertained that it is still here."

"Why wouldn't it be? Nobody has been here in twenty years. Didn't you say that?" Merula asked, puzzled.

"Yes, I suppose so. I can't be sure. I am worried that . . ." He rubbed his forehead again.

Merula came into the room and sat down on a chair. She put her candle on the table beside her. There was light enough in there already from several lanterns he had lit.

Royston said, surveying her, "Why are you still dressed?"

"I was too tired to get into my nightgown." She didn't want to tell him she had been too afraid to be in that still dark room in this eerie house. "I just wanted to sleep."

"Which explains perfectly why you are sitting here now," he said ironically.

Merula looked down at her hands. She didn't want to say she was worried about him. He'd probably balk at the idea that he needed anyone to look after him, even if only a little. "How can one sleep when everything is so . . . unclear and strange?"

Royston sighed. He sat down on the floor beside the

crates and crossed his legs. Raking his thick black hair back with one hand, he said, "I guess you have never felt before as if you were all alone in the world."

Merula tilted her head. "I have always had my uncle and aunt and Julia, if that's what you mean. Julia is older than me, and she loved me like her little sister from the day I arrived at their home. But I did feel at times like I was alone. I'm not really a part of their family. I mean, they are not my parents. I don't know who my parents are."

She had never spoken about her past like that, so candidly, and she winced briefly, but Royston nodded. "They died when you were a baby?"

"I assume so. I was delivered to my aunt and uncle to raise." She lifted her hand to touch the neckline of her dress, under which the pendant with the only clue she had to her past was hidden. "I have no idea why my parents would have left me with family if . . ." She fell silent and bit her lip.

"You did consider the possibility," Royston concluded. "You are not sure if they are really dead. You wonder if they abandoned you, and if they did, what for."

"And where they are, if they are still alive. If they ever think of me."

She said it spontaneously and regretted it at once. Men would not understand, and Royston would probably consider her melodramatic.

But to her surprise, he nodded again. "It would be odd

if you had never wondered about that. One gets to thinking after . . ."

He looked about him with that sad pensive look she had
seen on his face as they had arrived here.

"Are your parents still alive?" she asked.

He shook his head. "My father died three years ago.
We were never close."

"And your mother?"

It took him so long to reply, she was sure he wouldn't
respond at all. Perhaps her question had been too personal.
Perhaps she had assumed a confidentiality between them
that wasn't really there?

But Royston did speak at last. "She died here."

"Here? In this room?" Merula looked about her.

Royston shook his head. "On the estate. It was an
accident."

"I see."

His curt words seemed to be hiding a much longer and
more complicated story, but she didn't know how to ask
about that. She just sat and looked down at her hands. "It
must be difficult for you to come back here, then. I appreci-
ate that you were willing to do that for the case." *For me as
well.* "Thank you."

He made a dismissive gesture. "Not at all. I should have
come here earlier. I mean, the place needs a little cleaning.
You must think it is very dirty."

"I can imagine why, when no one has been here in such

a long time." She looked at him with a frown. "Didn't your father come here either?"

"No, we went away right after the accident and . . . neither of us had been back. At least, he never told me that he ever came back."

Royston looked at the crates surrounding him. "He might have been here. To remove things."

"You mean things that belonged to your mother? Things that had sentimental value to him, perhaps?"

"Or things that could prove something."

"Prove something?" Merula echoed. She stared at Royston. "About her accident?"

She was wide awake now, and her mind was working. "What kind of accident was it, anyway?"

"She drowned when she fell into the pond at the back of the estate."

"I see. Must have been a deep pond. And it must have been dark or nearly dark. Else you don't just fall into a pond on grounds you know."

"Very astute," Royston said.

It sounded cynical, and Merula blushed painfully. She rushed to say, "I don't mean it to sound as if I'm analyzing a case. Your mother's death is not a case, of course."

Royston looked at her. "Don't apologize," he said tightly. "Analyze it for me. It's not logical that you fall into the pond near your own home. A pond you know well. Go on."

Merula was undone by his mood, his strange tone, but she responded, "I'd say it must have happened while it was nearing darkness. And I'd almost think she would have been upset or otherwise undone. Not watching carefully where she was going."

"Blinded by tears?" Royston asked. It sounded sarcastic again, as if he didn't believe her assumptions at all, and still something nervous quivered under his words.

Merula was determined to explain her reasoning. "Well, I imagine a woman leaving her house as night closes in. She is walking fast, upset or agitated, and stumbles, falls, maybe hurts herself so she can't climb out of the pond again. Was no one with her? Didn't anyone hear any cries?"

"No, but you can't blame them for that. It didn't happen at nightfall when people might still be around. It happened in the dead of night. The grounds were completely abandoned."

"Your mother left the house in the middle of the night?" Merula asked bewildered. "She must have been upset indeed." *And not confiding in her husband . . .*

Royston leaned his head back and stared up at the ceiling. "She wasn't found until the afternoon of the next day. The doctor thought she had fallen into the pond and drowned. That is what they told me. I was only ten. I thought later they might have kept from me that . . . she . . ."

He faltered.

"Killed herself?" Merula asked softly.

Such a topic was very inappropriate to address, but she couldn't ignore the emotions that had gripped Raven upon being back here. She didn't want to act distant and polite as if they were just acquaintances. He had helped her escape arrest at the fatal lecture; he had helped her escape the burning conservatory. He had selflessly thrown himself into the investigation to clear her uncle's name. She wanted to do something in return. And discussing his mother's death honestly, without pretending she didn't understand the implications, was the least she could do.

Royston said, "There have been whispers. Because she was ill before she died. It started in the city, and she was told to recuperate in the countryside. My older brother was in boarding school already, so she took only me. But it got worse once we were here. She was terrified."

"Terrified?" Merula echoed, not fully understanding. "Of being ill? Do they think she killed herself because she couldn't accept that she wasn't going to get better? Or perhaps because she was afraid to lose her beauty? I heard of such a case in our acquaintance. My aunt spoke about it with a close friend. Julia and I were not supposed to learn of it, but we did anyway."

Julia had said that she could understand the fear of losing your beauty, your husband's love. That a woman's face was the most valuable asset she had. Merula had protested that perhaps a man's affection began when he saw a beautiful face but that it had to become more than that as time went by. That a man could also love a woman who lost her beauty. That he might even love her more as he knew she was slipping away from him and wanted to hold on to her.

Julia had called this romantic nonsense.

It was the only time she had ever called Merula romantic.

Royston said, "My mother was not physically ill. And I like to think my father would have still cared for her even if she had been. But it was . . . all in her mind, as he put it. And he had no patience for that. He believed she was imagining things and creating panic, also for the servants and for me."

"Do you remember panic?" Merula asked.

Royston kept staring at the ceiling. "I don't know. I remember an uneasy feeling, like not being quite sure what was going to happen. I remember thinking it was odd that my father was with us so little. He had to go to the city for business, and often he didn't come back until late if he came back at all. He didn't like it here."

"So your mother was alone most of the time? Also on the night she died?"

"My father says he came to the house in the morning. Around eleven. But I heard a male voice that night. I heard arguing."

Merula sat up, staring at him. "You think your father was here the night your mother died? And that they fought, even?"

Royston looked at her, pain pinching his mouth. "I don't know anything for certain, Merula. And my father is dead now. As she has been for many years."

Merula looked at his tense expression. "Did you ever discuss the night of her death with him? Before he died?"

"Yes, but in the wrong way."

"How do you mean?"

Royston sighed. "I was only ten when she died. I didn't really know what to think of it. I was told she was dead, that I could not see her again. I was taken away from here in a rush, back to the city. I think . . . for some time I blamed her."

He threw Merula a sad look. "For leaving me behind, just sneaking away like that. Then, when I turned eighteen, I got a bundle of papers in the mail. I have no idea who sent them to me. They were notes written by my mother. Some quite legible and sensible and real. Others scribbled in a rush, full of mistakes, of panicked thoughts and fabrications."

"Fabrications?" Merula repeated, unsure what to make of this word choice.

Royston sighed. He obviously had to force himself to repeat what he had read in those notes. "That she was hearing hands knocking on her windows at night, that she found a dead bird under her bed, that she saw blood smeared on her mirror. She was obviously dreaming things or perhaps even hallucinating. I wondered as I read all of it if she was addicted to some drug like opium that induced these fanciful thoughts."

Merula tilted her head. "Why had she written those things down?"

"To prove she was hunted."

"Hunted?" Merula echoed, perplexed. "By whom? What for? And who did she want to prove it to?"

"She wrote several times that she was afraid of someone

taking me, her little boy, away from her." Royston swallowed. "I think she was worried she was going to be proclaimed mad."

"I see." Merula considered this in silence for some time. If people had known about his mother's "fanciful thoughts," they might have thought them the result of some nervous illness, indeed. The onset of insanity?

Royston said, "Are you afraid now?"

She looked at him. "Of this house? Because it happened here?"

"No. Of me." Royston held her gaze, his eyes deep and dark. "She was my mother. She died probably out of her mind with fear. You know how madness creeps through families, transmitted by blood."

"You think you will go insane?" Merula frowned at him. "I have rarely met anyone who could think so logically and who is given so little to panic and irrational thought. Even in that burning conservatory, you were not afraid."

Royston laughed softly. "But I am afraid now. As I sit in this quiet room and listen to the silence in this house, I wonder if the hands she heard on that window were in her head and if someday I will start hearing them too."

"And what if they were real?"

He turned his head to look at her. "Excuse me?"

"What if they were real? What if there were hands knocking on her windows and there was a dead bird put under her bed and someone did smear blood on her mirror to make her afraid? To make her lose her mind?"

"What for?"

"I don't know. Revenge? Hatred against your family? Wanting to tear you apart? Take you away from her? I don't know, but I do know that it is far more likely that the things she described were real than that they were in her head, as you put it."

Royston looked her over. "It is the middle of the night, we are at an old, creaking, abandoned country home, I just told you my mother lost her mind here and even ran out into the night and died, and you are discussing this with me as if there is a rational explanation for all of it? You don't want to run away screaming yourself?"

"Not really, no." Merula half smiled. "As long as there is no dead bird under my bed, you will not hear me scream." She folded her hands in her lap. "There was a moth pinned to my dress this afternoon. Did you consider me mad when you heard that story?"

"No, but I know we have enemies who are persecuting us. And Bowsprit saw the moth. It is all real. What my mother described in those notes . . ."

Royston inhaled hard. "I went to see my father. I asked him what it all meant. He told me to destroy those notes and make sure no one knew my mother had been going insane. He said it would ruin my reputation and my prospects of marriage. That no woman would ever have me if she knew I'd go crazy one day. I asked him about the dead bird, the blood on the mirror. He said there had never been any."

"But how could he be sure if he spent most of the time in the city? Is it so impossible that someone was playing cruel tricks on her, driving her to distraction while she was all alone here? All alone except for you, of course. Did you ever see someone lurking about the house? Or trying to get in?"

Royston shook his head. "But we had servants then. There was a strange old gardener. He was also a poacher, so he could have brought in dead animals. His daughter cooked and cleaned for us. She was odd, too. I caught her one day in my mother's bedroom with my mother's dress on. She was twirling around in front of the mirror and laughing, laughing, until tears gushed down her cheeks."

"She might have been the unstable one, driving your mother to distraction to take her place. To become mistress of this house."

"My father would never have allowed her to come near my mother's things."

"She might have believed, in some fanciful idea, that your father would marry her."

Royston stared down at the floor. "I asked my father what he believed had happened to my mother. He refused to answer at first, but when I pressed him, he admitted he believed she had killed herself because she was crazy. That he had tried hard to believe the accident theory but in his heart had always known the truth."

"What did he say about the night before her death? The male voice in the house and the argument?"

"He said he knew nothing about that. But later he said to me that my mother might have had a lover and that I shouldn't talk about that either."

"So he made you afraid with all kinds of speculations but told you nothing that you could rely on."

"I started telling myself that it didn't matter. That whatever had happened, it was too late to save her." Royston's eyes were sad. "That is what I really wanted when I was eighteen. To save her. But there was nothing left to do. She died, and I wasn't able to do anything to prevent it."

He looked at her. "That is why I am helping you now, Merula. I told you in the carriage ride from Havilock's to your uncle's that hasty conclusions destroy people's lives. My father never believed my mother, and in not believing her, he might have driven her straight to her death. Whether she killed herself or she died running away from whatever she was so afraid of, the fact remains that my father didn't believe her and didn't help her. He thought she was just going crazy. But what if she wasn't? What if she was really in danger? What if someone put the blood on the mirror and the bird under her bed, just as you suggested a moment ago? If someone had looked into it and caught the culprit, she might have survived. That idea won't let go of me. I can't let your uncle take the blame for something he didn't do or let you be harmed. It must stop. *I* must stop it."

"It won't bring your mother back," Merula said softly.

Royston didn't reply. He sat motionless, his eyes fixed on the crates. Slowly a tear appeared in the corner of his eye and trickled down his cheek. He didn't bother to wipe it away.

Merula's heart clenched for his hurt. She wanted to get up and wrap her arms around him and tell him it would be all right. But she knew it would not. His mother was dead. She had died near this house, afraid and alone, abandoned by the man who had married her but had not believed her. Who had stayed away from her as if she were contagious because he believed she was going mad.

Royston blinked. "I never wanted to come back here," he said. "Because this house is an accusation. Against my father, but also against me. We did nothing to prevent her death."

"You were only ten years old," Merula protested, shocked that he could think that way. "What could you have done? She probably tried not to let you notice any of it, as she wanted you to be happy."

"Yes, she always wanted other people to be happy. She was kind and considerate and never asked anything for herself. That killed her. That selflessness."

He banged his fist on a crate. "Here are her things, left behind and abandoned like she was. And I find someone has been through them and . . . I don't know if it was my father. If he knew more than he ever told me. I'm not even sure if . . . he was here the night she died."

"You're not sure if he was involved in her death," Merula said, her heart heavy but knowing she had to put into words what Royston himself would not.

Could not, perhaps.

He nodded. "What if he really believed she was losing her mind and people would find out and point the finger, at her, him, me, my brother? He meant it when he said that our prospects had to be protected. He might have killed her also for my sake!" His voice rose. "My father was so proud of our family name, of our heritage and our future. He would never have let anything threaten that."

"You think he killed her to stop the rumors about her mental condition? But I'm sure he could imagine people would whisper about it and draw their own conclusions."

"The inquest ruled it an accidental death. I have wondered if he paid someone for that ruling. My father always had a lot of power around these parts."

Merula shook her head abruptly. "You don't know he was involved, Raven. Why torture yourself thinking he might have killed her?"

She leaned over. "Isn't it far more likely that someone else killed her? The same person who persecuted her? Who put the dead bird under her bed and all?"

Royston gestured around him. "And that person also went through her things? Looking for what?"

"We don't know." Merula studied the crates. "What were you looking for, anyway?"

"More notes. Some were sent to me, but I've always thought there had to be more."

He took a deep breath before continuing.

"Still, once I received the notes, I didn't come here to look for them. To look for more evidence of how she died and why. Even eight years later, it might have been easier to solve it than it will be now. So much time has passed. I left for France to have a good time and forget about . . ."

He jumped to his feet and paced the room. "I let her down, again! I didn't save her when I was here with her and I didn't save her memory either when I could have. I was . . . I don't know what I was."

"I can imagine that the argument with your father shook you." Merula watched his tense posture as he walked. "Perhaps you were afraid of discovering he was your mother's killer. What would you have done then? Get him arrested? Or let him go free?"

Royston halted and looked at her. "People say I'm just throwing away my money on useless things. But I couldn't care less. I am doomed anyway. My mother dead by who knows what devious means and for what unspeakable reason. My father possibly involved. Either he was a coward who let her die or he might even have had a hand in her death. For my sake! I, the product of the match between these two unfortunate people. Each mad in their own way? I don't know. I run around, traveling to places one should see and trying to make my name with inventions and all, before it ends in disaster. Before I start seeing blood on mirrors as well. Because I'm crazy or because I'm guilty. In the end, does it even matter?"

Merula looked at him. Her heart ached for him, for what he had been through as a boy when his mother died, and later when he had received those notes and become so confused as to what he should believe. But she didn't want to just be sweet and considerate to him. He needed to be rallied to fight.

"If I sat here and talked like that, saying that in the end I would end up in prison and I would die by hanging, because of the butterfly—hatching it, bringing it, releasing it, getting my whole family into trouble, on the brink of disaster—would you believe me? Would you say I was right? No, you would fight me and urge me to defend myself and prove it was all different from what I believed. Or have been led to believe. Now do the same for yourself. Yes, your mother died, but we don't know how and who was involved. Believe that she told the truth when she wrote those notes about being persecuted."

Royston looked at her. "There are two options and each has its own horrors. Either she was truly going mad and I might be about to follow her, one day or the other, or she was being persecuted and nobody helped her and she died all alone. Maybe she did jump into that pond in fear, running away from someone who drove her mad. Her death might have been an accident or suicide or whatever they want to call it, but I want to know if she was being followed that night. I want to know if someone was there when she died. Whether he or she helped her along by holding her under or just watched as the whole terror came to its inevitable conclusion. I need to know. But I have no idea how to find out. They're all gone now. The people who were once here.

I'm too late. My questions will go unanswered. That is what I deserve for not acting sooner."

"Raven . . ." Merula got up from her chair and walked over to him, putting her hand on his arm. "I'm sorry that the situation forced us to come here. I wish it was all easier and . . ."

Royston looked into her eyes. "I've not been able to save her," he said, "and I'll never forgive myself for that. But I *will* save you. I swear it to you. I *will* save you."

Merula held his gaze, sensing the pain and the determination coursing through him. She knew he meant what he said and that he would do anything to help her survive this plight.

But she also knew that with the mysterious butterfly conspiracy and their invisible enemies so close to them yet still so far out of reach, nothing was certain. His promise warmed her, as did the certainty that he'd be with her, supporting her. But in the end, none of them could make any promises that either of them would ever be safe again.

CHAPTER 11

In the bright morning sunshine, the house didn't seem as lonely and sad as it had the previous night upon their arrival. Merula opened the curtains in the dining room and let the light flood in across the dusty table, the chairs, and the sideboard along the wall. She smiled as she saw the twinkle of a rainbow in the edges of the mirror.

Galileo came in, holding a book in his hand, from which he read something to himself in an indecipherable murmur.

Her "Good morning" was met with silence as he seated himself at the table, putting the book in front of him as he continued to read in deep concentration.

Merula shook her head to herself and was about to go out and explore when Bowsprit appeared with a tray full of plates, cups, a polished coffeepot, and sandwiches. "I packed food before we left the city," he explained. "It is not much of a breakfast, as we have no sausages and no scrambled eggs, but at least we have something to keep us going."

He nodded at Galileo. "What is he up to?"

"I have no idea. But we could use a significant discovery." Merula accepted a sandwich and a cup of coffee and seated herself to watch Galileo read.

After a while, she asked Bowsprit, "Where is Royston?"

"I think he went for a ride on horseback." Bowsprit looked disapproving. "The horse is borrowed, so I hope he is careful with it. He can ride like a madman when he is in the mood for it. The horse, however, might not have any experience with cross-country rides."

Merula shook her head and sipped the hot coffee. She didn't want to show worry but hoped Royston wasn't still in the same grim mood in which she had found him in the room among his mother's things. She glanced at Bowsprit, but as he and Royston had met later in life, he probably knew nothing about the events that had transpired here.

Galileo looked up and said, "Oh. Hello there. Good morning." He peered around him as if he had suddenly found himself in a strange place. "Breakfast? Right." He reached for the sandwich Bowsprit had put before him and took a bite. "Good. Yes." He looked down at the book again.

"What is that?" Merula asked. "Can it explain anything about Lady Sophia's condition?"

"I couldn't sleep and looked around in the library. Found this fascinating book about animal superstitions. Ravens being portents of death and all."

"Does it say anything about dead birds bringing bad luck?" Merula asked, her heart skipping a beat.

"Enough," Galileo confirmed. "What exactly it signifies depends on what kind of bird it is."

"And that book comes from the library here?"

"Yes. Had to blow off all the dust before I could dive in."

"So it belonged to Raven's father?" Merula asked.

"Yes, it had an ex libris in front bearing his name," Galileo said. "Several pages have been marked, so I think he found those particularly fascinating."

Her heart positively pounded now. "And what are those about?"

Galileo leafed through the book. "Ah, here is one. The dead magpie signifying that something valuable was about to be taken away from the finder. Magpies are thieves, you know that."

Merula nodded. "And you just picked that particular book off the shelf?" she asked, a tremor in her voice.

Galileo shook his head. "It was on the writing desk. Hidden in a ledger."

"Hidden?" Merula echoed.

"Yes, well . . ." Galileo flushed. "I don't want Raven to think I pried among his father's things. I was just having a look at the books, and when I saw the ledger, I was interested in when it had last been used. How long this place had been empty, you know. So I opened it and found it was hollow and contained this book. I just had to read it. The link between animals and superstitions is fascinating, as it is different for every culture. One people might consider an animal a sign of good luck, while others believe it is unlucky."

The door opened and Royston came in, a healthy color in his face. "That was great exercise," he said with a satisfied sigh. "Ah, breakfast. Bowsprit, my man, you know how to make something out of even the direst circumstances."

"I try, my lord," Bowsprit said with a smile. "Coffee?"

Without waiting for a reply, he poured.

Royston said, "Lovely weather too. But we can't sit around and picnic all day long. We have to decide what we are up to next."

Throwing himself down on a chair, he sighed. "I just wish I hadn't paid that little man five pounds for his useless information. Lady Sophia choking on an almond at a garden party three years ago. From now on I will refer to it as the most expensive almond in history."

"What did you say?" Galileo asked. "An almond? Lady Sophia choked on an almond?"

"Yes, some neighbor of hers—a merchant he calls himself, but I wager he is losing money these days with his opium habit, and maybe gambling as well—attended a party three years ago where Lady Sophia displayed the same symptoms as at the lecture: turning red in the face, gasping, collapse. But it turned out she merely choked on an almond. You know, thing going the wrong way, cough, cough, problem solved."

"That is amazing!" Galileo cried. "It could explain everything."

"No, it could not. Because at the lecture there were no almonds. Or other nuts. And she never ate sweets. So she can't have choked on a sweet, either. We checked all that already." Royston sounded impatient.

"No, I mean, the almond," Galileo said, still waving his hand enthusiastically.

Royston stared at him. "Are you deaf? I just told you there were no almonds at the lecture."

"I know. But that doesn't matter. Three years ago Lady Sophia collapsed, you said. She turned red in the face, had difficulty breathing . . ."

"Yes, because the almond she choked on was hampering her breathing. Somebody probably gave her a good pat on the back to get it out of her windpipe, and then it was all solved."

"No, no, no." Galileo rose, his chair shoving backward so wildly it almost fell over. "People *thought* she almost choked on an almond. But that might not have been the case. Her strained breathing, the rash on her face, could be the result of a response to the almond."

"Excuse me?" Royston said. "I don't follow."

Galileo kept waving his hands. "This is all very experimental, but there are all sorts of things that people have a response to. Foods mainly. They eat them and then their nose starts to water or they have to cough or they get a rash or they even lose consciousness. It is something in the food that affects them."

"Like poison," Merula said, with wide eyes.

"Yes, like poison, only it is not poison. It is the food itself that is doing it. They are sensitive to something in the food while other people can safely eat it and do not respond. We have to find a word for it, I suppose." Galileo grimaced. "I am not up on all the details, as it is more of a medical thing, but it does have a very interesting chemical component. I mean, what exactly in the food causes their bodies to respond? There is so much about food that we do not know yet."

His face got a dreamy expression, as if he was pondering all the opportunities for research and amazing discoveries ahead.

Royston said impatiently, "What are you trying to say about Lady Sophia?"

Galileo sank back on his chair and said, "The information that man gave you could be the key to her death. You thought he meant to say a nut in her food got into her throat. But the nut caused her to respond. That means that if later in her life she came into contact with almonds again, she might have the same symptoms. Difficulty breathing, a rash, fainting."

Merula sat up, her hands on the table, trying to work out what it all meant. "So Lady Sophia believed that she had almost choked on something small and round and hard. That explains why she mashed all of her food. She wanted to avoid another incident. But in reality it was not the physical quality of the nut itself, its shape or its solidness, that caused the problem. It was something *in* the nut. A part that could also be in other things? I mean, almonds are in other things, are they not?"

Galileo nodded. "In pastry, for instance."

"So Lady Sophia might have eaten almonds in some other form and that caused her collapse?"

"Yes, that is possible."

Merula clapped her hands together. "That must be it. Her bluish lips were a result of her not being able to breathe properly, but Sir Edward thought it meant she had been poisoned with actual poison."

"If this is true," Royston said, "the investigation of her body will not show any traces of poison like strychnine or cyanide."

"But that won't clear my uncle per se," Merula said, "as they can argue the butterfly's poison is not known to them and can't be traced."

Royston said to Galileo, "We heard what she ate before she left for the lecture. I'd have to ask the butler again in detail, but I don't think a dish with veal would contain any almonds. How long would it take between contact and a response, anyway?"

"I would think it varies from person to person."

"So that does not help us at all." Royston's initial enthusiasm faded fast. "We'd have to prove she had eaten almonds in some form. That she actually had a response to an almond before, beyond just choking on the nut itself. It will be difficult. I mean, how can we establish a firm relation between all of these things? Won't it be too subtle for a jury?"

Subtle, Merula thought, subtle . . .

Bowsprit reached into his pocket. "Perhaps I can help, my lord. I took the liberty of going into the village, as I was aware it has a telegraph office."

"Such a small village?" Galileo asked in disbelief.

Bowsprit smiled. "It was set up here especially for a certain local resident, who must be able to travel to London at the beck and call of a certain lady."

"You mean Queen Victoria?" Royston asked in awe.

Bowsprit laughed. "Nothing quite so elevated, my lord. The lady in question is married, and whenever her husband leaves, she informs her lover, who rushes to her side. It is common knowledge that they don't even send the telegrams to the house anymore but simply fly a banner on the roof of the telegraph office, which can be seen from the estate."

"You are making all of this up," Royston said.

Bowsprit didn't confirm or deny this but simply produced a piece of paper from his pocket. "I took the liberty of telegraphing to the office in London, where your response about Lord Havilock's time in India should come in, to ask for any news. This is what came back."

Royston pulled the missive from his hand and read. "Aha!" he shouted. "My friend writes that Havilock had to leave India after he almost killed someone. Beat him half to death after a loss in a polo game?"

He shook his head. "Does show he has a violent streak. And he referred to this incident blandly when pressuring Lady Sophia to return his zoological specimens."

"Yes," Merula said, "but a man who grabs another man and beats him over a lost game shows that he is hotheaded and doesn't think about the results of his actions. I mean, what was there to gain? The game couldn't be won anymore, and Havilock just got himself sent off, out of India. His threat against Lady Sophia fits that image: it's quite crude and not intelligent. But the death of Lady Sophia has something . . . smart and methodical about it. Especially if we assume it has something to do with her response to almonds. Then it was almost ingenious."

"Not like Havilock at all, is that what you're saying?" Royston asked. "Hmm, yes, I see your point. And how would Havilock have known of the almond incident that happened at the garden party three years ago?"

"Maybe he was there?" Galileo suggested.

"No, he was in India then," Royston said. "He could have heard about it, of course, but would he have understood what it meant? That requires more . . . medical or chemical knowledge."

Merula nodded. "You just used the word subtle. And that's the key. If Lady Sophia's death was no accident but part of a coldly calculated plan, then it was subtle. And Havilock's actions are not subtle at all."

They all sat and thought about this in silence.

Merula went over everything she had seen at the lecture.

Lady Sophia's attitude, her mannerisms, the look on her face, her symptoms right before the collapse. She had been so busy waving her fan. Had she been faint already? Had she waved air into her face to fight the faintness?

Or to be able to draw breath? Had the response to an almond or almonds already started to hamper her breathing?

Images whirled in Merula's mind. The fan moving, the ostrich feathers ruffling in the breeze created by the motion, Foxwell wanting to take the fan from Lady Sophia's hand but her holding on to it.

The collapse, the screen being brought, the anxious waiting, the doctor's arrival, the speculations of the fearful guests about poison in the room. Poisonous wallpaper. Being in the same room with it being enough to . . .

She sat up and looked at Galileo. "This response that people have to certain foods, this sensitivity, does it only occur when they eat the food, actually have it in their mouths and throats and swallow it down, or can it also happen through inhalation?"

"Particles can be on the air and can be inhaled, and inhaled particles can cause a response. Bad or favorable. Some lung problems are cured by burning herbs in the fire and inhaling the scent of the burning herbs."

Galileo leaned back in his chair, apparently ready to expound, but Merula said, "The fan. It was the fan. It is so clever, so . . . Lady Sophia inhaled the almond scent. She started to feel unwell. She wafted more air into her face, but that was also full of almonds. She kept waving, desperate to stay conscious."

"Again waving more air into her face that was, to her, poisonous." Royston stared at Merula. "That is brilliant."

"She worsened her own symptoms," Galileo cried. "She just kept adding more stimuli. She applied the fatal dose to herself."

"Unknowingly." Merula nodded. "How terrible when you think about it. Poor woman."

"But wouldn't she know the scent of almonds?" Royston asked. "You always hear it is so distinctive."

"Not all people have a great sense of smell," Galileo said. "Besides, ladies perfume their fans. I bet you it was so full of her favorite perfume she wouldn't have smelled anything on it. Almonds or whatever else."

"So the killer must have introduced almonds to the fan somehow." Royston gestured with his hands. "Almonds are solid, but I assume that you can somehow also turn them into a liquid form?"

"Almond essence," Galileo said with a nod. "You don't need fancy equipment or intricate chemical knowledge to make it. All you need is almonds and alcohol to soak them in. The alcohol takes on the essential ingredients of the almonds. The longer you leave it, the stronger it gets."

"And you could mix it with perfume and put it on a fan?" Royston asked.

"Yes. I wouldn't advise anyone to just start soaking almonds, though. Apart from some people's sensitivity to nuts, there is cyanide in almonds, and in soaking them, you might be brewing your own poison. It would be dangerous to keep around in a household."

"The killer didn't care about the risks of the cyanide," Royston said slowly. "He or she needed an almond scent that Lady Sophia could inhale. A special poison, as it were, to kill Lady Sophia in the most ingenious manner."

"But who knew that Lady Sophia would have a response to almonds?" Merula asked with a frown of concentration. "The cook who was dismissed for the almond incident at the time, no doubt. Other servants, perhaps? Guests at the party . . . Wouldn't they have believed it was a simple matter of choking on something she accidentally inhaled? They can't have concluded anything more."

"Unless they had the knowledge to do so." Royston rubbed his hands together. "Now we are getting somewhere. We have to find out who had such knowledge. And if the fan was really treated with almond essence."

"I could analyze it," Galileo said, "if I had access to it."

"Buckleberry can help us get it. It must be at Lady Sophia's house. I don't think the police saw any reason to look closer at it."

Merula frowned. "It fell to the floor when Lady Sophia collapsed. I can't remember if it was still there later. What if the killer took it away?"

Royston gestured with his hands. "We won't know that until we have asked for it. Bowsprit and Galileo, you go into London first thing and see if Buckleberry can get his hands on the fan. Tell him he will certainly get his bearer bond if he helps us with this. Then take the fan to Galileo's if it's still safe there and test it. Let us know what you find."

Bowsprit and Galileo left the room at once. The book lay on the table forgotten.

Merula looked at it, her throat suddenly tight again. "Raven," she asked slowly, "that dead bird your mother found under her bed, what species was it? Did she mention it in her notes?"

"Yes. I had expected it would be a crow or a raven. A big black bird. But it was actually a magpie."

Merula's stomach filled with ice. "Your father, did he know anything about birds? Did he like to study them, look at them, read about them?"

"Not that I can remember. How come?"

"That book . . ." She pointed at it. "Is it his?"

Royston went over and looked. "I can't remember having seen it around the house. But the library is extensive, and it was a long time ago. Why do you ask?"

"Galileo found it hidden away in the library. He mentioned to me that it's about animals and superstition. It has marked pages. One of them describes the dead magpie as a portent of something valuable being taken away."

"A threat to my mother," Raven said in a low voice. "Referring to her sanity."

"Or her marriage," Merula added, "or you, her child."

Royston stared at her. "My father had that book? He marked those passages? He . . . drove her mad?"

"We don't know that. You never saw him with the book. The book was hidden, so someone else might have put it there."

"That mysterious someone we want to have been here to clear my father . . ." Royston laughed softly. "Perhaps he was a mean man who liked to make my mother suffer. I do know he was jealous and could accuse her of betraying him. He might have believed she had a lover and this was his way of punishing her for what he believed to be true."

"We don't know," Merula repeated softly. It hurt her that he was torturing himself with all of these speculations, questions he could no longer find an answer to, as both his mother and his father had died.

"No, we don't know anything, and that is the worst." Royston stood and stretched his shoulders. "When I came back from riding, I felt better for a while, but now I feel again as if the weight of the world is on my shoulders. We have to solve this thing surrounding your uncle. You need answers."

He looked at her, pale and tired. "Believe me, Merula, there is nothing worse than having to suppose a thousand things and not knowing one of them for sure."

CHAPTER 12

The atmosphere in the house was dark and brooding, and the tension of waiting for Bowsprit and Galileo to return seemed unbearable. Merula walked around the rooms for some time, staring at the furniture covered with sheets and trying to picture Raven there as a little boy. His mother, his father. A happy family, put under strain by a stranger?

Or a family where the tension had come from within, where jealousy had eaten its way into the very heart of their lives?

Had Raven's father become so obsessed with his wife's supposed infidelity that he had started to keep an eye on her, only pretending to have gone to the city but hanging about the house, watching her and after a while also scaring her with dead birds under her bed and blood on the mirror?

What would the purpose of such actions have been?

Driving her back into his arms? Seeing if she would confide in him?

Or torturing her, punishing her for the loss of her love for him, as Raven had supposed? Who knew what went on in a mind driven mad by jealousy and the fear of losing a beloved wife?

Yes, love could have caused it all, Merula supposed.

Still, listening to her own footfalls on the floorboards, she could not completely dismiss the theory that another had done it, for a reason they could not understand.

Or could they? The image of the girl twirling in front of her mistress's mirror and laughing hysterically would not let go of her. Had she been obsessed somehow? Had she started to believe she was entitled to this house, to her master and the child? Had she done those evil things?

Her being in the mistress's bedroom had proven that she could go there freely. She could have put the dead magpie under the bed.

She might never have read that book in the library. But she need not have. As a local, having grown up with a granny who told stories or listened to folktales around the village, she might have known about the superstition surrounding magpies. Knowledge was conveyed in many ways other than books. And it was just as powerful.

But the deviousness of putting that book in the library, half hidden, so it would seem that the master of the house had tried to hide the evidence of his machinations against his wife . . .

Wasn't it too clever and too ingenious for an infatuated local girl?

She had to ask Raven who had benefited from his mother's death. It was an unfeeling question, but it might point them in a certain direction. With Lady Sophia, it certainly had.

Simon Foxwell.

He had tried to take the fan away from his aunt. Had he known she was going to collapse and wanted to make sure the fan would not be studied more closely?

But why would anyone suspect a fan of having anything to do with her collapse?

And had Foxwell really wanted Lady Sophia to die? If the suggestions made to them were true, Foxwell had already been able to sell off bits and pieces from the zoological collection. He hadn't needed to kill Lady Sophia for that. He had alienated her from her former friends so that he didn't have to fear she would believe any stories about the collection being sold off. And she herself never came near it, so discovery of his actions would have seemed unlikely as well.

What could have forced Foxwell to murder her?

Besides, if Galileo was right in assuming the almond essence for the fan had been homemade, it had taken time. As he had explained, you had to soak the nuts in alcohol for weeks to get a strong concoction. That meant it hadn't been an impulsive decision from the killer but a plan long in the making. Why?

What had provoked it?

Oppressed by the silence in the house, Merula left it and

walked across the grass to a formal garden in the back. At least, it had been a formal garden once. The traces of flower beds were still visible, but everything was covered with brambles and weeds. Some had grown as tall as she was, and the thorns clawed at her arms, attaching themselves to her sleeves. Still, underneath that tangled mess, something was blooming. A few roses had survived and showed their white and yellow flowers, albeit suppressed by the intruders.

Merula smiled at them. "Well done," she said softly. "I hope that one day . . ."

She halted and considered. Did she really think Raven could ever live here? That he could take on a gardener to restore these gardens and that he could live in that house, with those memories? That he could live near the pond where his mother had drowned?

A strange need to see it drove her to walk on, searching for a body of water. She almost felt that if she could see it, stand near it, she could imagine the state of mind Raven's mother had been in when she had come out that night. That she could understand what had happened there.

She wanted to understand it. She wanted to give Raven some answers, as he had said, so sadly, that it was the worst thing not to know.

"Merula!" The hoarse voice came from behind. Before she could even turn, someone grabbed her by the shoulders. She gasped.

Strong hands spun her around, and Raven, deathly pale, looked down at her. "What are you doing here?"

"I want to find the water."

He stared into her eyes. "I should never have brought you here. The atmosphere of this place is getting to you. Seeping into your very soul." He shivered.

Merula shook her head. "There are no evil places. Just people who did evil things there."

Raven squeezed her shoulders. "Why didn't you stay in the house? I was looking for you, and when you weren't there . . ."

"I'm sorry. I didn't mean to frighten you. I only wanted to see the pond."

"Where my mother died?"

"Yes."

"Why?"

"I hoped I could deduce what happened that night."

"Deduce . . ." Raven laughed. "As if it could be done like that."

He stared past her. "I've tried to deduce it, as you call it, many times. Especially after I received her notes suggesting someone had been terrorizing her. But I could never make it all fit."

He let go of her and stood awkwardly, dangling his arms. "You won't find the pond."

"Excuse me?"

"You won't find the pond. It's no longer there. My father had some workers fill it up with earth. He didn't want to keep it. As it was the place where she had died, I suppose."

Or to remove possible traces of what happened. Traces of his presence on the scene?

Merula shivered as she realized it was a real possibility in her mind that Raven's father had killed his mother. Knowing that would not make it better for Raven. He was already afraid that his mother had suffered from delusions and that one day he might suffer the same fate.

But what if he had to conclude that instead his father had been a killer?

Of course, it didn't mean he had to become one as well, but . . .

Didn't you often see that a character trait from the father was present in the son as well? Easily inflammable temper. Tendency to gamble. Fear of heights even, or something else quite innate. Not taught, but present deep inside the human mind. Inborn, perhaps? There was so much about human nature and psychology they didn't yet understand.

Could a killer be born with the need to kill? Could he be more prone to do something evil at some point in his or her life? When provoked, when put in the right situation?

Raven studied her expression. "What are you thinking about?" His gaze held hers insistently. "Are you afraid to be alone with me, here in this place?"

Merula said, "I don't know. Part of me tells me there is nothing to be afraid of, as you saved my life and have proven to be a true friend to me. But part of me also knows there is so much I don't understand. About you, your family, about life in general."

Raven laughed softly. "Life in general," he scoffed. "Why not start with something smaller, my dear Miss Merriweather?"

Merula didn't look away. "I feel like a fool," she said, "in this whole investigation. I'm just groping in the dark, hoping I can catch something. I don't understand people or their behavior. I don't understand why they crave wealth, as I 've always known I would never have it and I've accepted that."

"You could marry a rich man."

Merula laughed. "With my past, my . . ." She gestured. "I know I'm not a great beauty like Julia. It isn't bad for a woman to be plain if she has a title or a fortune attached. At least, that is what Aunt Emma always says. I think I would feel bad if I had a title and a fortune and men came to me for that, thinking it didn't matter how plain I looked."

"You are far from plain," Raven said. "And far from a fool. You have acted very astutely in this case. I didn't want to pay that former neighbor of Lady Sophia for his information, but you persuaded me and it turned out to be very important indeed."

He held her gaze. "I've never met anyone quite like you. The women in my acquaintance are all . . . Well, some of them know what they want and how to get it, but in an unappealing way. As if they are hunting men. Then there are some who simper and cry constantly, or faint over every little thing. I don't have patience for that. Now you . . . you have been in fear for your life and you never cried."

Merula took a deep breath of the clear fresh air. "I don't have time to cry. I have to save Uncle Rupert, and the rest of the family, from ruin. It's all my fault, and even if it was not, I'd still want to help them. They took me in and gave me everything I have today."

She leaned back on her heels. "I hope that we can prove a connection between almonds and the fan."

"Even if we can, we still have some problems. We'll have to convince people that a healthy woman can die of contact with almonds."

"I'm sure there are doctors who can give testimony to such cases. Galileo knew about them."

Raven nodded. "I think I heard something about a man who is trying to prove that all kinds of things make people sneeze. Feathers and fur from animals and other things. It is also a response of the nose to something irritating."

"I see."

Raven smiled sardonically. "I was asked to invest in his research, but I didn't see an immediate practical purpose for it."

"But you did see such a purpose for the hair tonic for balding gentlemen?"

Raven winced. "My friend assured me it was going to be a sensation. Indeed, it was when skulls got burned!"

Merula studied him with a frown. "My uncle told me that your brother bribed the police to get you out of it."

Raven looked sour. "Yes, my brother is rather concerned for the family name. Or I suppose it's his wife putting him up to it. My sister-in-law merely married for the title and the money attached. I can't see how she ever managed to snare my brother, as she is about as interesting as a dead canary and that would probably be an insult to the canary."

Merula said, "She must have some hidden charming side that your brother discovered."

"Or he just let himself be talked into the relationship. You have no idea how that goes. You visit a few parties and you speak with a woman there. Rumors abound of an attachment while you never meant anything of the sort. Then you have to ask for her hand to prevent her from being ruined. It's just a trap!"

Merula laughed. "So you make sure you will never get trapped like that?"

"Not if I can help it," Raven said. "I don't want to tie myself down. Besides, I don't know if I would put any woman through the ordeal of being married to me." He forced a laugh. "My untidy habits, my peculiar friends, not to mention my spending."

"You make light of it, but you are truly worried about your past. Your mother and the implications of her death."

Raven looked at her. "I can't deny that. There are several choices. My mother was mad. My father was obsessed with the idea of her infidelity and killed her. Both would not be very palatable to a young lady contemplating living under the same roof with me. Not to mention having children."

He rubbed his hands together. "As my mother's death was ruled an accident, I guess I could simply leave it at that. My future wife wouldn't need to know. But I would know it and feel awkward about it. I wonder if you can start a marriage with a lie."

"An omission," Merula corrected.

Raven looked at her with a sharp, probing gaze. "You'd advise me to make such an omission?"

She shook her head. "Not at all. But you speak about it in such strong terms, making it all so black and white. Is it not possible you could meet someone and grow to care for her and she for you, and then at some point you might tell her the truth and . . ."

"No! After she had grown to care for me, I'd be afraid to tell her and risk losing her." Raven's eyes flashed. "She'd have to know up front. Or not at all."

He turned away from her and stalked back to the house.

Knowing there was no pond to find and suddenly aware of the deep menacing silence even in these woods, as if no birds lived there and no critters ran through the under-growth, Merula went after him at a trot.

★　★　★

Galileo burst in with something in his hand, wrapped in paper. "We have it. And it is true. It was treated with a solution of almonds. Alcohol too, but that could also have come from the perfume she sprayed liberally on it."

"This fan," Raven asked, "how did she get it?"

"Ah, I asked Buckleberry about it," said Bowsprit, who had followed the excited scientist at his usual sedate pace. But the look in his bright eyes betrayed that he was also happy about their discovery and was convinced it had moved the case along. "He thought it was rather new. He said he would ask the maids about it. They usually knew when the mistress had bought something. But Lady Sophia was rather fond of beautiful things and liked to spend money."

"Meaning it might be hard to determine," Raven said with a worried frown.

"We will hear back," Bowsprit assured him. "Now what can we do with this knowledge?"

"We must discover who knew of Lady Sophia's adverse reaction to the almond at the party." Raven paced the room. "Try to imagine the scene. If your hostess collapsed, that would make an impression. But if you believed it had been a nut getting into her windpipe, you'd not think twice about it. Those things happen, especially at parties. So we have to assume the person in question knew something about medical things."

"You mean," Merula said, "that he or she would have realized it was more than just a choking incident? That Lady Sophia's response indicated she responded badly to almonds and that such a response could be provoked again?"

"Exactly. So we'd be thinking along the lines of a medical man, or a nurse, or someone with chemical knowledge."

"Sir Edward, who treated her at the lecture, had been

in the army as a doctor. He explained that he knew the symptoms of poisoning. Would he also have recognized the adverse reaction to the almond, had he been there at the garden party?"

"We have to find out who was there that night. All the guests." Raven looked at Bowsprit. "Can you get in touch with one of the servants and see if there is something of a guest list left? In some households, everything is recorded carefully. Menus of the night included."

"I can try," Bowsprit said.

Raven looked at Merula. "You and I are going to hire a cook."

"A cook?" Merula echoed.

"Yes. We are once more the Duttons from Walking woods, and we are looking for a cook. But not just any cook. The cook who used to work for Lady Sophia."

"Her name was Bridgewater, Buckleberry told me," Bowsprit said. "I asked him about her without telling him everything we're suspecting. You never know whom he might mention it to."

"Very good. We can try employment agencies in London. After Mrs. Bridgewater was sent off, she had to have found a new employer somehow."

"Perhaps she knew someone in another household and found a new position that way. She may not have gone through an agency."

"I know, but we have to start somewhere. Bowsprit can ask, when he's asking for the guest list of that fateful night, if the person knows where the cook went. We will all have to do our bit."

"What about me?" Galileo asked.

Raven waved at him. "You guard that fan with your life. It is concrete evidence that we can use."

Galileo looked about him. "So I will be staying here?"

"Yes, for the moment." Raven nodded at Bowsprit. "Ready? Then we are off."

CHAPTER 13

The employment agency had two waiting rooms, one for the clients who were hiring and one for the people seeking employment. They were on opposite sides of the corridor and, although the doors leading into them were identical, Merula had concluded that the rooms were not. A glimpse into the other room had taught her that it had benches along the wall and nothing giving it atmosphere or charm, while the room in which they were now waiting had an intricately carved sideboard along the wall, a few good oil paintings, a rich carpet on the floor, and two sofas and two armchairs to sit on. There were no small trinkets, though, so the owner seemed to consider it wise not to let anything lie around where it could be taken along by either of the parties involved in an agreement.

Raven shifted his weight on the sofa beside her. "We are probably wasting our time," he whispered. "The other two knew nothing and only kept us for ages recommending people on file with them for whom we have no need. I can't afford to end up actually hiring a cook."

Merula suppressed a smile. The door opened, and a page boy escorted them to a room down the corridor. The heavy oak-paneled door led into a large sunlit room with a big desk, behind which a competent-looking lady sat leafing through some papers. She greeted them with a nod and gestured at the chairs in front of her desk. "You came all the way from Walkingwoods to hire a cook in London?" she asked with a piercing look over her pince-nez.

"Not just any cook," Raven said. "Some years ago, we were guests at an excellent party in the countryside, with Lady Sophia Rutherford. We talked about cooks, and Lady Sophia confided in us that her cook had created all those amazing recipes herself. Now, recently, I have had the good fortune of being promoted at the bank where I work."

The mention of a bank took some of the skepticism from the woman's eyes and replaced it with respect. And interest.

Raven continued, "My wife and I will be expected to receive distinguished guests to dinner, and as we are somewhat new to all of this, we are quite eager to make a good impression. We remembered the cook, and of course we asked Lady Sophia whether she was intending to part with her. To our surprise, we learned the cook had already left. Lady Sophia wasn't sure with what family she was now. You must forgive her, but the death of her husband put a lot of strain on her."

"So I have heard," the woman said. If she knew about

Lady Sophia's death—and with the newspapers writing about it the way they did, she could hardly not know it— she concealed it well. "Now you are trying to find this particular cook?"

"Yes. A Mrs. Bridgewater. We have it on good authority you can help us."

Merula thought this statement was quite bold on Raven's part, but the woman smiled and said, "Over the years I've provided Lady Sophia with many servants. Indeed, her butler and her companion came through me. I've never heard a bad word about them. However, her cook for her country estate didn't come through me. And her new employment wasn't arranged for via our agency either."

"That is a shame," Raven said. "But I thought I heard Miss Knight had come to Lady Sophia through the Grunstetter Agency?"

"By no means. She came through us."

Merula was surprised, as Miss Knight had boasted to Buckleberry that she had come from the best agency in London, and according to Buckleberry this had been Grunstetter, where Raven and she had indeed found Miss Knight trying to find a new position after Lady Sophia's death. Why had Miss Knight not returned to the agency that had arranged for her placement in Lady Sophia's household?

To find out more, Merula said hurriedly, "Miss Knight is such a pleasant woman. So capable."

As the woman didn't seem to want to respond, Merula pushed harder, "So patient with Lady Sophia. I must confess

I find people who discuss their health incessantly quite loathsome, but she seemed to be able to reassure Lady Sophia."

"Normally," Raven added, "it is quite hard to persuade people who believe they are ill that they are not, or at least not as ill as they believe, but Miss Knight was so good at it. Lady Sophia relied on her."

"That is probably," the woman said with slight disapproval in her tone, "because Miss Knight worked as a nurse before she came to Lady Sophia and knew what she was talking about. I don't think much would have escaped her. And she is not a woman who indulges silliness. Lady Sophia's nervous streak demanded a steady hand."

As if she realized this might sound odd, the woman added, "Those were her husband's words when he came to get a companion for his wife. I recommended Miss Knight, as she seemed exactly the pleasant but firm character needed. I've never heard a single complaint about it. And it has been ten years."

"Yes, indeed, an ideal match," Raven said. He glanced at Merula a moment. "Miss Knight a former nurse . . . I'd never have guessed. But now that you mention it, she does have that bit of cheerful determination that suits someone in that profession so well."

Merula wagered he was thinking the same thing she was. Having been a nurse, and one who noticed every little thing, as this woman assured them she did, Miss Knight had to have noticed the almond incident at the garden party and drawn her own conclusions about it.

Still she had apparently not warned her mistress against the dangers of almonds.

Nor had she explained to her that her weird habit of mashing her food was unnecessary. Wasn't that odd?

Or had Miss Knight perhaps tried to explain, but Lady Sophia hadn't wanted to hear a thing about it? She had been said to be rather headstrong and stubborn.

Raven thanked the woman for her time and they left. In the street he took Merula's arm and pulled it through his with vigor. Walking side by side with her, he said, "A nurse! So she can have known about it. It makes her the ideal suspect in the household."

"But would a nurse kill?" Merula objected. "She was trained to cure, something deeply ingrained into her being. And what for? Why would she want to murder Lady Sophia?"

"Buckleberry told us Lady Sophia had accused her of theft. Their relationship was under strain, ever since Foxwell had come into the household."

"Yes, but . . . is that enough to kill for? The missing earring was never found among Miss Knight's things. There's no proof at all that she did steal. It was Lady Sophia's idea, but we already know she imagined a lot of things. Or was led to believe them. Foxwell might indeed have tried to turn Lady Sophia against Miss Knight. Julia mentioned to me that Miss Knight had shown an interest in Foxwell. Perhaps he was so insulted by her behavior toward him that he decided to get her into trouble?"

Merula thought about this theory with a deep frown between her eyes. "I can't imagine a nurse would kill someone for an accusation that had not materialized. She might understand how to do it, but she would also realize others might have the same knowledge. Could she be sure it would not be detected?"

Raven nodded. "Yes, and consider this: the fan was returned to the household after Lady Sophia died, and Miss Knight took no trouble to remove it or even destroy it. You'd think that, if she knew it held a clue about the murder method, she'd have disposed of it. Still, we have to keep her in mind."

"Of course. We must keep all options open. Including the missing cook." Merula sighed, stretching her shoulders. "Is it time yet to meet Bowsprit and hear what he learned? I could do with something hot to eat."

Raven seemed about to say something when he suddenly pulled her into an alley. "What?" she asked.

"A policeman coming in our direction. Looking about him."

"Might be after a boy who stole an apple at the grocery store. Why would he be looking for us?"

"I'll let him pass before we move on," Raven decided.

They waited, and then when Raven had checked the street on both sides, they continued to walk. "Our chances of ever finding that cook are minimal," Merula said slowly. "It was three years ago. She might have left the area. Why stay around here?"

"Perhaps, but she is the only person we know that knew of the almond incident, and her dismissal might have given her a reason to hate Lady Sophia and want revenge."

"After three years?" Merula asked in disbelief.

"Yes, well, you know how things go. At first she told herself she'd find another position. She did, but she got dismissed again. Or she couldn't find anything and had to take up work below her station. She had time to think about her sad fate, the injustice of it, as she had never meant to do Lady Sophia any harm. Not at the time, that is. Now she's thinking that Lady Sophia has a wonderful life, while she lost everything."

"You know absolutely nothing of the kind. It is all speculation. Oh, there's another police officer." Merula nodded in the direction of the man who was coming down the street toward them.

Raven immediately dragged her into a tobacconist and took his time buying pipe tobacco while he kept glancing over his shoulder as if he expected the policeman to be a fan of pipes as well. At last, when they came out again, the street was full of people but no uniforms.

"I wonder," Raven said, with a glance about him, "if they are also using informers. You know, people who look like they are going about their business, selling something or sweeping, while they look out for us."

"You're getting overly suspicious," Merula said with more conviction than she felt. "Ah, there's the restaurant. I hope Bowsprit is already waiting for us. I can't wait to learn what he discovered." She glanced up at the front. "What does vegetarian mean?"

Raven smiled at her. "Meatless. You can't order any dish here that contains meat or fish. I've never been in any such place before. But Bowsprit swears by it. He claims it is not only delicious but also very good for your health."

Merula gave him an incredulous look. "Bowsprit struck me as a very practical man. And because of his seafaring, he traveled everywhere. I thought he'd eat anything. Sheep eyes and tentacles of the octopus. Not that he wouldn't even want to eat beef."

Raven laughed. "You sound almost disappointed. Bowsprit is an educated man. He likes to read, and somehow he got his hands on a leaflet about this whole vegetarian idea. I guess it is in line with all the other nonsense we hear. About sleeping with your window open and all to let the fresh air in. And burglars, I'd say. I keep my window firmly shut at night."

"You have a point there," Merula agreed.

As they entered the establishment, she took a deep breath to determine what scent was on the air. Was it cabbage?

Her nose wrinkled. It was considered a poor man's food, and now here she'd actually have to pay money to taste it?

Still, she saw some fashionably dressed ladies sitting at a table and some men, most likely merchants at their lunch, in a corner. Bowsprit was gesturing at them from a table in the back.

Raven ushered Merula over, whispering to her, "I hope

the police aren't fond of vegetarian food as well. If we're caught in here, there is nowhere to go."

Merula made no reply but took a seat beside Bowsprit, who leaned his elbows on the table. "I have a list of all the guests at the garden party," he said weightily and passed a paper across the table to Raven.

He looked over it. "Like I thought, Havilock is not on it. He was in India then. I don't see Sir Edward either."

"It would have been illogical," Merula said. "If Sir Edward had been present when Lady Sophia suffered a similar collapse, he would have said so at the lecture. But he didn't seem to know what to do. He was quite agitated and upset."

"Perhaps he was so upset," Bowsprit said, "because he cared for her. I heard that before Lady Sophia met her husband, she was close to being engaged to Sir Edward. But as he didn't have a title yet, at the time, her parents liked Lord Albert Rutherford much better for a son-in-law. Sir Edward stayed friends with the couple, also after his own marriage. There were rumors that, when Rutherford died, Sir Edward tried to get closer to Lady Sophia again."

"That could explain her appearance at his lecture," Merula said, "even though she usually avoided such occasions. Perhaps she even brought a new fan to impress him?"

Raven looked doubtful. "Sir Edward is a married man. Surely a woman as dedicated to decorum as Lady Sophia wouldn't have encouraged his interest in her?"

Merula shrugged. "As long as they met in the presence of others, there was nothing improper about it, and nothing Sir Edward's wife could complain about, I suppose. I'm sorry for Sir Edward that the woman he cared for died under his hands, while he wasn't able to do anything to save her."

Raven nodded with a grave expression. His hands tightened on the list in front of him. "I don't see anyone on this list who was also at the lecture. We seem to be stuck with our elusive cook."

Bowsprit said, "I already ordered the beet soup. What can I get for you?"

Raven looked about him as if he were in a foreign land and asked hopefully, "Is there anything that at least looks and tastes like meat?"

Bowsprit said, "You could try mushrooms. They seem to have a similar structure to meat."

"Mushrooms? I've always been told they are poisonous," Raven exclaimed.

Merula shook her head. "Some kinds are, but not all. You have to know your species, though, if you're going to pick them in the wild. Poisonings because of mistakes with identification are quite common."

Raven grimaced. "Thank you, I will not risk my life. Give me that beet soup, then." He glanced at Merula. "How about you?"

"The cabbage with cheese is delicious," Bowsprit enthused, and Merula said, "I'll have that." She smoothed her dress, glancing around her. "I have never eaten in a restaurant before. Aunt Emma calls it uncivilized."

"But she does eat at the houses of friends?" Raven asked.

Merula nodded. "Of course."

"Then what is the difference?"

"I don't know. I think this is quite exciting." Merula smiled, then sobered as she looked at the list of guests to the summer party where Lady Sophia had had the almond incident. "Can you deduce nothing useful from that list?"

Raven shook his head. "Miss Knight must have been right when she said Lady Sophia had lost contact with most of her friends."

"It is odd," Merula persisted, "as you told me her late husband was a respected member of the zoological society. Wouldn't people have attended that party who'd also come to a lecture like the one Lady Sophia died at?"

"You have a look then." Raven passed her the list.

Merula read the names, which were almost all foreign to her. "Foxwell is not on it," she said to make some kind of observation. "He wasn't yet living with Lady Sophia then, I assume. Or no: even if he had been living with the family, he would not have been on the list as a guest."

"So could he have known about the almond incident?" Raven asked.

Merula sat up. "Yes, I think he could have. Julia told me when we met at the exhibition that Miss Knight was friendly to Foxwell. As if she hoped he would take an interest in her. If they spent time together, she might have mentioned the almond incident to him. As a reason for Lady Sophia's eccentric behavior, for instance."

"Why would she have? When we talked to her, she didn't mention it to us. After her mistress collapsed and died, surely such an earlier incident would have been refreshed in her mind, especially with her nurse's training?"

Merula sank back against the chair. "Yes, that is odd," she admitted.

Bowsprit said, "One of Lady Sophia's footmen told me that as word of Lady Sophia's death got out, the shops where she ordered goods all hurried to send messages to Foxwell about the outstanding bills. It seems he is under pressure to pay quickly or risk rumors that there is not as much money in the estate as everyone expects. He was even seen leaving the house with some large object covered with a blanket. The footman supposed it was some valuable, like an antique clock or painting, he was going to sell off."

"Or a zoological specimen," Merula said. "Did the footman know where he was going?"

Bowsprit shook his head. "I've asked at some pawnshops if zoological specimens have been offered to them, but none of them knew of any."

Raven said, "I think it makes more sense to assume Foxwell would sell directly to a collector. And as long as we don't know to whom . . ."

Merula was still pondering the mention of unpaid bills and asked, "Was the ostrich feather fan among the items purchased but not yet paid for? Then we'd know the name of the shop where it was bought and could go there to ask questions about it."

Bowsprit said, "I can try to find out."

Their soup and cabbage with cheese were brought. Raven put his spoon into the red substance and gave it a critical look.

Merula laughed softly. "It's no different than any other soup, I suppose. Give it a chance."

Raven carefully tasted it. "Not bad," he said with a surprised half smile. "Rather spicy even."

"They like to use spices here," Bowsprit nodded. "Influences from the East, I imagine."

Merula was glad her cabbage didn't have too much spice. The cheese was melty and delicious and a great combination with the cabbage. She said to Raven, "I would like to try this once again. Some other time when we don't have to . . ."

He silenced her by putting his hand on her arm. He nodded at the door. A policeman entered, looking back and saying something to someone behind him.

Bowsprit was on his feet already. "This way," he hissed.

They abandoned their table and followed him to a worn velvet curtain that concealed a door. They stood in the kitchen, several cooks giving them rather surprised looks.

Bowsprit put down some money, calling "For our meal" while he went ahead of them to a door that led into a back alley.

A foul stench of waste filled the air, and Merula held her hand over her face as they hurried across cobbles wet with dirty water. At the end of the alley, Bowsprit looked this way and that.

"Hey! You there!" a voice called. "Halt! Police!"

They broke into a run, pushing past a maid carrying several hatboxes and a group of children sharing sweets from a paper bag.

On the corner, Bowsprit, who was well ahead of them, almost ran in front of a brewery cart, the driver swearing at them as his horse neighed in panic. They managed to cross behind the brewery cart and in front of a brougham, ducking into another alley where the sounds of hammering resounded.

Passing an open door, Merula glanced in and saw an old man putting together a coffin. Several finished ones stood along the wall.

Shivering, she hurried farther, waiting for a hand on her shoulder. But there was no hand and no shouting. As she dared to slow down a moment and glance back, she saw no one following them. Apparently the policemen had lost them at the moment of crossing the busy street.

"Raven!" she tried to call between strained breaths. "Wait for me!"

Bowsprit was out of sight, and Raven was about to turn the corner, but he looked back and then waited for her.

Panting, she leaned against the wall.

"You have to practice running," Raven said. "Every morning after breakfast. The grounds at Raven Manor are big enough for it."

Merula didn't have the energy to reject this eccentric proposal or even laugh about it. Her head was light, and she saw black spots in front of her eyes.

Raven stepped closer to support her. "They might not have been after us," he said in a cheerful tone. "They might just have thought it suspicious that we ran. They might have taken us for thieves or something."

"I hope so." Merula wiped the sweat off her forehead. "We need to find that cook, but how can we if we can't move about anymore?"

Raven patted her arm. "We will find the cook," he said. "Bowsprit has asked around, and he might hear something. Think of how far we've come already. We figured out how Lady Sophia died."

Leaning closer to her, he said, "*You* figured it out. You thought of the fan. It was genius."

She looked up at him. "It won't help Uncle Rupert if we can't determine who put the almond essence on the fan."

Standing here, hot and tired and feeling more like a fugitive than ever before, she felt so small and inadequate, unable to ever solve this conundrum.

Raven held her gaze. "We'll find that cook. I promise. Now come on before they catch up with us anyway. What was the address of the next employment agency?"

CHAPTER 14

No one had heard of a Mrs. Bridgewater who had been the cook of Lady Sophia Rutherford, and with a heavy heart Merula sat in the carriage on the way home to Raven Manor. The sun was already sinking, casting everything in a fiery red glow. In a field, a deer was looking for something to eat, and high against the skies a bird of prey circled, searching out his dinner on the ground below.

At the bridge leading across a brook onto the road to Raven Manor, a small boy was waiting. He stepped onto the bridge, blocking their way, and halted them with a weighty gesture. "You can't go there," he said. "The police are there."

"What?" Raven called. He leaned out of the carriage door to look at the boy. "What are you saying?"

"I got a pound," the boy said with an exultant grin, "to wait all afternoon and night, if I had to, and tell a coach that came to pass here that the police were at the house."

"Galileo's way of warning us," Raven said to Merula

with a grim expression. He asked the boy, "What are they doing at the house?"

"Nothing. Just watching it. That's what he said."

"Is he still at the house?"

The boy shrugged. "I don't know. He had many boxes with him."

"So he managed to sneak out with his things," Raven said pensively. "Where can he have gone?" He looked at the boy again. "Did the man with the boxes tell you where he was going? Or what we were to do?"

The boy shook his head. "Just that the police were watching the house. Oh, and that the owl always finds a place to roost."

"A place for the night," Raven muttered. "Owl . . . What can he have meant by owl?"

He thanked the boy, and Bowsprit turned the horse around. He asked Raven, "What do you want to do now, my lord?"

"Owl." Raven stared ahead. "Galileo gave us a hint with this word owl. A hint as to where he is hiding out. But I don't understand the clue. Do you?"

He looked at Merula.

She shook her head. "I think it's meant for you to understand. You grew up around these parts. Is there a place here where you can see owls? Or something named after an owl?"

"Naturally." Raven's expression lit. "There's an old factory where they used to make cigars. They were called

Athenas. Athena is the Greek goddess of wisdom and her symbol is the owl."

"Of course. Do you know where this factory is, exactly?"

Raven gave Bowsprit some instructions, then leaned back against the padding. His expression was grave again. "They found Raven Manor. It means they are well informed and rather desperate to catch up with us. Your uncle must have admitted under pressure that you are the butterfly expert, not he. They must believe you can give them vital information as to how Lady Sophia was killed."

"Or they think I killed her," Merula said, her stomach full of ice. "They want me because they believe I am a murderer. They want to catch me to convict and hang me."

Raven grabbed her hand and squeezed. "I won't let it come to that, I promise." He rubbed his thumb over the back of her hand. "We have come too far to lose now. Lady Sophia died because someone consciously put almond essence on her fan. Someone knew that once the fan was used and the essence inhaled, Lady Sophia would become unwell. Struggling for breath, she would wave the fan more vigorously and inhale even more of the lethal scent. She worsened her own symptoms; she hastened her own death. It is so devious that, if only for that reason, I want this person caught and brought to justice."

Merula caught the intensity in his voice and wondered if he was also thinking of his mother, of the fears she had endured, of how she had been hunted by someone who had tried to drive her mad, who in the end made her rush away from her home into the night, into the arms of her killer.

It was indeed devious.

It made the blood boil with fury.

In the dusk, they saw the contours of an old factory building, the last rays of sunlight glinting in the cracked windows. As they got out of the carriage, a crow called out in the distance. The eerie silence drove a shiver down Merula's spine. What if the boy had also mentioned the owl to other people? What if this was a trap of some kind?

Raven seemed to wonder the same as he stood and looked around him, carefully, his body tense, his hands formed into fists.

Bowsprit said, "I will go see if I can find Galileo. You stay here near the carriage. At the first sight of danger, you flee with it. Don't wait for me. It is most important that you stay free to complete the investigation." He walked away from them with firm steps to try the door leading into the building.

Raven watched him with a doubtful expression. "He has a point, of course, that we have to stay free, but can I just let him go in there alone?"

Merula shrugged. "Bowsprit is a resourceful man. He saved us at the vegetarian restaurant."

Raven had to smile. "Yes, he even remembered to pay for our food. A real gentleman."

Then they heard a call and a call back. Two owls, it seemed, in the dusk. But then Bowsprit was already gesturing at them to come over, and they ran up to him. Inside the factory building Galileo was waiting, his many "boxes," as the boy had called them, strewn about. "I thought you'd never come," the chemist called. "I was certain you had been caught and it was left up to me to solve this whole thing."

He breathed a sigh of relief. "There you are now. We must go back to London. We must find a safe place there."

"Where?" Raven asked, glancing at Bowsprit as if he expected his valet to have the answer.

But Merula said, "With Lamb's mother. She lives in Rotherhithe. The police don't like to come there, as they say it's full of cutthroats and disease."

"Yes, an ideal hiding place," Raven said ironically.

But Merula said, "Lamb's mother knows I helped Lamb to care for her. She'll take us in."

"But earlier," Galileo said, "we suspected that the police had found out about my house via this girl Lamb. What if you walk straight into the police's arms by going to her mother?"

"I don't believe Lamb told the police anything," Merula said firmly. "And we have no choice. We can't go back to Raven Manor, and we can't stay here either. This building looks as if it's about to collapse."

"It won't just collapse," Galileo protested. "Besides, who says the police haven't issued a reward for information about us? If Lamb's mother is a poor woman, as you suggest, she might be tempted to turn us in for the reward money."

"She would never do that," Merula said, her voice more

certain than she felt. "If we want to get back to London before midnight, we must leave now."

"The lady has a point," Raven said. "We have to find that cook, and we can best do that from London."

"Julia might also have discovered something very interesting about Foxwell, finances, or other people involved," Merula added, rallying herself into believing this. "We have to combine all our information and see who is at the heart of it."

Galileo picked up a box or two. "Carry this to the carriage, then," he said with a sigh of resignation. "But I tell you that if this girl Lamb and her mother can't be trusted, we are going to be in a lot of trouble."

★ ★ ★

Merula had never actually been to the house of Lamb's mother and had to go by memory of little things Lamb had told her about her upbringing. The alehouse nearby where her father spent all of their money, the lodgings for sailors who carried strange tattoos from all the ports where they had been, the sound of church bells in early morning inviting people to start the day with praise. And the next-door neighbor who was a butcher who gave the pig bladders to the children to turn into balls to play with.

"This must be it," Merula said softly, pointing at the chipped door. At the next house over, a straw dog licked a bucket that was stained with something dark. Probably blood from slaughter.

Raven said, "Are you sure?"

Merula lifted her hand as a chime filled the air. She pointed up at the tower of the church high over the houses, then down the street where windows were still lit and the raucous laughter of drunken men drifted out a half-open door. "That is the alehouse. This must be it."

Not allowing doubt to seize her, she knocked on the door. It took some time before it opened a crack and a suspicious face peered out. It was an old woman in a mended nightdress, her white hair pulled back in a braid that hung over her shoulder. "What do you want?" she asked in a hoarse voice.

"I am Merula. Your daughter Anne's mistress."

The elderly woman's face changed at once. "Miss Merula! I had never expected you to come here. And at this hour." She peered worriedly down the street to where the alehouse was. "Come in quickly."

"This is my friend, Lord Raven Royston," Merula said. "And a friend of his. And his valet. I will explain why we are all here."

"Come inside first and do the explaining there," the old woman said.

They all stepped inside, the men bowing under the low door beam. In the small living room, two chairs stood at a table with a cloth over it. A chipped vase held some flowers. Over the open fire was a shiny polished kettle. Everything was simple and old but neatly cleaned and arranged to give the small space some atmosphere. The old woman said,

"I can't offer all of you a place to sit." She studied Raven. "A real lord, who would have thought it?"

"I must be frank with you," Merula said. "Anne must have told you about the . . . problems?"

"Your uncle's arrest, yes, Miss. A terrible thing. Anne is certain he is innocent."

"Yes, we know it, but we must prove it. The police, however, believe in his guilt. We cannot face them until we have evidence it was different from what they believe. Can we stay here? Can you hide us until we have found that evidence?"

Anne's mother stared at them. "Hide you? So the police are looking for you?"

"Yes." Merula held her gaze. "I'm honest about it, as I don't want you to get into any trouble. The police seem to be looking for me. And also for my friends because they have helped me. But I must stay free a little longer. We know how Lady Sophia was killed, just not who did it."

The old woman crossed herself. "May death stay far away from my home," she said softly.

Then she studied Merula with sharp eyes. "Anne told me how you made it possible for her to leave the house at night. How you even gave her money once for coals."

Merula looked down. "It was nothing much. I have such a good life; I've never had an empty stomach or a cold night. I just wanted you to have food and warmth as well. Anne works so hard to provide for you. I've seen her hands chapped from cold water and her face all red with exertion from doing heavy chores. She never complains, though. She is always cheerful and grateful. You should be proud of her, not me. I did nothing really."

"Anne told me so often," the old woman said, "Miss Merula is different from the others. Miss Julia doesn't see me. But Miss Merula does."

"Julia does see the servants, too," Merula protested, but inside she knew Julia mainly saw them as convenient presences to do chores for her and make her life easier. She doubted if Julia had ever wondered how they lived, what they did on their days off, or what kind of future they had. To defend her cousin, she said, "Julia has just led a very sheltered life, and she can't imagine how it would be outside of that. But she is never cruel to the servants."

Mrs. Lamb nodded. "I heard from other families whose girls are in service that the mistress beats them with a ruler on the fingers when they are too slow. One girl broke her hand and couldn't work any longer. But that is not the mistress's problem."

She sounded bitter.

Merula said, "Aunt Emma would never beat anyone, let alone a girl."

"Still, she wouldn't agree to Anne going out at night," Mrs. Lamb said. "You make that possible, and Cook. I'll help you. No matter what the police are after."

She nodded firmly. "But my house is too small for all these men." She cast them a disapproving look. "Back there's a warehouse for wood. You can sleep in the attic. Lord or no lord."

Raven made a mock bow. "I'm much obliged."

A knock sounded at the door. They all froze. Merula's heart seemed to skip a beat, then thundered on.

Mrs. Lamb went to the door to ask, "Who's there?"

"Me, Mother. Who else?"

Mrs. Lamb opened the door, and Anne stepped in. Seeing Merula, she raised her hands to her face and cried, "Miss Merula! I was just thinking about you. Wondering how you were."

"I need a place to stay, Anne," Merula said quietly, "and your mother has let us in. How is Aunt Emma?"

"At first she was in bed, crying all the time, but today she let a lawyer come. Heartwell listened at the door to hear what they were talking about."

Mrs. Lamb shook her head in disapproval. "Butlers always think they're entitled to know what their masters are involved in. But they're no better than other servants."

Ignoring her mother's comments, Anne continued, "Heartwell came to the kitchen afterwards, and he told us, after Cook asked him several times, that the mistress was certain Lord Havilock was involved in the death at the lecture and that the lawyer had told her it would be hard to do anything about Lord Havilock because he had powerful friends and wasn't easy to touch. He even suggested that the master should plead guilty to the charges and hope he would not be condemned to die."

"What?" Merula clutched her hands to her chest. She felt queasy. "Plead guilty of murder? Of course they will never let him live. How could they if they believe he killed a lady? Will this lawyer not do anything else? How about Newbury and the others who have a claim against Foxwell to get specimens back? If they take legal action, surely that must prove that others had a motive to murder Lady Sophia."

"I don't know anything about that," Anne said with sad eyes. "After the lawyer left, the mistress cried her heart out. She even talked about leaving London."

"Fleeing the scandal." Merula understood. "But if she leaves, it will be as if she also believes Uncle Rupert is guilty." She stared at Anne. "Does she believe that?"

Anne shook her head. "I don't think so. Miss Julia does not believe it for certain. She asked me to tell you something." Her sad eyes acquired a glimmer of hope. "I'm so happy you are here, Miss. Now I can tell you right away. Miss Julia didn't want to write it down so I could give it to you. She said that it should not become known widely."

Anne hesitated.

Merula said, "I'm sure none of us will talk about it unless we have to, for the case."

Anne nodded. "She said to tell you Mr. Foxwell does not have money of his own. That he lied about that. She was quite cross about it. And she cried too. I don't know what for."

For seeing her hopes dashed that Foxwell had honestly liked her, Merula thought. Julia was smart enough to work out that if Foxwell had lied about his fortune, he had also lied about other things.

For a moment, Merula thought of Miss Knight, the companion, and Foxwell's tale to Julia that the woman had wanted a relationship with him but not he with her, naturally.

Had he lied about that too?

Had he first flirted with Miss Knight, perhaps even taken certain liberties, and then dropped her and thought up the missing earring to have her dismissed, removed from the household?

Some men seemed to think they were entitled to do with their servants whatever they wanted.

"Did Julia say anything about Miss Knight?" she asked Anne. "Lady Sophia's companion?"

"No, not now. But I do know she doesn't like her. Once, a few weeks ago, she asked Heartwell all kinds of questions about her."

"Heartwell knows Miss Knight?" Merula asked in surprise.

Anne shrugged. "Heartwell seems to know everybody. Miss Julia wanted to know how long she had worked for Lady Sophia and if she was beautiful and accomplished. Heartwell said she played the piano well and spoke French. Miss Julia didn't like that at all."

Merula suppressed a smile. Julia hated French and had never managed to learn to speak it well, although she could read it a little. Julia also neglected to spend time on the piano as Aunt Emma demanded, saying she played well enough not to make a fool out of herself if she was asked to play something at a party. But Aunt Emma reiterated often that Julia could be much better at music or languages if she only invested the time now spent on Regent Street buying hats or meeting with friends to take tea and gossip. Usually oblivious to her mother's censure of her frivolous pastimes, Julia must now have felt that a simple companion was ahead of her in accomplishments. No wonder she had been cross.

She asked Anne, "Did Julia see Miss Knight as competition for Foxwell's favors?"

Anne shrugged. "It's not for me to say, Miss. But Heartwell joked to the footmen that Miss Knight was moving up in the world, or at least that she wanted to, and they seemed to think it was very funny."

"So maybe she did want Foxwell," Merula mused.

Raven shook his head. "She can want anybody she sets eyes on, but the other party has to accept her. And I can't see Foxwell becoming engaged to his aunt's companion. Not even if Miss Knight had been ten times more beautiful and enticing."

Merula had to agree with him there. "But what if she put pressure on him because of something she knew? Something related to the zoological collection?"

"Blackmail to get him to marry her?" Raven asked with a dubious expression. "I'd sooner think he would have killed her then, if she was such a threat to him. Besides, she told us freely about his supposed sales from the collection. If she used that knowledge to put pressure on him, she'd have kept it to herself."

"I suppose so." Merula sighed. She smiled at Anne. "Give my love to Julia and tell her I'm doing everything I can to clear Uncle Rupert. Tell her I've made progress. Also tell her to be careful. When we met at the exhibition, someone was near us who doesn't wish us well."

Anne's eyes went wide. "How do you know that? What happened, Miss?"

"The details don't matter. Just tell Julia to be careful. And if she can, to persuade my aunt not to leave London. We might be able to clear Uncle Rupert soon."

Anne nodded. "That is good news indeed, Miss." She turned to her mother. "You should be in bed, I'll get the guests settled in." She leaned down and kissed her. "You're cold. Get into bed now."

As the old woman shuffled off, Merula said apologetically, "We're sorry to have disturbed her. But there's nowhere we can go. The police also turned up at our other hiding places."

"They'll not come here," Anne said with confidence. "They think there's disease here. A fever took some sailors last week. Their bodies have been burned to prevent it from spreading." She shivered. "I wonder, if they burn your body, if you can still feel it."

Galileo said, "It's an interesting question if there's sensation after death. When the soul leaves the body, does that mean the body can't feel anymore? Blood circulation has stopped. Dead bodies don't bruise. But if that also means that the dead can't feel anything . . ."

"Please stop talking like that," Merula said. "The poor girl won't dare walk back to the house later with such talk."

Galileo looked hurt. "I'm merely posing it as a scientific problem."

Raven said, "Yes, well, pose it at some other time." He said to Anne, "Your mother said we can't sleep in this house and must go to a warehouse for wood at the back?"

Anne nodded. "I'll take you." She gestured to them to follow her.

Raven winked at Merula. "You'll get a bed, I'm sure. For us it will be a hard floor. But at least we're still free. Take heart, and we'll continue in the morning."

She smiled at him, then, as they were gone, wrapped her arms around herself and sighed. She was bone weary, and her head was full of all the information they had collected over the day. Had Miss Knight been in love with Foxwell? Had she first tried to win him, then put pressure on him somehow? Had he spurned her anyway? Had Miss Knight then killed Lady Sophia with the fan, hoping that Foxwell, as the heir benefiting from the death, would be blamed for it and would be tried and hanged?

It was a bitter revenge for being rejected, but who knew how bitter Miss Knight had become during her long years of serving Lady Sophia?

Perhaps the wrongful accusation of theft had driven her

over the edge. Had made her decide to punish them both for treating her so shamefully?

And there was Havilock, with his need to sell part of his collection but the inability to get his prize pieces back from Lady Sophia. His threat to her, referring back to a violent incident in India. A man who liked to assert himself when he felt cheated.

But how would he have had access to the fan?

And Foxwell, such a clever manipulator of people, not afraid of telling a convenient lie to get his way. If he had been able to sell off zoological items without Lady Sophia knowing about it, he need not have killed her for money.

Unless he had grown tired of getting a little here and there and had wanted it all, without having to wait for her natural death. Once Lady Sophia was out of the way, he would also have been free to marry whomever he wanted, without having to endure Lady Sophia's censure of his choices and the fear that she would disinherit him if he didn't do what she asked.

Disinherit . . . Was it possible Lady Sophia had been about to cut him from her will? Could they find out about that?

Anne came back in. She frowned. "Can a lord really sleep on the floor?"

"I'm sure Raven won't suffer any ill effects from a night or two on the floor," Merula assured her. "He isn't spoiled like some others. In fact, I think he quite enjoys this whole investigation."

"They say he is a troublemaker. You have to be careful around him." Anne seemed to want to say more but feel awkward about it.

Merula smiled at her. "You may speak your mind, Anne."

"Your aunt would have a fit if she knew you were here staying with my mother. And traveling in the company of men without a companion. You are not titled, so it doesn't matter like it would for Miss Julia, who has to marry a duke or an earl, but . . ." Anne wrung her hands. "It isn't proper. There will be talk about it."

"Anne . . ." Merula reached out and touched the girl's arm. "My uncle is in prison. How much talk do you think there is about that? We are just about ruined. I have to do everything I can to prove his innocence. I can't sit at home with Aunt Emma and wait until somebody else does something. Besides, the police are looking for me too, because of my involvement with the butterfly."

"You shouldn't have brought them to England, Miss. All of these foreign animals. They must stay where they are."

"But don't you want to learn about them? Discover new and fascinating things about them?"

"Like how they kill people?" Anne shivered. "I'm glad they destroyed the insects with fire. I would be afraid to work in the house knowing they were still there."

Merula bit her lip. She couldn't understand how Anne could want her butterflies dead, but on the other hand, she could understand the servants' fear of the unknown and of the idea that death had lived so close to them and could have struck out at them as well.

She said, "Other people are not allowed to burn my uncle's property, Anne. They should not have done that."

"Perhaps not, but they only tried to help us." Anne looked at her. "I'm sorry for you, Miss, and for your uncle. But if the butterfly killed Lady Sophia, it had to die as well. Like a rabid dog."

"It did *not* kill Lady Sophia. We know how she died. Just not who did it." Merula held Anne's gaze. Galileo had been worried Anne could not be trusted. That she had given away information about her whereabouts earlier. She asked softly, "Did you know where I was staying earlier? Did Bowsprit tell you when he asked you to fetch my clothes?"

"No, he was very emphatic that no one should know. Making himself important, I wager." Anne looked hurt. "I would never tell anyone where you were, Miss. Not even for money. That newspaper man offered me money, but I said no."

Merula widened her eyes. "A newspaper man asking for me?"

"Yes. He didn't look like he could write a very good story, though. He was snooping everywhere. I saw him several times when I was out on errands."

Merula thought about this. Had someone pretending to be with some newspaper and offering money for information somehow discovered that she was staying with Galileo?

Had that same person followed them to Raven Manor? Did it have to do with the mysterious butterfly conspiracy?

She was relieved that Anne hadn't know about her whereabouts and could not have betrayed them, not even accidentally. Smiling warmly, she said, "Please believe me when I say that someone wanted to kill Lady Sophia and used an ingenious method to do it. It had nothing to do with the lecture, the butterfly, my uncle, or me. Lady Sophia died at the lecture, yes, but if she had gone to the opera that night, she would have died there and people there would have been suspected."

"I don't understand," Anne said in a trembling voice. "What killed her then?"

"Her own fan."

Anne blinked. "Her fan?"

"Yes. I can't explain it all now, but her fan was treated with poison and Lady Sophia inhaled the poison and died. We have to find out who put the poison on the fan."

Anne shuddered. "I had no idea such things could happen. What is the world coming to?"

Merula gave her an encouraging pat on the shoulder. "Don't worry about it, Anne. Lord Royston will help me solve it. And perhaps you and your mother and your friends here in the neighborhood can help as well. We are looking for Lady Sophia's cook. A Mrs. Bridgewater who worked for her at her country estate until about three years ago. She was dismissed after an incident at a party. We'd very much like to talk to her about this incident. It might help us discover who killed Lady Sophia."

Merula was not about to reveal they suspected the cook herself of involvement. "If your friends here know Mrs. Bridgewater, it would be very good if we could meet her without her knowing in advance what it is about. We'd like to hear her memories without them having been influenced. You know how it goes. Things in your mind change when others have told you their thoughts about it."

"Yes, Miss. I'd be happy to help. Now you must go to bed. You look so tired. I'll show you where you can sleep, and then I'll go back to the house. Cook warned me not to stay away too long. She says we have enough trouble as it is."

"And so we do," Merula muttered as she followed Anne to find her place for the night.

CHAPTER 15

The next morning, Merula freshened up with the cold water in the jug left on the windowsill and made sure her dress looked its best. Going down, she found the room empty and decided to take a look outside. At the butcher's, the windows were wide open, and a voice shouted from the inside, followed by the sound of a hand striking flesh.

Merula flinched and hoped it was the man at work with the dead meat, not a living being, least of all a human child.

She smelled fresh bread and walked down the narrow street to detect where the scent came from. An old woman came walking up to her, laboring with a bucket full of coal. When she was ten feet away, the bucket's handle broke and it tumbled over, spilling the coal into the street. The old woman cried out, and Merula went over at once to steady her. "Don't worry," she said quickly. "I will gather it again."

She leaned down and picked up the pieces of coal, putting them back into the bucket.

The old woman watched her in mute surprise.

When the bucket was full again, Merula wiped her dirty hands together. Without a handle, it would be difficult to carry. She could lift it and hold it against her, but it would ruin her dress.

"Let me do that!" a voice called, and a cheeky lad of about fourteen appeared by her side. He gave her an appreciative look and picked up the bucket as if it weighed nothing.

The old woman pursed her lips. "If you had seen the bucket fall, James Jones," she snorted, "you would have put as much coal as you could under that shirt of yours instead of helping me gather it again."

James pulled a repentant face. "Cold porridge is hateful," he said, "full of lumps."

"Can't afford no coal again," the old woman concluded, shaking her head.

The boy carried the bucket for her, Merula by his side to watch that he didn't take any from it. As they reached the old woman's home, no more than a door and a single boarded-up window squeezed in between two bigger houses, the boy put the bucket down in her hallway.

To Merula's surprise, the old woman took two coals from the top and gave them to him. "You find some firewood to go with this, James, and then your little sisters can have a warm breakfast."

He thanked her and ran off.

"He's a good lad, I suppose," the woman said. "He can't

help it his father died. Went to work in the fields, fell off a cart, got trampled."

She told it as if it was a mere observation, not a sad family tale. "She doesn't want to remarry, but she'll have to. A woman needs a man's protection. Especially her. Pretty little girl, she is."

The old woman looked up at Merula. "About your age, she is."

Merula gasped. "That can't be. She can't have a son that age if she's as old as I am."

"James is her husband's boy, from his first marriage. Wife died from lung trouble. Very sad. He remarried, and together they had the girls. Twins. Three they will be around Michaelmas."

Merula couldn't quite imagine having three-year-old twins at her age, but she supposed most girls here married young and started families right away. "You were generous with the coal," she said.

The woman shrugged. "Like I said, James is a good lad, even if he is a little wild sometimes. He needs a man around to see that he doesn't get into trouble with the law. Yes, she will have to remarry." She suddenly studied Merula. "And what is a fine lady like you doing here? Lost?"

"I'm staying with someone. I need to . . . be away from home for a while."

The old woman tutted. "They say that the rich people have all the pleasures and none of the trouble we have here, but I think rich people have their own troubles. Bless you for helping me with the coals, girl. You have a good heart."

"Merula!" Raven appeared beside them, his shirt undone at the top, his hair whipped up by the wind. He looked like a rake from one of the romantic tales Julia loved to read.

He said, "What are you doing here? It isn't safe."

The old woman cocked her head. "If your husband finds you, he might shoot you. We had something like that last month. Lady hiding here with her lover and her husband came and shot them both. Scotland Yard made sure it didn't get into any newspapers. Seems she was an influential lady."

"I'm not married," Merula rushed to assure her. "And I'm not doing anything illegal either."

Raven hitched a brow at her and said to the woman, "We'd better be looking out for some breakfast now. Good day."

Ushering her along with his arm around her shoulders, he whispered. "Nothing illegal! You're wanted by the police. Had you forgotten?"

"She thought I had run away from my husband and was hiding here with . . ." *You.*

Merula found this whole idea inexplicably painful and thought it better not to expound on it. "I only wanted to assure her there would be no husband coming to shoot us."

"No, there might just be conspirators who want to deliver another threat." Raven clutched her tighter. "I don't understand how you got it into your head to leave the house alone."

"I'm sorry," she said demurely. "I didn't mean to startle you."

Raven exhaled and let go of her. Straightening up, he walked beside her with his hands folded on his back. "You're just a naïve girl who needs to be protected against her own whims."

"You're not my brother or any relative of mine. You can't tell me what to do." Merula whipped back a lock of her hair, and Raven, looking at her to retort, burst into laughter. "Right now you look like a naughty toddler who fell into the coal cellar."

Merula looked down in horror at her smudged hands and fled ahead of him to the house so she could wash up.

When she came down again, still feeling rather silly, everybody was seated around the table, Mrs. Lamb and Raven on the chairs while Bowsprit sat on the floor cross-legged and Galileo perched on a barrel, reading through some notes on a crinkled sheet of paper. The table with the neat cloth held three plates, a basket with bread, a small piece of cheese, and some bacon. Mrs. Lamb sat smiling as if she enjoyed playing hostess to them all.

Raven stood to give his seat to Merula and encouraged her to take some bread with cheese. Wondering how much of it was to last perhaps all week, Merula denied wanting any cheese and ate her bread bare, praising Mrs. Lamb for her strong coffee. Mrs. Lamb explained she had got some via a niece who cleaned at a coffeehouse. "She doesn't like being paid in beans, but we all love it," she said with a crooked smile.

Merula praised the coffee some more and then the neat little house and especially the lace curtains that were so white. "That is because Anne knows how to wash them right," Mrs. Lamb enthused. "Anne learned so much since she went into service. I was worried about her at first, having heard the stories, but I'm glad now."

"Nothing happens in our household," Merula assured her. "Heartwell is a very decent man. A little garrulous perhaps, but he doesn't allow the footmen to dally with the girls."

Mrs. Lamb seemed to want to say something, then decided against it. "Anne has done well for herself," she concluded and leaned back against the worn pillow.

Merula decided that once this whole ordeal was over, she'd have to think up a way to reward this sweet old woman for her hospitality. Perhaps a new pillow would be a good idea? Or some extra food?

But it would have to be done in such a way that Mrs. Lamb didn't feel as if it were charity. She had her pride.

"It is unfortunate," Galileo observed, "that almonds are not treated like strychnine or cyanide. Chemists who sell poisons are usually careful with them and remember to whom they sold them. Or they even keep a poison ledger registering their sales. But almonds are easy to buy and considered quite innocuous. I don't think we can trace who bought the almonds that delivered the essence."

"For the moment, I would be insanely happy," Raven observed sourly, "if we found a way to speak with the elusive Mrs. Bridgewater. But I suppose you can't expect to find her in a city of millions. Disregarding your theory"— he nodded at Merula—"that she left the region."

"You have to talk to Polly," Mrs. Lamb said with a nod. "She knows so many people. We all joke that if you know someone and you talk to Polly long enough, she knows someone who knows them too. She makes you feel like everybody is everybody's cousin. In the third degree at least. She runs a boarding house."

Merula felt excitement rush through her veins. "Is there any way to entice this Polly away from her boarding house so we can talk to her in private?"

Mrs. Lamb shrugged. "Her daughter usually comes to help her clean in the mornings. I know Polly has a sweet tooth. She's especially fond of that terribly sweet thing. Nougat or something."

"I see." Raven threw Bowsprit a look. "I think you will have to go and buy half a pound of the best nougat you can find and invite Polly to come sample it here. Include some with nuts, so we can start a conversation about almonds."

Bowsprit jumped to his feet. Although he had looked content sitting there, he was obviously glad to be able to do something. When Raven reached into his pocket, he said quickly, "It's taken care of, my lord." He then left the room.

Raven retracted his hand, and Merula wondered if Bowsprit worried about Raven showing he had money on him in this place. The people here were mostly poor, and the kind of money that Raven carried with him to purchase a book or tobacco meant to them the difference between cold porridge with lumps or a decent breakfast.

Or perhaps no breakfast at all? What would it be like to have children and no idea how to feed them?

Mrs. Lamb gestured at the cheese on the table. "Don't you want some, Miss?"

"It's fine this way," Merula said, chewing on the bread. She smiled at Mrs. Lamb. "Thank you for taking us in. We didn't know quite where to turn."

Mrs. Lamb shook her head. "That one like you should end up like that. And your good uncle at that. In prison while there are so many crooks running around free. We never did like the police here."

She folded her arms over her chest. "You can rely on us to keep you away from them. Any way we can."

★   ★   ★

Bowsprit returned with the nougat—white and pink ones—a few minutes before their guest arrived. Polly was a tall thin woman with a shock of black hair combed back from her narrow face. She had lively eyes and was quick to burst into roaring laughter. Merula heard her in the street even before she came to the door. "I tell you," she said to Mrs. Lamb, who had gone in person to fetch her, "that I've never seen a man run so fast."

She entered the room and saw Merula. "Well, well, look who's here. You're Anne's young mistress, aren't you? Anne described you in such detail, I'd recognize you anywhere. Besides, who else of that fine family would set foot here?"

Merula winced under the implicit condemnation of her family. She forced a smile. "Pleased to meet you."

Polly seated herself on the barrel where Galileo had perched earlier and studied Raven. "I daresay you are the gentleman who tried the experiment with the steam-powered coach. It all exploded, didn't it? I have a memory for faces."

Raven flushed and looked chagrined that Polly knew of this debacle.

Merula wondered if Polly had laughed heartily about it as she just had about the man running fast.

Polly now spied the nougat on the table and made wide eyes. "My, that is a lovely sight."

"His lordship bought them as a treat," Mrs. Lamb said, "but I don't like very sweet things. I told him that you do."

Polly eyed the nougat greedily, then looked at Raven. She seemed to realize that her remark about his steam-powered coach had been a little risky, considering he was the giver of these sweet delights. Smiling, she said, "I've always liked a man who took chances. No invention would ever have been made if those men had not taken chances. Maybe they failed at some point, but in the end they made what they dreamed up. I'm sure you will one day have your steam-powered coach, my lord."

It was a gracious retreat, and Raven accepted it as such, answering her smile and saying, "As these nougats are just going to waste, lying there untouched, I suggest you see if they are as good as the salesman told my valet."

Polly didn't have to be asked twice and put a pink nougat in her mouth. She closed her eyes in concentration. Her entire expression contorted in what was probably meant to convey total bliss.

Merula, for her part, was worried the woman's mouth was glued together with the sticky mass and she'd never talk again.

But Polly had already opened her eyes again and mumbled around the nougat, "Delicious. Best I ever had."

"I think you should also try the other flavors," Raven suggested.

Polly leaned back and stretched out her feet, obviously intending to enjoy her task.

Raven said, "I hope you don't mind the nuts, though. Some people hate nuts."

Polly shook her head to indicate she didn't.

Raven said, "Some people really fuss about everything." He glanced at Merula. "This lady acquaintance of yours, screaming and shouting when a nut only came near her."

"Well, there was a good reason for that," Merula took up the tale. "She had had a very bad experience once. I think it was three summers ago at her house in the country. At a party, she almost choked on an almond."

Polly, who had been sucking and chewing on the nougat as if her life depended on it, shot up straight. "I heard that," she managed to say around the lump. "The almond was supposed to have been put in on purpose. But it was an accident, I swear. Poor Mrs. Bridgewater."

Merula felt as if she had been punched in the stomach at the woman's casual mention of the name. So Polly did know her.

Raven feigned ignorance. "Who?"

"Mrs. Bridgewater. She was the cook there. A very nice, competent woman. Would never have hurt her mistress. For the life of me, I can't imagine how the almond got in that dish. Must have fallen in in the kitchen. Or some hired hand for the night made a mistake. Who knows? But Mrs. Bridgewater was dismissed. Dismissed, for an almond!" Polly grimaced and reached for another chunk of nougat.

Raven said, "I can imagine that, having been dismissed like that, it was hard for her to find another job as cook."

"Hard?" Polly let the nougat hover in front of her mouth so she could express her indignation out loud. "Hard? Impossible, you mean, my lord. Lady Sophia hadn't given her a reference, and the party had been attended by many friends of hers. They all made sure Mrs. Bridgewater couldn't find a position anywhere. She had to work in an inn at first, serving, but the innkeeper thought she was too old and not fast enough like the young girls were. She then ended up in a laundry, standing with her hands and arms in water all day long. Most women sicken eventually from that harsh work, but with her it went really quick. First her hands got all swollen and painful and she couldn't do much wringing anymore, and then it was her lungs. Wheezy breathing, coughing. She didn't get a wink of sleep at night. But she had to keep working, to earn some money for herself and her daughter."

"She had a daughter?" Raven asked.

"Yes, a bright girl who was destined to become something big. Her mother didn't want her to be just a maid or something, but get a good job that would take her places. She put everything she had into that. Poor thing. All the work just killed her."

"She's dead?" Merula asked, dejection rippling like cold water across her back. That was why they hadn't been able to find Mrs. Bridgewater.

Polly nodded. She popped the nougat into her mouth and mumbled, "Died within a year after leaving Lady Sophia. That cruel woman drove her into death, all for an almond."

Raven looked at Merula. It sounded like Mrs. Bridgewater had had every reason to hate Lady Sophia. But she was dead.

"How about her daughter?" Merula asked, clinging to the next best suspect. "Did her mother's death mean she couldn't become what she had wanted?"

"Oh, no. She's doing right well for herself. She's a milliner, Miss. Makes hats for fancy ladies. Maybe you have bought one made by her once. She works for the best shop on Regent Street."

Merula sat up. "What shop would that be?" Her heart beat fast. Bowsprit had mentioned unpaid bills. Lady Sophia had loved beautiful things . . .

Polly gestured with her hands. "Something fancy it's called, in a foreign language. I think French?'

"Le Bonheur?" Merula asked, naming the shop where Julia loved to order.

"Yes, something like that." Polly chewed. "This one is even more delicious than the other one, my lord."

"I'm glad you like them," Raven said. "So Mrs. Bridgewater's daughter works at Le Bonheur and makes hats there?"

"Yes, and other things. What are they called?" Polly waved her hand again, spreading her fingers.

Merula took it as a gesture to stir the good woman's memory, but after a while she understood what that waving hand was supposed to depict. "Fans?" she asked.

Polly nodded. "Big ones of exotic feathers," she said. "I think she once mentioned they make the handles from mother of pearl." She clicked her tongue. "I can't imagine owning anything like that. But some of her customers have a closet full of them. For every occasion a different one. Well, if you can afford it . . ."

Raven looked at Merula. Merula saw the intensity in

his eyes. Her own stomach wriggled with the same nervous hope. If Lady Sophia had been a customer at Le Bonheur, Mrs. Bridgewater's daughter could have made her fan. The fatal fan that had caused Lady Sophia's sudden death at the lecture.

Would Mrs. Bridgewater's daughter not have had every reason to hate Lady Sophia for driving her mother away from the safety of her household into an uncertain future? Could she not claim that Lady Sophia's cruel dismissal had caused her mother to sicken and die? Could she not blame Lady Sophia for her mother's demise?

Would it not have been very tempting, especially as she had known about the almond incident, to tamper with the fan and let Lady Sophia die, because of almonds, the same thing that had destroyed her mother?

It all fit.

Polly continued, unaware of the importance of what she had just unveiled. "I daresay your cousin is a customer at that place, Miss. You might have seen Mrs. Bridgewater's daughter there sometime. She is a handsome girl, blonde and tall, with lovely skin and big blue eyes. Really smart, they say, which is why she is also allowed to help customers, not just sit in the back making the things."

"I see," Merula said. Had the daughter recognized Lady Sophia one day? Had she realized that a chance for revenge was within reach?

Had she sat over the fan, smiling to herself that she could at last do something about the injustice of old?

Merula's throat constricted at the idea of having to go see a girl who was building her life, who had already lost her mother and might be all alone in the world, to find out if they could accuse her of murder and have her locked up to await trial and death by hanging.

It was gruesome, but to save her uncle they had to produce another suspect. A likely one. And here they had the perfect combination of a compelling reason to hate Lady Sophia *and* direct access to the fatal fan.

Polly said, eyeing the nougat pieces, "They are quite good, my lord."

"I suggest you take some home with you," Raven said.

"Take all of them," Mrs. Lamb said, "I don't like the sweetness of them."

Polly gratefully accepted the paper bag in which the sweets had arrived at the little house and put them in, popping another one into her mouth in the process. She mumbled something about her daughter loving them too and that she'd better be going to see how the cleaning was coming along.

After she left, Raven said, "Those sweets were well worth their price. It seems as if we have our killer within reach."

Merula nodded, although her heart was heavy. "We have to go to Le Bonheur to see Mrs. Bridgewater's daughter and confront her. We have to find out if she handled the fan."

Raven looked at her. "*If?*" he repeated incredulously. "You doubt that it was her? But it all comes together now. Don't you see?"

"It seems so." Merula stood and smoothed her skirt. "I want to talk to her first and see what kind of person she is. If she could hate enough to do such a gruesome thing."

"Can you tell by just talking to someone? Maybe she is nice and friendly on the outside while her pain over her mother runs deep on the inside."

Merula wondered if, with those words, Raven was also describing himself: the gentleman who spent money on every corner, who liked parties and good food and wine, who was considered flighty and silly, while perhaps inside he was broken over his mother's death and the suggestion that it might have been foul play.

Raven said, "Off to Le Bonheur we are."

Leaning over Merula, he added, "Bonheur, happiness, luck. It doesn't seem like Lady Sophia was lucky in buying her fan there. Or that the young lady who made it will be very lucky once her misdeed comes to light."

CHAPTER 16

Le Bonheur was a beautiful large shop with two windows on either side of the door. They were filled with hats, both small models for everyday use and large extravagant affairs with feathers and pearls, the richest fabrics, and the highest contraptions.

Raven looked at them with distaste, muttering, "Waste of money, all of it."

"If you had a wife, wouldn't you want her to look pretty and sophisticated? She would have to represent a certain . . . level of living. She'd have to represent your wealth and standing to the world."

"I know, a sacred duty," Raven said sardonically. "I just wish women would not take it so seriously and spend quite so much good money on it."

Merula laughed softly as they went inside. In the solemn silence she began to walk more slowly, trying to spy the owner, who was usually at hand herself. But the woman was nowhere in sight, and from behind the silk curtain in the back they caught subdued voices.

"A client," Merula said to Raven. "who does not wish to be served in full view. We could have to wait a while."

But as she said it, a tall blonde girl came from the back, smiling at them. She was handsome, with big blue eyes, and Merula froze as she compared Polly's description to this girl.

"May I help you?" the girl asked. "Are you looking for a hat or fan perhaps? We can also do gloves, as we have excellent contacts with . . ." She fell silent, studying Merula more closely. "I know you," she said. "You came here before with Miss Julia DeVeere, Lady Emma's daughter. I'm so sorry that I did not recognize you at once."

"No need for apologies," Merula said. "I'm not here to buy anything, just to ask a quick question."

"How may I be of assistance?"

"You delivered hats and fans to Lady Sophia Rutherford, did you not?"

The girl winced a moment as the name was mentioned. An almost imperceptible stiffening of her shoulders, a tightness in her lively face. She said, "Yes, why do you ask?"

"Did you also create a fan of ostrich feathers for her? A rather large one?"

"Yes. That must have been five weeks ago now."

"Five weeks ago?" Merula glanced at Raven. That was odd. A woman who had a new wardrobe item to show off would usually take it along at the first occasion. Would

Lady Sophia have kept her new fan in a drawer for five weeks before taking it to the lecture?

"Who made it?" Raven asked.

"I did, sir. Well, that was, I did part of the work. We have someone who makes the handles for us and attaches the feathers. We then refine them with paint and other adornments."

"Scent?" Raven asked.

"Yes, also, if clients ask for it."

"Did you scent the fan for Lady Sophia?"

"Yes, with her favorite perfume."

Merula tried to detect something of discomfort in the girl at the turn the conversation was taking. If she was guilty of putting almond essence on the fan, she had to realize these questions posed a danger to her and be on her guard. But while she seemed slightly puzzled by all the questions, she didn't seem troubled by them.

Raven said, "Did you know if Lady Sophia wanted to use the fan for a special occasion?"

"No, sir. I assume she wanted to use it as soon as it was finished."

"She didn't want to take it especially to a zoological lecture, for instance, because the feathers of an exotic bird would look well there?"

"I have no idea, sir. The customers rarely tell us much about the social events they attend. They do talk among themselves sometimes, and one can catch a thing or two, but . . ."

"And you caught a thing or two about Lady Sophia?"

"She hardly ever came here. She disliked it. She had someone come to her home with items to show her. She then ordered them."

"I see. And have you ever been to her home?" Merula asked.

The girl nodded. "Twice. It's a beautiful place."

Full of wealth and luxury, while this girl's mother had died from her swollen hands and bad lungs, a consequence of being turned into the street by this vain, rich woman.

Raven asked, "On those occasions, did Lady Sophia recognize you?"

"Me?" The girl seemed taken aback. "She knew I worked here."

"No, I mean from an earlier occasion. Did she know you are the daughter of her former cook, Mrs. Bridgewater?"

Now the girl froze and looked at the curtain, behind which her mistress was helping the customer. She lowered her voice and said, "No, I don't think so."

"And your employer doesn't know that either." Raven looked at her with a probing gaze. "You kept it to yourself."

"My mother was dismissed for a trifle. She could not help it. She was ashamed of it though, and . . ." The girl's lips pulled tight. "Why are you asking about her?"

"Did you know for what trifle your mother was sent off? Did you understand what it meant?"

"She had supposedly put a nut in a dish, and Lady Sophia believed she could have died because of it. But it was just an accident. There might as well have been a bone in the fish. It was not my mother's fault."

"But your mother did pay a heavy price for it. She died." Raven looked at the girl. "Do you blame Lady Sophia for her death?"

"No. Not anymore. I used to when it first happened, but . . . what was the point? I couldn't change anything about it." The girl knotted her fingers. "I have a good life now. A job I love, a place to live. I try not to think about it anymore."

"Can you really not think about your mother? My mother died, and I still think about her."

Merula shrank under the heartfelt tone of Raven's voice.

As if she had also sensed the intensity of his statement, the girl looked at Raven. "I'm sorry for your loss, sir. But I also lost my father when I was just ten. And servants we knew lost some of their children. Death is a part of our lives."

"Sometimes death comes too early. It could have been avoided," Raven said through clenched teeth.

"How can you know that? I don't disagree with fate." The girl held her head high. "I accept it and I move on."

"Still, when you realized that the woman who had dismissed your mother and caused her to sicken and die was now a customer of yours, you must have thought about it. When you were working on her fan, did you not think of her and her white hands that were going to hold the fan, the same hands that had killed your mother? "

"You make it all sound so . . . dramatic. I did think about it, I won't lie, but I didn't . . ." The girl's eyes were worried now, a frown hovering over them. "Why are you asking all of these questions?"

"Lady Sophia is dead," Merula said. "You must have heard that she collapsed at a lecture and died. The police think it wasn't an accident. They treat it as foul play. Murder. The fan you made might have something to do with it."

The girl became deathly pale. "No," she whispered. "That can't be."

Raven supported her as she staggered and led her to a chair to sit down.

The girl refused, whispering, "I can't sit down there. It is for the customers."

She leaned on Raven, saying to Merula, "How can a fan have anything to do with her death?"

"She breathed in a scent that was on the fan and it killed her. You just admitted you scented the fan."

"Yes, with her perfume. But a perfume can't kill any-one, can it?" The girl pushed a hand to her face. "How can this be? What is happening to me now?"

Merula wasn't sure what to think. Was the girl guilty and was this just a very good act to elicit pity and escape justice?

Or did she really not know anything about the almond essence on the fan?

Raven had said a hasty conclusion had ruined the life of his mother and others, including himself, the little boy who had been left motherless, struggling with questions and doubts and fears for the future. Could they just accuse this girl without having tried to find every possible answer to the puzzle?

"You said you made the fan five weeks ago," Merula said. "How did it get from here to the house? Did you take it there?"

"No, we had the parcels delivered. Lady Sophia always had them delivered. As I said, she rarely came here herself. Just . . ." The girl halted and frowned.

Raven asked, "What is it? What do you remember?"

"Well, I think the fan was picked up here. It was not delivered to her house, in fact." The girl stared ahead, her face scrunched up in the deepest thought. "It was picked up here and paid for. I remember clearly, as it was unusual. Lady Sophia always had all of the things delivered. But this was picked up. By her companion."

"Miss Knight?" Merula asked.

"Yes. I recognized her right away. When my mother was still Lady Sophia's cook, I went there to visit her on the estate. I've seen Miss Knight there."

"And she has seen you," Raven added with a quick look at Merula. "Did she mention she remembered you?"

"No. But she already knew I worked here. I had been to the house, as I just said. She saw me there."

"So Miss Knight knew you were working at this shop and that you had prepared the new ostrich feather fan for Lady Sophia."

"Yes. We talked about the scent on it briefly. Miss Knight said Lady Sophia liked heavy perfumes, but they gave her headaches that she then complained about."

Merula looked at Raven. "Miss Knight knew that the fan was made here, that it was scented."

"With a heavy scent," Raven added, "that would disguise whatever else."

Merula looked at the girl again. "Five weeks ago? You are certain?"

"I usually remember the more extravagant pieces we make. But I can look up the date. We write everything down. One moment please." She disappeared into the back.

Raven whispered to Merula. "How devious. Miss Knight recognizes the daughter of the dismissed cook as working at the milliner's now. Perhaps she didn't think up a plan right away, but the information lingered in the back of her head."

Merula added, "Then Foxwell humiliated her, rejecting her affection. Lady Sophia accused her of theft. She wanted to get even with both of them. She knew of the almond incident. As a nurse, she had the knowledge to recognize Lady Sophia's ill response to the almond. Not choking per se, but a response to the almond itself. A response that could be provoked again."

"The collapse would never be connected to the fan," Raven added, his eyes sparkling with fervor. "And even if it would, then there would be a scapegoat in place. The daughter of the dismissed cook, carrying a grudge, preparing the fan. So perfectly planned in every little detail."

The girl came out the back. "Five weeks ago, like I said," she enthused. "Miss Knight picked it up and took it along."

"But I bet she didn't give it to Lady Sophia right away," Raven said to Merula. "She had to treat it with her own little scent first."

"What are you saying?" the girl asked.

Merula touched her arm. "Don't worry about it. You have done nothing wrong. Lady Sophia died because someone wanted her to die, and we now know who it was. The police won't come here to bother you. I'm sorry about what happened to your mother. But I'm glad you made a good life for yourself. I hope you will be very happy."

"Thank you," the girl said, perplexed.

They left the shop and stood on the pavement looking at each other. Raven said, "We need to make sure we're right. We need to know that Miss Knight treated the fan and not somebody else. Foxwell, for instance. We have to ask Buckleberry if he knows when the fan was given to Lady Sophia. Where it was before the night of the lecture."

Merula nodded. "Bowsprit can contact him and bring the information to us."

Raven looked at her. "I don't really understand Miss Knight's motive though. Do you? What did killing Lady Sophia solve for her? It meant she lost her position, for a companion is no longer needed when the lady she has to accompany is no longer there. She'd have to find a new position. She'd move away from the household where she could see Foxwell. Assuming she did fancy him."

Merula said, "Maybe she wanted to go away because Foxwell hadn't reciprocated her feelings for him."

"But she could have taken her leave."

"Then people would have wondered why. Now they pity her and will want to help her find new employment."

Raven pursed his lips. "Is it a strong enough reason to kill? You said before that a nurse is dedicated to healing people, that she would not easily take a life. I agree with that idea. She would only kill if she had a really good reason. But I can't see what it might have been."

Merula shrugged. "Let us first fit all the pieces together. Then we can see what to do with what we know."

★　★　★

Bowsprit reported to them that Buckleberry had been there in the hallway when Lady Sophia had been about to go out to the lecture and that the companion had given her the fan then. There had been a moment's discussion, as Lady Sophia had wanted to know why she had not been informed sooner that her fan had arrived from the milliner's, but Miss Knight had said it had come in that afternoon.

"On the day of the lecture?" Merula said. "That was a lie. Miss Knight had already had it for weeks."

"To treat it," Raven said. "This is conclusive for me. It was her."

"But," Merula said, "where did she keep the almonds as they were soaking in the alcohol to create the fatal essence?

Her room in the house would not have been private. I mean, any servant could come in and see something."

"She might have put it in a closet underneath something. I don't suppose the servants go through her things behind her back."

Bowsprit lifted a hand. "If I may, my lord. Buckleberry mentioned earlier that Miss Knight never received any letters at the house, nor did anyone ever call for her. He had the distinct impression she had an address elsewhere. Perhaps a room in a boardinghouse."

"But why keep a room if you are never there?" Raven gestured with his hands. "That only costs good money. She had a day off, I assume, but that doesn't explain keeping a room somewhere."

"There is only one way to find out," Merula said. "We must lure her into a trap."

"What?" Raven stared at her.

"I'll tell her I know she did it and I want money to keep my mouth shut. Then she will have to do something. Deny, or pay up."

"No, no, no," Raven said. "It's much too dangerous. I'm not letting you do anything of the kind."

"But I have to save my uncle. And the police aren't looking for any other suspects. The lawyer even said Uncle Rupert had to admit the murder and throw himself at the mercy of the jury! We have to force Miss Knight's hand in some way. If she tries to attack me or hurt me, we can prove she has something to hide."

"If I may again, my lord," Bowsprit said. "There was a parcel delivered to the house holding a poison bottle. There was also a death's-head hawk moth attached to Miss Merriweather's dress when she spoke with her cousin at the exhibition. Did Miss Knight do that? Or somebody else? Can she be in a league with others?"

"Exactly. It is much too dangerous to confront her. I won't have it."

Merula straightened up. "Oh, so we go to the police and we tell them that Miss Knight picked up a fan at the milliner's and went home and soaked almonds to make an essence and scented the fan with that and then gave it to Lady Sophia as she was about to leave the house so she would inhale the almond essence and get unwell and die at the lecture where my uncle would get accused of murder? They will never believe that."

"It does sound . . ." Raven sighed.

"Besides, they are looking for us. For me, in any case. As soon as we walk in, we'll be arrested. We can't turn to the police. Not unless we can prove Miss Knight killed Lady Sophia."

Raven hid his face in his hands. "I hate to admit this," he said, smothered, "but you are right. Still, I think you shouldn't confront her. She's smart, and she won't let you get away. Bowsprit just said there may be others involved."

"But I'm not alone either. You can follow me and watch and see what happens. If she does try to hurt me, you can prevent it."

Raven shook his head, but Merula continued, "It's our only chance. I'll write her a note saying I want to meet her in the park. I'll have it delivered to Lady Sophia's house. Miss Knight will realize that I'm on to her and she'll come. Believe me."

CHAPTER 17

Merula thought of these self-assured words as she walked up and down in the park, seeing gentlemen on horseback, nannies with their charges, and even a hotel page boy smoking a cigarette while he probably should have been on duty. Everything around her was lively and bustling, but inside her it was cold and still.

If Miss Knight had killed Lady Sophia, she was a ruthless woman who had calmly handed the fan to her mistress, knowing it would kill her. Her motive was still unclear. Perhaps she was simply mad and capable of anything?

And that was the woman Merula was about to meet.

"Miss Merriweather."

Merula swung round to see Miss Knight standing behind her as if she had materialized out of nothing. A chill went down her spine as she imagined that that woman's hand had attached the moth, the portent of death, to her dress at the exhibition. She had not seen her, let alone recognized her.

"You wrote to me that you wanted to talk to me about an urgent matter," Miss Knight said, smiling pleasantly. Her brown eyes were warm and intelligent, not like the eyes of a cold-blooded murderer. But then Merula had never confronted a murderer before and was only speculating about how she'd look. Maybe the talent of a murderer was the ability to be so clever and calm and confident, without for a moment acknowledging her own wickedness and the sacredness of life?

"I'm sure," Merula said in a slightly trembling voice, "you know I'm in a desperate position. My uncle is accused of murder and, as I helped him with his research into the butterflies, the police are looking for me too. I haven't been home in days. I feel hunted, dirty, all alone."

"You're hardly alone with Raven Royston helping you," Miss Knight said in a vicious tone, as if it irked her that a handsome man had come to Merula's aid.

Merula tried to look forlorn. "He abandoned me as well. He is just a coward who believed that I would fall into his arms so he could take advantage of me. When I did nothing of the sort, he told me he couldn't risk his reputation for me and left London."

"Aren't all men the same?" Miss Knight said with a peculiar little smile around her lips. "They want one thing and when they can't get it, they're gone."

She observed Merula closely. "He is a handsome man. Were you not tempted to give him what he asked of you?"

"I don't bargain with my person," Merula said curtly.

"Money is another matter, of course. I'm sure that Royston would be willing to assist me again if I had some financial advantage to offer him. That is why I wrote to you."

Miss Knight hitched a fine brow. "You think I have money? And I would feel the need to assist you?"

"Whether you have money or not is no concern of mine," Merula said. The other woman's callous tone encouraged her to also show a cold side. "You live in a rich household, and I'm sure you can lay your hands on something valuable. Doesn't Foxwell sell off zoological items? Perhaps you could as well?"

"I don't have the contacts." Miss Knight folded her hands on her back. "I'm afraid my time is rather short, Miss Merriweather."

"Almonds," Merula said. And she saw a flicker in Miss Knight's eyes. The briefest flash of a response.

"Excuse me?" the companion said.

"You know very well what I'm referring to. I'm willing, however, to forget all that I know when I get some money to survive the predicament I am in."

Miss Knight studied her with narrowed eyes. "Money won't get your uncle out of prison."

"My aunt will take care of that. She has powerful friends. My uncle may have been arrested, but he can't be convicted without solid proof that the butterfly killed Lady Sophia, and there is no such proof. They won't find any poison in her body."

Miss Knight didn't say anything. She just continued

watching Merula with those brown eyes that seemed so kind and interested.

Merula said, "I know you will want to leave London. And I won't keep you here. I just want some money in exchange for my silence."

She was sure as she said all this that Miss Knight would never fall for it. She was relying on the connection between almonds and the death to stay hidden or, if discovered, prove to be so fragile it couldn't lead to anything.

Miss Knight said, "A park is not the best place to discuss this. I have a room where we can talk freely. I also have some money there. I'd like to know what your plans are so I may assist you. I can imagine your uncle is fairly protected, but you are not. I should have realized sooner that your inquiries into the case were not for his sake, but for your own."

Merula wanted to protest that she wasn't selfish, but she gathered that Miss Knight could understand that sentiment and that it might be the only thing that prevented her from walking away now.

"Show me where it is," she said.

The two women walked side by side, away from the park, through busy streets. There was nothing to say until they reached their destination. To Merula's mind, it took forever, and with every step she got more worried regarding what she was about to do. She trusted Raven and Bowsprit to save her at the crucial moment, but she could not even be sure they were still following her and Miss Knight. What if they were seen by a police officer and arrested?

What if she was on her own once she got to Miss Knight's room?

What if Miss Knight decided not to attack her at all but simply give her some money? Would it be enough proof of her guilt? She could simply argue she had wanted to help a person in need.

So Merula actually had to hope Miss Knight would attack her, not knowing in what form the attack might come.

They went up two stairs to Miss Knight's room, a simple affair with little furniture and a fireplace where a low fire burned. Miss Knight took the teapot off the side table and poured two cups of tea. She handed one to Merula and sat down with the other.

She took a long sip and sighed. "Nothing quite like tea to calm down." She looked at Merula with a smile.

Merula sat down as well, picking up the tea. It had a strong herbal scent, perhaps chamomile or something with lavender. She held the rim of the cup to her mouth and pretended to sip.

Miss Knight said, "What is your plan? Can you go back to your uncle and aunt?"

"Hardly," Merula lied. "Men burned down the conservatory. My aunt blames me. She never liked having me around. I'm not her daughter."

Miss Knight nodded. "I suspected something like that." She sipped from the tea again. "I could help you leave the country. That would be best for all involved."

"What could I do abroad? How would I live? I have never done manual labor."

Miss Knight's expression flashed with contempt a moment. "It won't kill you."

Merula leaned back against the chair. "It killed Mrs. Bridgewater."

"Lady Sophia killed Mrs. Bridgewater. She was a cold, evil woman. She drove a wedge between people."

"Between Foxwell and you?" Merula asked. "Julia believed he loved her, but I never thought he did. I have always thought he was pressured by Lady Sophia to make a match she approved of."

"But she didn't approve of your dear cousin Julia," Miss Knight spat hatefully. "She didn't approve of anyone. Sometimes I thought she was herself in love with Simon's handsome face and desperate to keep him to herself."

Merula kept her hands round the teacup. Miss Knight's spiteful suggestion struck her as highly improbable, but who knew what a jealous mind could begin to believe? Had Miss Knight killed Lady Sophia to remove an alleged rival? "Lady Sophia wasn't a fool."

"She was. She was afraid of everything. It was pathetic to see how she mashed her food, how even the slightest lump in something could drive her wild with fear."

"Because she believed an almond getting into her windpipe had almost killed her. But you knew better. You knew it had never been the obstruction of the nut. It had been the nut itself, its vital qualities. Yet you didn't tell her. You didn't try to alleviate her fears. Or, should I say, you consciously let her be afraid of things that wouldn't harm her so the thing that *could* harm her could strike her when she least expected it?"

Miss Knight smiled softly. "We were talking about you and your future, Miss Merriweather, not about me."

Merula said, "But you fascinate me, Miss Knight. You are so clever. You thought of everything. You put the fan into her hands the moment she was about to leave the house. She would die under someone else's roof and while you were miles away. You'd never be implicated."

She held the woman's gaze. "How could you know that some poor idiotic neighbor with an opium addiction would remember the dismissal of the cook over the almond and would mention it to me, just because he had heard about a reward for information?"

She apologized to the neighbor inwardly for denigrating him so, but Miss Knight had to be played. As the woman felt superior to other people, she would recognize that feeling in others and agree with it. By sounding just as cold and selfish as Miss Knight, Merula might convince her to take her seriously.

Miss Knight held her gaze. "Opium is very dangerous. Too much of it can kill you."

Merula stared at her. Her breath stuck in her throat under the woman's suggestive tone.

Miss Knight nodded slowly. "Oh, yes. I know of him. Or should I say, I knew of him? I'm sure his obituary will

Vivian Conroy

not mention his addiction and just say nice things about the old fool."

She clicked her tongue. "Ah, greed, Miss Merriweather. It can be deadly."

Merula's mind raced. Had Miss Knight killed the neighbor? After he had talked to them? Was that poor old addicted fool dead because of this case?

This woman was more dangerous than Merula had first thought.

Merula pretended to take a deep draft of her tea. The cup almost slipped from her sweaty palms. She said in a squeaky voice, "You must understand, I have nothing against you. I only need some money. I can't turn anywhere else. I'm an outcast."

Miss Knight watched her. "Why would I believe that if I gave you anything, you wouldn't come back and bleed me dry?" She leaned on the table with both hands. "It would be very unwise to try and play games with me, Miss Merriweather. You have no idea who you're dealing with."

Merula put the cup down and touched her forehead. She suppressed a yawn. "I've had so little sleep."

Miss Knight smiled. "You could lie down on my bed for an hour. I don't mind."

Merula said, "That's not necessary." Then she sagged to a side, almost toppling off the chair.

Miss Knight did nothing to help her as she slipped to the floor. Looking down on her, she said, "I applaud you for working it out, Miss Merriweather. I thought the almond incident was forgotten and even if someone remembered, they would not connect it to her death now. But you did. That was smart. But you should have thought twice about coming here with me. I am a nurse, after all."

Merula groaned. She started to grope around her, tried to drag herself to the door.

Miss Knight let her move a few inches and then leaned over her. "This is no good," she whispered. "You won't get far. You'd better stay here. Die here. This room is rented under a fake name. I guess you might be buried under it. I hope you like it. Else it would be a shame. But that is what happens to busybodies."

At the last word she kicked Merula viciously in the side.

Merula felt pain splash through her. She didn't have to fake the cry that seemed to ring through her head. Where were Bowsprit and Raven? Why weren't they doing anything to save her?

Miss Knight crouched beside her. "You little meddling bitch," she spat. "You believed you could snare a lord to help you, that you could outwit the police. You believed you could even outwit me and get money out of it. But I don't intend to pay you or anybody else. All I earned is mine."

She continued in a low, almost soothing tone, "I even warned you. The empty poison bottle, the moth left on your dress, exactly the intellectual clues I thought you and your little band would enjoy."

"How . . ." Merula spoke in a halting, croaking voice, "did you find out I was staying with Galileo so you could deliver the parcel there?"

"I watched Lord Havilock's house that night. I wanted to be sure that a doctor was called and that a dead body would be removed. I saw you and Royston leave in a rush, almost as if you were fleeing the scene of the death. I thought it couldn't hurt to follow you and see what you wanted. Royston was already suspected of having endangered people's lives in several instances, with his exploding engine and his bad hair tonic. I wondered if he was somehow afraid to be accused of Lady Sophia's death and thought how I might best use that to my own advantage. I saw the men enter your uncle's house and saw the fire break out and watched you two escape from the conservatory with a bundle. Obviously you were fugitives, and that was very interesting. Again, I only had to follow you to know where you had gone and why. Galileo's address is infamous among household personnel, as nobody wants to work there or even go there for an errand. They are all so afraid of his poisonous creatures."

Merula whispered, "But why kill Lady Sophia at all? Did you hate her so much? For Foxwell's sake? Now that he has her fortune, he can marry any woman he likes. It won't be you."

Miss Knight hissed, "You have no idea what I wanted. Foxwell? Marriage?" She seemed to compose herself with an effort and laughed softly as if the insinuation hadn't hurt her at all. She got to her feet and looked down on Merula. "Forgive me that I can't talk more, but I have things to do."

She went to the table and reached for Merula's cup of tea that was still standing there.

At that moment, the door crashed open and a figure flung himself through the room. He grabbed Miss Knight's shoulders and pulled her away from the table. She fought viciously, kicking at the table as if trying to topple it.

"Bowsprit!" a voice called. "Secure that cup of tea. It will contain traces of poison."

"What are you talking about?" Miss Knight protested. "It is a simple herbal concoction. Very calming."

"Which is why Merula lies crumpled on the floor!" Raven cried. Still struggling with the woman, he glanced at her. "Merula! Merula!"

Bowsprit picked up the teacup and sniffed at it.

"That won't prove anything," Raven cried. "Some poisons are odorless."

Miss Knight cried, "Just herbal tea. I drank from it as well. I poured both our cups from the same teapot." She pointed at it standing on the side table.

"Yes," Raven said, "but I wager that in Merula's cup you had already put the poison. She couldn't see that there was something inside already when you poured the tea." He repeated to Bowsprit, "Hang on to that cup at all costs."

Miss Knight wrestled to escape from his grasp. "Are you all insane? Let go of me! Help! Someone help me! I'm being attacked. Help!"

At the door, curious faces appeared, peeking in. Raven called to them, "Alert the police. This woman should be arrested for murder."

People shrank back upon hearing the word murder.

Miss Knight said viciously, "They will not call the police for you. They don't want anything to do with murder. Besides, if the police came, they'd arrest *you*. They are looking for *you*. Not me."

"That will change when they have analyzed that tea," Raven said grimly. "It will contain whatever you used to sedate Merula."

He looked at her again, despair in his features.

"Why is she not moving?" he spat to Bowsprit. "You hold this woman so I can go see what is wrong with Merula."

Bowsprit gestured at the teacup. "What to do with this? If it spills, our evidence is lost."

Raven groaned. "We should have brought Galileo as well. We are short a pair of hands."

As he spoke, a policeman appeared in the doorway. He stared from Merula's form on the floor to Raven holding Miss Knight and Bowsprit with the teacup. "What is going on here?"

"The tea is poisoned," Raven declared. "This woman here is a murderess who feared exposure and tried to kill Miss Merriweather before she could tell. Please ensure the liquid in the cup is tested for poison."

"These men forced themselves into my room with the dead woman," Miss Knight cried. "They believed I was out for the day and wanted to put her in my room so I would be blamed for murder. I do not know her at all."

"Dead?" Raven cried. "No! Merula cannot be dead."

He let go of Miss Knight and fell to his knees on the floor beside Merula, touching her face and neck. "Why can't you find a pulse when you need one?" he muttered.

Released, Miss Knight threw herself at a cupboard in the corner, extracted something from between the shelf and the cabinet wall, and ran to the fireplace to toss it into the flames.

In a flash, Merula was up on her feet and stopped the woman, knocking the item she carried out of her hands. It fell to the floor.

Miss Knight roared with anger and lashed out at Merula, hitting her full in the face.

Merula staggered back, against Raven, who locked her in his arms.

Merula pointed at the item on the floor. "Secure that! It is important."

The policeman came into the room and bent to pick it up. "It is a notebook," he said in a surprised tone. "What can it mean?"

Miss Knight was at the door already, intending to rush through it, but Bowsprit had put the precious teacup back on the table and placed himself in her path. She knocked into him hard and sank to her knees, gasping for breath.

"If you'd be so good as to handcuff this woman," Bowsprit said to the policeman, "we will explain to you what is in the notebook." He threw a warning look at Raven and Merula as if to say, *You'd better know what to do now.*

Merula moved away from Raven, wincing, as every movement hurt her side where Miss Knight had kicked her. Perhaps she had bruised a rib?

She reached for the notebook in the officer's hand and opened it. "Here are . . ." She let her eye run quickly down the notes, hoping she could make sense of them. The policeman would believe them and arrest Miss Knight only if they could prove she had been involved in something criminal.

On the pages before Merula were four columns. In the first, names of people. In the second, items. In the third, figures. In the fourth, names again, with short comments.

Merula had no idea what it all meant.

But Miss Knight had wanted to destroy the notebook, so it had to be related to criminal actions somehow and perhaps even to Lady Sophia's death.

Merula's still dazed brain registered one thing about the items listed. They were all valuables. Mainly jewelry, such as rings and brooches, but also silver vases.

Her eyes raced across the numbers beside the listed items. Could those be their monetary value?

Yes . . .

Her heart beat fast as she struggled to fit the pieces into a meaningful whole. Valuables, money asked for.

Or paid?

She then read the last column better. It wasn't just

names but also short notes. *To pay a gambling debt. Must cover for extravagance of husband.*

Her eye fell to a word in the *Items* column. *Gold earring with ruby.*

Earring.

She looked up at Miss Knight. "You really are a thief. You stole from Lady Sophia and you sold off the items at pawnshops, every time giving a different reason to explain why your mistress wanted to get rid of her property, discreetly."

Her gaze flicked back to the first column. The names of these people . . . all influential, all of the highest classes.

"You were not alone in this, either," she said. "That's why you rented a room here. Servants brought their spoils to you and you sold them. You gave them some money and kept the rest yourself. It was a whole ring of thieves. And once Lady Sophia became suspicious of you, you had to make sure she could not accuse you openly and dismiss you. With such an accusation, you'd never work in a good household again. You had to kill her. You knew of the almond incident. You knew that if she was exposed again, she might die. You were not certain, perhaps, but you wanted to try. You treated the fan with the almond essence. You knew the vapors would be released and Lady Sophia would inhale them."

Miss Knight stared at her impassively. "I don't know what this madwoman is talking about. A butterfly killed Lady Sophia when it sat down on her arm. A butterfly hatched by you. You killed her."

"Ah," Raven said to the policeman, "How remarkable that the woman just declared she doesn't know Merula and now she seems to know so much about her."

The policeman stared at Merula. "You are the butterfly lady? The whole city is looking for you!"

Merula said, "I will gladly accompany you to the station to tell you all I know. But please be assured that this woman led a ring of thieves and that she killed Lady Sophia."

The policeman looked at the notebook. "I do know," he said, "that some of these items have been reported missing, and we have been asked to look out for them. I would like to know why they are on this list, then." He looked at Miss Knight.

Merula said quickly, "She used different pawnshops and different reasons so she would not be caught. It is all listed here and in her handwriting."

The policeman said, "You are all coming along to tell us what you know."

Bowsprit lifted the teacup. "And this must be analyzed."

As the policeman led Miss Knight from the room, her neighbors in the corridor whispering about her, Raven took Merula's arm. "You had me scared a moment," he said. "When you were lying there on the floor, I thought you had really drunk the tea and been poisoned."

"I smelled that it was herbal but had no idea what was in it. Laudanum has no taste, so it could have been in there. Or anything else she might know about as a nurse. I pretended to drink, but I did not. Then I acted as if I were getting drowsy and even collapsed off my chair. When she believed she had full power over me, she showed her darkest side."

"Good girl." Raven squeezed her arm. "You were very convincing. She was certain you'd be dead any moment and could no longer betray her. Claiming we had killed you and tried to blame her was very smart."

Merula sighed and winced as her ribs hurt again. "That kick of hers was anything but an act. My side burns as if it's on fire."

"Perhaps some ribs are broken," Raven said with a worried look. "You should be in bed, not going out to the police station to make a statement."

"You can't keep me from it. I don't want to miss this for the world." Merula straightened up, suppressing a groan. "I will be sore for a day or two. But that doesn't matter. Uncle Rupert will go free now. All will be solved."

Light-headed with happiness, Merula walked to the door and out of the damp room among the whispering neighbors who would have a tale to tell for time to come, of the master thief who had lived among them and who had been so clever, leading a ring for years without being caught. Until one day she had begun to fear that her whole scheme was in danger and had decided that only murder could save it.

CHAPTER 18

"Uncle Rupert!" Merula ran to hug her uncle. He looked pale and gaunt from his time in prison, but his eyes twinkled as he said, "I heard you had an adventure of your own, girl."

Holding her by the shoulders, he added, "You should not have taken so many chances for my sake. I heard it was an entire conspiracy."

"The butterfly conspiracy," Julia said, spreading her hands as if she were unrolling a banner with those words on it. "I still shiver when I think of that awful woman walking past us at the exhibit and pinning that ugly thing to your dress."

Merula had told her story to Julia, several times even, as her cousin wanted to know all the details as if she was sorry she herself had not been involved in these exciting events.

Merula had left out a few things that might be too shocking for Julia's sensitive mind—such as the creatures in Galileo's house—and those that she considered a private matter. Foremost, how Raven's mother had died and how much pain he still felt about that.

A hint of sadness stabbed her as she realized she had not seen Raven for days now, and she missed him. She had grown used to being around him, and it was strange to be home again with Aunt Emma, Julia, and the servants as if nothing had happened. She had a feeling her adventure had changed her and made her see life in a different way.

She had experienced what it was like to practice her skills, to go after a goal, and to be persistent in the face of danger. It was something she had never quite felt before. The idea that she was good, a genius even, as Raven had said, and could accomplish things, things that mattered.

Uncle Rupert said, "I'm sorry they destroyed all your work, Merula. We must see to restoring the conservatory."

Aunt Emma said, "No, I will not have it. Butterflies have caused us enough trouble."

"But butterflies had nothing to do with it," Merula protested. "There never was any butterfly conspiracy. The ring of thieves merely used that name given by the newspapers to scare me."

"That woman might be arrested now and about to stand trial," Aunt Emma said, "but the others we do not know. They may not like what you have done." She looked at her husband. "I wish Merula had not been involved at all."

"I will be fine," Merula said.

Uncle Rupert smiled. "I think I have good news for

everyone. Emma, you do agree it would be best for Merula to be away from London for a while?"

Merula wanted to protest that she didn't want to leave at all, but Uncle Rupert winked at her so she didn't speak up.

Aunt Emma said firmly, "I would encourage it."

"Wonderful. For I received an invitation this morning that I think will be excellent for Merula. A little time away from London to recover from all the anxiety. And spent in a beautiful place."

Merula looked at him with a questioning expression.

Uncle Rupert added, "It even has some zoological interest."

"Ah, there we have it," Aunt Emma cried. "It has to do with disgusting dead animals again. I won't allow it."

"A renowned zoologist has a house in the countryside with a collection full of rare specimens. His kraken, especially, is legendary. A deep sea monster with long arms that could drag a whole ship into the depths of the sea."

Julia gasped and shivered while Aunt Emma pulled her most reproving face.

Uncle Rupert said, "The man is rather solitary, living like a hermit, but he has agreed to receive a visit from a friend. Merula can come along and have a look at this kraken. The house is in Dartmoor, where you have moors, the sea, clean air. You could recuperate completely."

"And who is going with her? Who will take care of her? She can't simply live with a man on his own. That would be disastrous."

Uncle Rupert said, "Merula won't be alone there. She is traveling with someone I trust. A real gentleman and his valet."

Merula perked up. Could it be true? Could it? The thought of seeing Raven again and traveling with him and exploring zoological novelties made her heart sing.

Aunt Emma said, "I still don't see how it would be proper. I assume the gentleman in question is not married? His wife can't be a companion to Merula?"

"I've thought about a companion for Merula. Lamb can become her maid and assist her with everything."

"But Lamb's mother . . ." Merula protested, not sure how she could explain that the old woman needed support and Lamb could not leave for weeks on end.

"I'm sure we can find a way to take care of Lamb's mother," Uncle Rupert said with a twinkle in his eye. "Now you'd better decide about everything you need to take along, for I understood from this rather impatient gentleman that he wants to leave tomorrow."

"And who might he be?" Aunt Emma asked, still looking icy.

"Lord Raven Royston."

"That disaster magnet, as you always call him?"

"Used to call him. I changed my mind now that he and Merula solved the case of Lady Sophia's sudden death and brought the murderer to justice. Remember, dear"—Uncle Rupert tapped Aunt Emma's arm—"without them I would not be standing here."

Aunt Emma muttered something, but she didn't repeat that Merula couldn't go.

Merula clapped her hands together and resisted the urge to do a little dance through the hallway. She couldn't wait to see Raven again, and Dartmoor, where she had never been before.

It wasn't just a name to her, though, as it had always been the only connection she had to her parents. They had perhaps once been in a little place in Dartmoor. That place marked on the pendant on a chain that had been left with her as a baby. She felt for it, safely hidden under her clothes. As her fingers touched the metal, she felt connected for a brief moment to her past. To the people she had never known and could not help wondering about.

Would her journey into Dartmoor also provide an opportunity to learn more about her parents?

It would make an already exciting prospect even more inviting. With a smile, she hurried up the stairs, wincing as her hurt ribs ached, making their presence known again. She was not fully recovered yet, but that would come. The fresh air would aid that, and so would spending time with Raven, looking back on the case and looking ahead. That he wanted to travel with her, take her to his friend, to see the kraken, was simply wonderful.

At the top of the stairs, Merula turned and looked down to where Uncle Rupert was standing. Aunt Emma straightened his tie, rebuking him, but with a tender tone in her voice.

Julia watched them with a wide smile.

Merula laughed and ran to her room. Her family was reunited again. And soon she'd be reunited herself, with the man who had become her ally in solving Lady Sophia's death and whose friendship had outlasted that case. There lay something ahead for her and Raven, with Bowsprit, Lamb, and the other friends they had made along the way. Something exhilarating. Something good.

Something that made her feel more alive than ever before.

ACKNOWLEDGMENTS AND AUTHOR'S NOTE

As always, I'm grateful to all agents, editors, and authors who share online about the writing and publishing process. A special thanks to my amazing agent, Jill Marsal, whose enthusiasm for the zoology aspects of this series shone through from our very first conversation about it; to my wonderful editor, Faith Black Ross, who made the whole process from manuscript to published book so smooth and easy; and to the talented crew at Crooked Lane Books, especially cover designer Melanie Sun for the evocative cover.

The first seed for this series was planted when I read Sir Arthur Conan Doyle's Sherlock Holmes story *The Speckled Band* and realized the amazing potential of animals and natural history for murder mysteries. Further inspiration came from watching Sir David Attenborough's *Natural Curiosities*, where he draws on many exciting sources—biographies, treatises, encyclopedias, correspondence, and so forth—to explore misconception, confusion, and conscious deceit in the development of zoology. My mind spun with what-if scenarios, and the Royal Zoological Society was born—a fictional society comparable to real-life institutions founded in the nineteenth century dedicated to the study of natural history—along with my heroine Merula Merriweather and her colorful allies who confront mysterious deaths connected to novel discoveries in the field of science.

Researching the Victorian age through the modern conveniences of the Internet is a joy in itself, as I was one moment watching footage of a still-operating Victorian sweets machine and the next reading up on lethal wallpaper, a subject both intriguing and terrifying, as people did die, even children, although researchers still debate whether the wallpaper was really to blame or not. That inhalation of only a few particles of an agent one is severely allergic to can kill is proven by many contemporary scientific studies, and the interest in adverse responses to foods, but also to fur, pollen, and so forth, began to soar in Victorian times, making it likely that Galileo would know about this and could arrive at the conclusions he did—although he couldn't use the word "allergy" to denote the condition, as it hadn't been introduced yet (Galileo's remark that "we have to find a word for it" is actually a playful reference to that!). And, yes, there was a very real, very large vegetarian movement in London at the time, even though, after reading the recipes of those days, I'm not too sure those dishes were as healthy as people believed at the time.

But before I lose myself in too many details of Merula and Raven's world, I want to thank you, reader, for entering it with me and invite you to join us on our next adventure in misty coastal Dartmoor, where a creature of legendary proportions is rumored to spread death from the deep.